SOHUT'S PROTECTION

A.G. WILDE

Sohut's Protection

Sohut's Protection © A. G. Wilde 2020

This book is dedicated to my mother, who, bless her heart, missed my eyebrows waggling when I said I write books about humans being "taken" by aliens.
I love you, Mom!
Everything I know about surviving, I learned from you.

DISCLAIMER

This work of fiction is intended for mature audiences only.

All sexually active characters portrayed in this book are eighteen years of age or older.

SOHUT'S PROTECTION

You have to be really unlucky to be captured by aliens twice...

Well, here I am.

The Queen of Unlucky.

When I'm taken from Earth, my life takes a sharp turn. The alien ship crashes on a strange planet and before I know it, I'm taken again. These new "owners" are just as bad as the last ones and it doesn't take me long to realize my chances of survival are dim.

I only have one chance to escape—so I take it.

I'm doing a good job of surviving too. That is...until the aliens send a hunter to track me down.

As soon as I lay eyes on him, I know he's there to find *me*.

I can't run; I can only hide—but I can't hide forever.

It's a fight for my freedom...

...but it's my heart that's in trouble of falling into the hunter's trap.

Sohut's Protection is a full-length standalone sci-fi romance featuring a heroine with the will to survive and a hot, charming, and possessive hero who would do anything to protect the one who steals his heart.

If you like sexy aliens, adventure, and steamy romance, check out Sohut's Protection.

This standalone book contains:
- Steamy scenes
- HEA
- No cheating
- No cliffhangers

PROLOGUE

Hudo III
A little over, a year ago

WHAT'S WORSE THAN ONE GREEDY ALIEN?

Two greedy aliens.

"They will be most pleased with what we've retrieved."

The aliens' conversation drifted toward the back of the rattling cart, and Cleo resisted the urge to growl at the two green beings.

They were some version of an alien species of orc: big and green with the tusks to boot.

For the entire journey, they had been discussing just how many credits they would get from their wares and...wait for it...she was pretty sure *she* was one of the wares.

Heck, if she wanted to sell herself, she could have easily done so on Earth. She didn't need to be kicked straight across the universe to end up in some cage.

...Earth.

She'd give anything to go back there. Anything so she didn't have to be *here*...wherever this was.

Above her, the pink sky looked surreal, but it was a definite indication that she wasn't home anymore—unless she was on the set of some weed smoker's music video.

Another jolt of the cart she was traveling in and her forehead almost banged against the metal bars of the cage she was holding on to for stability.

"The slizz alone will get us a teruva coin," one of the aliens continued.

"What about the human?" the other asked.

Mention of her made Cleo's spine stiffen a little and she gripped the bars even tighter.

Till then, they hadn't discussed the beings they were transporting in any specific way. It'd just been talk about credits.

She hadn't even known they were aware she was human.

"Not much. It looks too frail for labor…"

There was a pause.

"Who said we had to sell it for labor? Blurgens are frail but good for pleasure."

There was another pause.

If her lungs didn't start burning, she wouldn't have realized she was holding her breath, waiting for the alien's response.

"A pleasure creature." The alien let out a disturbing laugh. "Good point."

No.

Not a good point.

Not a good point AT ALL.

The cart rattled again, and it threw her upper body against the bars. Off to her side in one of the other cages, something cried out as it collided with the metal of its own cage.

Big ole Tweedle-orc-dee and Tweedle-orc-dum didn't even glance behind them at the sound. But she didn't need their obvious nonchalance to know they didn't care.

For the entire journey, they'd sat with their huge green leathery backs turned to the many cages behind them.

They didn't seem to care that she and the other creatures in the cages were on a huge moving vibrator—only, she wasn't getting any pleasure from this ride.

The rocky road the cart traveled over shook the cart bed so much that her teeth rattled in her head.

Gripping the bars tight, Cleo squeezed her eyes shut to stop her mounting headache.

Her cage was right at the back of the cart and she could see every rock and bump the wheels rolled over. Gripping on to the bars was the only way she was avoiding getting a concussion.

"What about the fuhol?" The aliens' conversation continued.

His companion grunted. "If it survives the journey, we sell it to the dragars and buy woogli smoke."

"You should give it some of that life fluid."

The alien took a swig of what she assumed was the "life fluid" they were talking about and swallowed eagerly, gulping so hard she could hear the sound even above the noise of the cart.

The one drinking grunted again. "Waste life fluid on that ugly beast's scales? I see you're still suffering from our last time sniffing woogli smoke."

At that, they both chuckled—a horrible wheezing sound that made Cleo's blood boil.

They'd mentioned scales.

As far as she could see, there was only one creature in the cart that had scales, and it was lying in the cage across from hers.

Blue iridescent scales fanned down to fishlike fins.

It was a mermaid—or at least, an alien that looked a lot like one.

Red hair much like her own obscured the alien's face. It was a real Ariel, if she were ever going to meet one.

The mermaid's skin glittered in the sunlight, the blue moving over the scales as if the color itself was alive.

But that was the only natural-seeming movement.

Apart from the mermaid's body jerking because of its own cage rattling, it didn't move otherwise, and Cleo shuddered to think that the creature was dead.

Its four arms hung limp at its sides, and its body was set haphazardly in its cage.

The aliens' conversation took on new meaning.

3

The mermaid needed water, and they didn't care enough to let her have any.

The cart rattled again, jerking Cleo against the bars, and she accidentally bit down hard on her tongue.

God-fucking-dammit!

Tears sprung into her eyes and she tasted blood.

With that last bump of the cart, her cage shifted even closer to the edge of the cart bed and she eyed the ground below through the blur of her tears.

There was no safety barrier between her cage and the ground.

For the greater part of the journey, she'd been worried about her cage falling off the back of the cart.

All it would take was one huge jerk and off she would go.

And with every jerk, the bolts that held her cage together rattled as if they would pop right out.

Maybe they would.

She was kind of hoping on it, but she didn't want her cage to fall apart just yet.

There was nothing but rocks and dirt as far as she could see.

This would be the worst place for her to try an escape attempt.

Squeezing the tears from her eyes, Cleo's gaze moved to the other cages as she checked to see if any other creature was as alert as she was.

Farther up, closer to the front of the cart, one cage had a pile of black fur.

Earlier in the journey, she'd thought that was exactly what it was —a pile of fur like a huge rug. That was, until she saw six black eyes looking back at her.

The fur animal had its eyes closed now, but a shudder still made her skin prickle just looking at it.

Monster tarantula, maybe?

She didn't see any legs, but she didn't want to find out.

Directly to her right, another cage had a little gray animal that looked like a Chihuahua with tarsier-like eyes and a tail like a howler monkey.

Its big brown eyes blinked at her as it too gripped the bars of its cage for dear life.

The animal looked so small and innocent; it made her angry that they were keeping such a thing in a cage.

"I hope you find a nice home, little one," she murmured to the thing and she didn't know if it understood her or not, but it kept its large brown eyes on her.

There were about six other cages, all with different species—some she couldn't see because of how they were lying—but there were no other humans.

She was the only one.

The sole lucky human.

Now, if only someone could tell her which raffle she'd accidentally won for this once-in-a-lifetime trip?

She'd like to return the ticket.

Her last memory of Earth was her finishing her shift at the bar she worked at in Cali. It'd been late and she'd just hopped out of her little Toyota, ready to hurry inside her apartment when she'd felt a strange pain at the back of her neck.

Next, she'd woken up to see a slug on a blue orb and a walking alligator.

Her first thought was that she'd been drugged—what she was seeing was impossible.

Only, the drugs hadn't worn off. She was still in the nightmare.

What's worse, the alien ship they'd had her on crashed.

What happened next was a blur.

She remembered the pain and the confusion, then she remembered the reinforced room she'd been locked in being opened.

The next image in her mind was that of Tweedle-orc-dum and Tweedle-orc-dee.

But she was alive.

She wasn't on Earth anymore, the pink sky alone was proof enough of that, but she was alive.

Her father's voice rang in her head.

Cleo, you have to learn.

You have to adapt.

Then you will survive.

Cleo cast her eyes in the direction of the orcs driving the cart.

They were still nattering about something, but their voices were so low, she couldn't hear what they were saying.

The fact they weren't concerned about the cargo they were transporting was probably a good thing.

With their lack of care, she could plan an escape.

Because she *was* escaping.

There was no way she was going to be sold like a box of stew...

Stew? ... She'd fix her analogies later.

Glancing down at the road, Cleo gulped.

The plan that was hatching in her mind was going to hurt like a bitch. But, if this was how the orcs treated their "wares" before they got to their destination, she didn't have high hopes about things getting better when they actually arrived.

What's worse, she wasn't becoming anyone's pleasure pet.

So, pain it was.

She could deal with pain.

She couldn't deal with death.

As awkward as it was to move in the cage, she tried to see over the aliens' shoulders.

She couldn't see very far ahead, but she could tell the air was getting more humid.

Possibly, they were approaching a change in the terrain.

...somewhere with vegetation, maybe.

Somewhere heavily wooded, hopefully?

She could only hope they didn't turn off the road before they got there.

Glancing down to her bare feet, she swallowed hard and moved her toes a little, feeling for the item she'd found and hidden.

When her toes moved over the piece of metal, she released a breath of relief she hadn't realized she'd been holding.

She'd found the sharp piece of shrapnel behind the cage not long after the orcs had loaded her into the cart.

She'd acted quickly, taking the metal and hiding it underneath her foot, not daring to move her leg should her captors notice what she was hiding. It's not like the simple brown dress she was wearing had any pockets she could hide the weapon in.

It was almost the length of her foot, but thin. She didn't know how she was going to use it yet, but having it was better than having nothing.

As the conversation of the two aliens kept droning on in the background of her mind, she focused on the mermaid in front of her once more.

She hadn't realized it before, but the scales of the creature looked considerably lighter in color than they'd done earlier.

It was almost as if the blue within the scales was fading. What's worse, the thing still hadn't moved.

It was dead.

She was sure of it.

A spike of sadness for the creature turned into iron that strengthened her resolve.

Right.

She wasn't going to let that happen to her.

She was going to get out of this...somehow...one way or the other.

A little whimper to her right had her glancing at the Chihuahua-monkey and it blinked at her with sad eyes as if it was having the same thoughts.

"I know little guy," she whispered as the animal's big brown eyes locked on hers. "Be strong."

SHE'D BEEN RIGHT about them heading toward lots of vegetation.

First, it was just a few small orange shrubs and one and two trees, but now, on both sides, there was a fully fledged jungle filled with yellow-orange flora.

It looked like she'd been dropped into a strange magical world, and if she wasn't in her current situation, she might have stopped to appreciate the strangeness of the view.

Instead, there was only one thing on her mind—getting off the damned cart.

The road only seemed to get bumpier the deeper into the jungle they went, and they'd been traveling for so long, she could tell the sun was starting to go down.

Cleo grabbed the bars of her cage, pressing her lips together as she did.

She'd probably have one chance to do this and only one.

From the dusty road to where they were now, her cage had drifted increasingly closer to the edge of the cart. If she put her weight on it, with the next big jolt, it would topple and she'd go tumbling into the jungle beyond.

At least, that's what she was hoping would happen.

She wasn't exactly Stephen Hawking.

Her gaze moved to the dead mermaid before her, and she swallowed hard.

The alien's scales were now almost completely white—a sickly white—and the more she looked at it, the more her resolve hardened.

She needed to get off the cart.

If she *did* manage to get out, she'd make a run for it and hope no alien jaguars were waiting for her in the bushes beyond.

It was her only hope.

Her father had been a man of the wild, able to survive anywhere and in the harshest of situations.

To her, he'd been like The Crocodile Hunter.

Fearless.

Everything Thomas Barlow knew, he'd taught her.

And now, as she stared into the yellow-orange jungle before her, she knew this might be the time all those skills he'd taught her came into play.

As her cage jerked again, tipping dangerously close to the edge, Cleo's heart caught in her throat.

It was almost time.

Gripping the cage tight, her pulse beat in her throat as things her father taught her replayed in her head.

If your surroundings are harsh and dangerous, you'll have three hours to survive without shelter, Cleo.

Three hours.

Maybe a little more with this metal weapon under her foot.

Why? Because she was going to use it to stab anyone or anything that stood in her way.

If she managed to survive the fall from the cart and reach the cover of the jungle, she'd have three days to live without water.

That's three days to find water if the aliens didn't come after her.

Staring at the orcs' backs now, she worried her bottom lip between her teeth.

They were huge and looked unfit.

She could outrun them.

She was sure of it.

Her father's voice came into her head once more and she swallowed hard.

If you find water, Cleo, you'll have three weeks to survive without food.

Fuck.

What she planned to do was hard enough if she'd been lost in the wilderness on Earth.

Only an insane person would contemplate executing this stupid, stupid plan.

The aliens operating the cart obviously didn't think she was insane enough to throw herself off a moving cart. Otherwise, they would have restrained her better.

Well, they didn't know Cleo Barlow.

Another jolt of the cart pushed her cage a little closer to the edge.

It was now or never.

Eyes on the green backs of the orcs at the head of the cart, Cleo took the piece of sharp metal from underneath her foot.

She'd have to hold it in her hand and hope it didn't cut into her palm during the fall.

Bracing all her weight on the side of the cage that faced the road, she waited.

With her weight and the help of gravity, the next jolt would no doubt tip her over the edge.

Beside her, the little Chihuahua-monkey stared at her with interest, as if it knew what she was going to do.

She eyed the thing. It looked cute in a weird way, but she didn't trust it.

She didn't trust any of these aliens.

She could only hope the little creature didn't raise an alarm and cause the big green aliens to look behind them.

Just one more jolt.

Just one more jol—.

She'd been waiting for it, but it was still unexpected.

—The sudden feeling of being off-kilter.

—The cage tilting past its center of gravity.

A yelp lodged in her throat as the cage tumbled from the cart and crashed into the ground below.

The pain was immediate as she landed on her shoulder, and she grit her teeth to stop from screaming.

Luck must have been on her side because the cage was rolling. Where she'd fallen off the cart was sloped ground and the metal contraption tumbled into the bushes.

She was vaguely aware of being thrown all around and not knowing which side was up or down. Her head banged against the bars and the sharp piece of metal she was holding dug into her palm.

Dizziness overtook her before the cage crashed into the side of a tree.

There was a searing pain in her head and her knee, and Cleo groaned as she tried to get her bearings.

The world felt upside down, as if gravity was not the right way around, and she soon realized why when the smell of soil drifted into her nose. Her head was against the bars now pressing into the soil and her hair was over her face, obstructing her view.

The soil had a strange metallic smell, not like the dirt on Earth, and it helped make her focus.

Still, it took her a few moments to realize her plan had worked.

Fuck, it'd worked!

A shout somewhere in the distance, no doubt from one of the green aliens, had her jerking into action.

The bars.

She had to force the bars free.

With the piece of metal in her hand, Cleo spun onto her back, her gaze moving over the bars at the top to spot one of the slackened bolts she'd seen earlier.

All she had to do was lodge the sharp metal she'd found between the bolt and the metal bar and hope to God phase two of her plan worked.

She could hear the aliens somewhere in the jungle arguing stupidly with each other, in no haste to chase after her.

Their mistake.

She'd be gone before they found her.

She only had to break free now.

As soon as she managed to lodge the metal between the bolt, she braced her legs against the bars at the top of the cage.

Straining, she pushed as hard as she could, willing the cage to budge even a little.

Her leg muscles protested with the effort, but the bars didn't even shift.

Goddamnit.

She couldn't fail now. Not this close to freedom.

Pushing harder, she willed all her strength into her legs as she applied more force to the bars. Her back was pressing into the bars below her, her spine against one of the bars themselves, and it felt as if she was going to cripple herself.

But she couldn't give up.

She couldn't.

She could do this.

She heard the alien's voices again, and this time they seemed closer.

"It must have rolled this way."

"You find it. I'll dump the dead fuhol. Looks like the slizz is dead too. Phekking, draxx. That's a teruva coin lost. I'll have to dump it as well."

"Why do I have to go for the human jekin?" It sounded like he was whining.

"You want to dump the dead ones then?" the other answered.

There was a disgruntled sound, and she assumed the alien was dragging his feet as he headed her way.

She had no idea how far she had tumbled, but she was sure they'd find her shortly if she didn't get her ass out of the frickin' cage!

But no matter how hard she pushed, the bolt wouldn't disengage.

In pure frustration, Cleo kicked the bars and the cells rattled. They rattled so hard, the sound echoed into the quiet jungle—but they budged a little.

She could hear the rustle of leaves as the green alien approached and she began kicking, not caring that she was making noise now.

She needed to get out.

She almost lost her balance as a part of the bar bent outward, the bolt flying off. The sharp piece of metal she'd lodged in the spot fell back on her chest, and she stared at the open space in shock.

It was open.

Open enough for her to squeeze through.

She didn't hesitate.

Righting herself as best as she could, she grabbed the sharp piece of metal and hoisted herself up.

Her head and shoulders fit through the space as she pulled herself through. Bracing her arms on the outside of the cage, she pulled her legs through next.

The sound of the bushes rustling was really close now.

He was coming.

She just about jumped from the top of the cage when she saw one of the burly green aliens appear through the undergrowth.

His eyes met hers and his giant maw opened in surprise.

Incompetent fool.

She couldn't help the glimmer of mischief and triumph that she knew appeared in her eyes.

They'd underestimated her. Costly mistake.

Without so much as a backward glance, Cleo began running.

Running for life.

Running for freedom.

And hopefully not running toward a sooner death than the one she'd been fated for before.

Behind her, she heard a loud cry that sounded suspiciously like one of the aliens being attacked by something fierce.

There was a rustle of bushes, but she wasn't looking back and she was stopping for nothing.

And so she ran.

She ran as fast as her weak legs could take her.

She didn't stop when branches ripped into her dress or when she stumbled over roots and fell.

She kept going.

Deeper into the jungle she went, as far away from the alien captors as she could reach. And when her lungs and her legs couldn't take it anymore, she stumbled, falling against the thick trunk of a tree.

Sliding down against the tree, Cleo leaned her back against it and sat on the ground.

It didn't sound like he was pursuing her.

She must have lost him.

That thought brought a feeling of relief and hanging right on to the tail end of it was a surge of fear.

Now what?

What's the next stage of the plan, Cleo?

Problem was, there was no plan.

She'd half expected her effort to free herself from the cage to fail.

Chest heaving as she took deep breaths, she tried breathing through her nose slowly and evenly so she could focus on listening.

At the back of her mind, there was the pressing thought that night was approaching.

She needed to find shelter.

Y-shaped branches, Cleo. Her father's voice rang true.

If she could find some branches of that type, she'd be able to create some kind of shelter on the ground.

As she began searching for the branches, she froze.

She could feel it—it was an unmistakable feeling, a sort of sixth sense—the knowledge that *something* was watching her.

That sixth sense had served her well for twenty-five years; she wasn't going to question it now.

As the hairs at the back of her neck stood on end, Cleo spun around slowly, the piece of metal she still gripped pointing outward.

Her eyes scanned the orange bushes, looking for a spot of green that would tell her the green alien had crept up on her without her hearing.

But there was none.

Nevertheless, the bushes moved a little and it wasn't because of the wind.

There was something there.

As the bushes rustled some more, Cleo took a step backward, fear crawling up her back.

A bunch of hanging leaves moved and a head popped out.

For a few moments, she just stared at the thing.

It was the Chihuahua-monkey.

The animal stopped moving and blinked at her with its large brown eyes.

It remained unmoving as it looked from the sharp piece of metal to her and back.

They stood like that for a few minutes, each unsure of what the other would do, until she slowly lowered her weapon.

She didn't realize the animal was tense until its pointed ears flattened and it sat on its haunches, watching her.

How it escaped its cage on the cart, she didn't know.

But it was obvious it had followed her through the bushes.

"Hey," she murmured to the animal, and its ears perked again.

Crouching, she stared at it.

"What are you doing here?"

The animal tilted its head at her, but it didn't make a sound.

Taking a step toward the thing, and against her better judgment, she outstretched her hand toward it, staying just far enough away that she'd be able to pull her hand back if it tried to bite her.

The animal's nostrils twitched as if it was smelling her, and then it moved cautiously toward her hand and paused.

She was just about to pull her hand back when it bumped the back of its head against her palm, much in the way a cat would.

A smile she didn't expect spread across her lips as the animal moved closer to rub its head into her palm some more.

That one movement settled the anxiety that had been growing within her.

"You're just lost too, aren't you," she murmured, and when the animal paused rubbing against her to blink its huge brown eyes at her, she smiled again.

It *was* lost. Just like she was.

"You look so innocent..." She studied the little thing. It was innocent and cute, and that pulled on her heart. "I'm going to take care of you."

It was a promise.

"I'm going to take care of you and me, little Chihuahua-monkey."

When the animal simply bumped her palm with its head once more, Cleo smiled again.

Three hours without shelter, Cleo.

Three days without water.

Three weeks without food.

She could do this.

She was Cleo Barlow, Thomas Barlow's spawn.

She'd been trained to face the odds and survive.

1

Present day
(Over a year later)

Walking through the undergrowth, following a path she'd now memorized, Cleo made her way to her lookout spot high up on the side of the mountain.

From there, she could see the road that cut through the jungle. It was the same bumpy road the orcs had been transporting her on so, so long ago.

Sometimes she saw carts rattling through, and the sight of them always sent her back to that day when she'd escaped.

Taking a deep breath now, she settled in the bushes, her gaze on what she could see of the road.

There were no travelers now—not that she could see—but she still remained hidden.

Such was her routine.

She made it a point to surveil the area at least three times a day without fail.

It was the only way she could keep tabs on her surroundings while remaining relatively safe.

Crouching low, she scanned the area far below.

Many times, she'd seen vehicles passing through, but never had the occupants ever spotted her.

She'd taken precautions for that.

If anyone happened to look in her direction, she was sure they wouldn't see her.

The mud she'd daubed over her body stuck to her like a second skin.

She blended into her surroundings like a gecko.

Camouflage, bitches.

Eyes narrowing, she kept scanning the area. Parts of the road were obscured by the vegetation, but she could see enough spots to tell what was happening down there from her particular location. And so, she kept an eye out for any movement.

On several occasions, she was sure she saw the green aliens that had been transporting her on that fateful day.

For over a year, they kept returning—she assumed, to search for her. But they never, ever ventured far into the jungle.

They always kept close to the road.

As a matter of fact, of the many carts she spotted taking the jungle road, none of the aliens ever stopped and entered the jungle itself.

She didn't mind. No intruders meant she was relatively safe, and safety meant she could live free.

And, surprisingly, she had been safe. So far, she'd encountered no dangerous animals lurking in the underbrush.

She sometimes heard them though...far in the distance, though they never ventured close enough for her to meet one.

And she wasn't curious enough to go looking for one either.

Gazing from the lookout spot, her eyes moved over the yellow-orange plant life.

Spots of purple and pink flowers dotted the yellow-orange, making the scene look like some sort of wonderland.

She was a modern-day Tarzan. She even had her own little pet monkey.

As if he knew she was thinking of him, the little Chihuahua-monkey stood upright on her shoulder and rubbed his head against her neck.

"Hey, Wawa," she breathed and he bumped his head against her gently.

He was her constant companion, the little soft thing, keeping her company when she'd otherwise have gone mad.

Balancing on his four legs, Wawa stretched his neck as his ears perked.

"What do you see, boy?" Cleo whispered, her gaze moving back to the road.

Wawa seemed focused on something at the bottom of the mountain, and it took her a few moments before she saw movement through the undergrowth too.

A vehicle of some sort was on the road.

Now and then it would go out of view, hidden behind the foliage, and then it would pop back into the open.

Her heart stilled a little and she didn't know why.

This vehicle was different from the others she was used to seeing.

It looked like a stocky milk carton on wheels—not like the usual carts that drivers traveled these parts in.

As the vehicle came to a stop, she eased forward a little, her eyes widening even as her brows dived toward her nose.

Vehicles didn't usually stop.

They were too afraid of those sounds she'd heard deeper in the jungle.

For a few seconds, she waited for the vehicle to continue on, but nothing happened.

That made her stiffen.

From the distance, visibility wasn't at its peak, but she could see enough to tell it was her original captors—either them, or more of their kind. Their green bodies were clearly identifiable in the transparent front windows of the vehicle.

But something wasn't right.

They weren't exiting the vehicle, but neither were they moving on.

Regardless that they'd failed at finding her for so long, it still made her anxiety rise whenever they came looking for her.

At first, she'd considered moving farther into the jungle but two things hindered that:

1. Dangerous things lived in the jungle's depths. She'd take their roars for a warning.

2. She wasn't an idiot to not realize she'd found the perfect spot to live in.

With Wawa's help, she'd found shelter, food, and water.

She had a comfortable house, the weather was good, she didn't go hungry and she had her own private pool.

The logic of survival demanded that she stay put unless she was *forced* to leave.

So whenever the green orcs came around, it made her anxiety rise. Life in the wild was as perfect as it was going to get. Leaving to venture deeper would most likely cost her the one thing she wasn't willing to give up: her life.

She didn't know how she'd been so lucky to survive this long but her luck hadn't run out and she was thankful for that.

Eyes still on the vehicle far below, Cleo watched for any movement.

For a good few minutes. There was none.

Usually, the green orcs would be out of the vehicle already and would be searching the undergrowth close to the road for any sign of her.

Instead, they were still in the vehicle.

Squinting so she could focus, she was sure they were moving their heads as if arguing about something.

A few more minutes passed before the vehicle opened and a figure stepped out.

It was a different type of alien entirely.

She couldn't make out the species clearly, but it certainly wasn't one of the orc idiots.

This alien was tall and...blue.

And yes, it was a he.

It had to be.

Even from the distance, she could tell the alien was male.

A tall, blue alien male.

He was humanoid in the fact he had two arms and two legs, broad shoulders...

Staring so hard, Cleo forgot to blink, and when the alien turned to scan the mountain on which she hid, she flattened herself almost immediately.

He was looking directly at her!

Surely he couldn't see her.

Cleo froze, not daring to move.

On her shoulder, Wawa stiffened too, almost as if he could feel her anxiety.

That was a coincidence, wasn't it?

The alien *couldn't* see her. Could he?

Her breath was stuck in her throat in the few seconds that the alien looked in her direction.

Shit.

Shit shit shit shit shit.

He was there for her.

She didn't know how she knew it, but she did.

This man, whoever he was, was there for *her.*

Anxiety began crawling up her spine and something in the back of her mind was telling her to run straight back to her cave, pack everything she could carry, and retreat deeper into the jungle without a backward glance. It would have to be a toss-up between facing this dude and facing the wild animals that roared in the nighttime.

Staring at the blue alien, the feeling building within her suddenly became overwhelming.

This was more than slight anxiety—his mere presence was creating full-on panic.

The big blue alien turned back to the vehicle and she got the impression he was talking to the green orcs.

That only took a few seconds before he slung a bag over his shoulders, turned from the vehicle, and disappeared into the undergrowth.

Eyes wide, Cleo watched as the vehicle pulled away.

They were leaving him?!

...

FUCK.

...

She couldn't breathe.

Somewhere deep inside her, there was a feeling of impending doom.

Trust your gut, Cleo. Her father's voice echoed in her head.

Trust your gut.

Her instincts never failed her before. They wouldn't fail her now.

This wasn't like all the other times the orcs had come looking for her.

This time, shit was different.

That big blue alien was trouble. She could feel it.

As she moved away from the lookout spot, hurrying through the bushes, Wawa remained alert on her shoulder and that alone sent a shiver down her spine.

The only other time Wawa had stiffened on her shoulder in such a way was in their first few weeks in the jungle.

If he was alert...if he was *worried*...it meant she wasn't over-reacting.

He knew that a dangerous enemy was near too.

2

"Reckless fools," Sohut muttered as he turned and headed into the dense growth of the great Koznia Jungle.

He doubted the Gori who'd dropped him off heard his remark. They were too busy driving away, rushing as far as they could from the trouble they'd gotten themselves into.

Not that what he'd said wasn't the truth.

The Gori were reckless fools.

Only idiots would have lost an animal the way they had done. To boot, they'd failed to retrieve the creature after so many moons.

His ears pressed flat against the sides of his head, the only indication of his annoyance.

He couldn't imagine the pure terror the animal must have experienced all alone in an alien world—and in the Koznia Jungle to add.

It must have been incredibly frightened before it died.

Shaking his head, Sohut walked slowly through the undergrowth as he contemplated this.

The Gori thought the creature was still alive.

He highly doubted that. A non-native species being lost in the Koznia Jungle was highly unlikely to survive.

The spined beasts alone would have quickly made the thing their dinner many rotations ago.

But no matter. If he didn't find the animal alive, he was sure there'd be *something* he could use to prove to the Gori the creature was indeed dead.

It's bones, maybe.

Senses primed as he made his way through the undergrowth, he scanned and noted everything even as he stepped over the twisting vines, shrubs, and small fallen trees in his path.

To any animals peering at him from their nests, he looked like a harmless visitor strolling through their domain.

To anyone who knew him well, they'd know that he was on the prowl.

Nothing escaped him.

Every slight movement of the leaves, he saw.

Every slight sound, he heard.

He was very aware of the tuli birds in their nests above him, silently watching, and the little zideks blending in with the bushes as he walked by. But he made no indication he knew they were there.

They were safe from him.

After all, he wasn't hunting *them*. He was hunting something different entirely.

Something that was probably already dead but...

Sohut perked his ears, ducking under some hanging branches as he did. So close to the road, he was probably safe, but the deeper he ventured into the jungle, the more dangerous it would become.

The beasts of Koznia didn't like intruders. Because of this, the jungle was untouched except for the reckless Torians that lived in its center.

Out here was...freedom.

It was so different from the Sanctuary he called home with his brother, Riv...different from the mines they'd grown up in too. The Sanctuary was free but out here was a sense of natural freedom you could only get if you went out into the wild.

It was unpredictable.

There was no routine to things, no restrictions.

Out here...he could forget for a few moments.

He could be of use.

Out here, he wasn't a mistake.

He could pretend he wasn't the reason his brother had endured so much.

Pretend his very birth hadn't been a curse upon his family.

He could forget he was the reason all things had gone to hell.

It was probably the reason he liked taking these jobs.

Where Riv preferred staying within the perimeter of the Sanctuary tending to the animals they cared for, he liked taking jobs such as this one that took him all over Hudo III.

They reminded him that he was alive, gave him purpose.

Back at the Sanctuary, Riv handled almost everything with precision. Riv didn't need his help or his company. His brother only tolerated him because they were blood.

And so, he spent most of his time away, taking odd jobs all across the planet.

This was just one of them and he'd do what he was hired to do.

He'd hunt the thing, find his evidence, collect his payment, and head back to the Sanctuary he called home.

Repeating the description of the animal through his mind, Sohut kept his eyes peeled.

The Gori said the creature had red fur covering its head, running down its shoulders and its back. Otherwise, it was pale and hairless all over, with long spindly legs, translucent eyes, and a flat face.

It was not like any animal he'd ever seen before.

And, he had to admit, it sounded quite...*strange-looking*.

He imagined it ran on all four legs and, for that reason, he surveyed the ground as he walked, looking for any strange paw prints in the areas where soft ground was exposed—just in case he was wrong and the thing still lived.

Absentmindedly, his forefinger moved over the single rectangular device that he held in his hand; the dark button at the top glistened whenever it caught the light.

It was a tracker, coded with the creature's DNA and programmed to restrain the animal with an energy band once activated.

It'd been a long time since he'd seen such a device, and he frowned now as he glanced down at it.

This particular tracker was a device used mainly by the High Tasqals in the Great Wars when the Tasqals had gone about enslaving whole worlds. A master race, the Tasqals called themselves, and they always had the strangest technology.

The tech he now held was rare.

How the Gori got their hands on it was a whole different question.

Never mind that—he reached back and slipped the tracker into his satchel—he doubted he'd need to use it anyway.

PAUSING FOR A BIT, Sohut looked up into the leaves and vines strung in their intricate natural patterns above.

He'd been walking for some time now, and the dark cycle was almost upon him, but the farther he went into the jungle, the more a feeling of unease began settling over him—and it wasn't because of the beasts he knew lurked in the shadows.

Long, long ago when he'd realized his love for tracking things, he'd gotten his nostril sensors enhanced and, now, the entire time he'd been walking, he'd been picking up a scent.

The scent was in such a pattern he was sure it was some kind of animal marking its territory.

The problem was, it smelled like...slizz.

He knew what his nose was telling him...but it was highly unlikely...almost impossible even, that he was right.

Slizz were rare.

They were like myths.

He'd only met one slizz once and it had been on the other side of Hudo III, right before it had killed three men and almost killed him too if it hadn't been shot down.

He wouldn't ever forget the smell of a creature that terrible, but he *had* to be mistaken.

What would a slizz be doing in the Koznia Jungle?

He had to be wrong.

Narrowing his eyes, he swatted some hanging leaves out of the way as he continued walking through the undergrowth.

He was trying to ignore the scent but couldn't. His instincts wouldn't allow him to.

Cursing underneath his breath, he began following the trail the scent marked.

Right through most of the dark cycle, he followed the scent around the mountain in a huge circuit that spanned even some flat areas at the base of the elevation.

Like an invisible barrier, it was warning all the creatures that dwelled in these parts that this was its territory.

And it was a clear warning—one he shouldn't ignore.

But he was Sohut U'xol Cal-Pholy...problem was...he *couldn't* ignore it.

Something deep within him told him the scent marking wasn't coincidental.

What were the chances of him tracking an alien creature only to find territory marked with the scent of slizz?

Pausing in the darkness, he lifted his head to look up at the trees before him that were rising up the mountainside.

Whatever he was hunting must have a direct correlation with this "defense" barrier.

He just *knew* it.

Dropping his satchel, Sohut paused at the edge of this invisible barrier. His ears pricked from the sides of his head as he listened for any sound.

Nothing.

If it was a slizz, he wasn't going to enter its territory in the dark. That would put him at a disadvantage.

Resting against the root of a huge tree, he knew what he was going to do.

The slizz's scent would keep the other predators of the jungle at bay, for now.

That meant he could rest for the dark cycle and cross the barrier when the sun rose.

A little sliver of excitement ran through him at the thought.

There was something across that barrier—something worth finding.

He could feel it as well as he could feel the frilli on his nose.

3

It'd been a day since, against his better judgment, he'd crossed the scent barrier.

Since then, the scent had steadily faded, making him believe he'd been right about it being a perimeter marking.

As he walked now, the terrain was rising on an incline. He was climbing the mountain and the farther inland he went, the more that feeling of something huge happening increased.

Walking through the undergrowth, he kept going for a few moments when his steps halted.

Yet, he wasn't quite sure why.

Turning his nose to the air, Sohut sniffed.

There was a smell in the air...a new scent...different from the territory-marking scent yet still somewhat mingled with it.

The smell was faint; so faint, he almost missed it.

For a few moments, he stood unmoving, processing the scent as it flowed into his nostrils.

It wasn't a spined creature or a mog.

It wasn't a tuli or a zidek.

It wasn't a fruiting or flowering plant...

This was the smell of a creature.

A strange creature.

Something alien.

The scent was a few days old but there was enough of it for him to know he'd never scented anything like it before.

Thank Raxu for the lack of wind under the canopy or the smell might have been too faint for him to notice.

Blinking rapidly, Sohut's brows furrowed and his ears stood up from the sides of his head as he scanned the bushes around him.

He knew he was alone...at least, as alone as he could be with the animals in the jungle around him.

No creature had crept close enough to him without him realizing it.

He still scanned the bushes anyway, his frown deepening when he finally lined up with the direction in which the scent was strongest.

Inhaling deeply, his ears perked even more as he processed just what he was scenting.

Maybe the Gori had been right.

He couldn't believe it...but maybe the creature they'd sent him to find still lived.

As he inhaled deeply once more, he took a step forward only to pause again, his eyes widening.

A curse slipped from his lips.

The creature was female.

Somehow, he knew that fact with clarity.

Phek.

Undeniably female.

Taking another breath, a groan rumbled in his chest that had him stiffening for another reason.

Horror couldn't describe what he was suddenly feeling as his gaze slowly fell.

The phlickin' phek?

Pressing against his trousers was his...*phekking draxx*...he was solid and hard.

His lips pulled back in a snarl, his fangs baring.

He was aroused by the *scent* of an alien *creature?*

Raxu in the phekking stars.

30

Growling underneath his breath, he stretched the muscles in his back, more than slightly perturbed by this occurrence.

This was something that never, ever happened before and he sure as phek wasn't going to acknowledge it.

Pushing the disturbing thoughts from his mind, he focused on his task and the scent that was drawing him farther into the dense growth.

Time to do the job he was hired to do.

It'd been three days.

Three days since she'd seen the blue alien enter the jungle.

Three days since she's been hiding in her cave.

It was the best place for her to remain out of reach but whenever she peeked through the vines and leaves covering the entrance to the cave, she didn't spot anything out of the ordinary happening in the jungle below.

But that was little consolation.

Whenever she looked out, she was looking over the tops of trees.

That didn't tell her what lurked beneath their branches.

Nevertheless, if she hadn't seen the blue alien enter the jungle with her own two eyes, she wouldn't have known he was somewhere within the dense growth.

Nothing seemed out of place and the thought made her uneasy.

She could have easily gone hunting for food and encountered the stranger.

Unaware of his presence beforehand, she'd have been at a huge disadvantage.

Cleo paced, her bare feet moving over the thick dried grass she'd laid as flooring on the rock floor.

She could make a run for it.

Fear was telling her to escape but there was just one problem.

Logic said she should stay.

And she was going to listen to logic.

On her shoulder, Wawa bumped his head against her neck as if he could sense her restlessness.

Living by herself for an extended period could have made her paranoid.

Maybe they hadn't sent the blue alien after her.

Maybe he'd entered the jungle in search of something or someone else?

Maybe she was just overreacting…

But there was that niggling feeling inside her that told her she wasn't overreacting.

He was there for *her*.

She was sure of it.

And what was she doing? She was waiting like a sitting duck.

If he somehow found her, she'd be caught without any defenses.

She needed to do something.

Taking a deep breath, she crouched by the small mouth of her cave and looked out.

There was a safe distance in her mind that the alien shouldn't cross, and that was an invisible line she drew right at her water hole. If he crossed that line, then she was in trouble.

He'd no doubt find her.

It'd take him some time to do so—her cave wasn't the easiest to spot—but she couldn't stay in her little hidey-hole for weeks on end.

She'd starve to death, but realistically, she'd probably die of thirst first.

Biting her bottom lip, she looked out into the jungle.

If the alien came close, she'd have to get rid of him.

There was no other choice.

Well, there was another choice but that one involved her getting eaten—and not in the way that would make her scream in pleasure.

Cleo's shoulders slumped as she let out a huge breath.

She couldn't sit and wait.

She had to go out.

If he was coming for her, the least she could do was try to defend herself.

CREEPING through the jungle was difficult when trying to be completely silent.

The dried leaves and branches she stepped on screamed like she weighed a ton.

Still, she mostly managed to be quiet.

And with Wawa on her shoulder, it was easy to not get caught.

She knew he'd become alert if they came too close to anything dangerous to them—blue guy included.

Hurrying through the bushes, she clutched the bones she'd gathered to her chest.

They were the bones of a large animal, she was sure.

Months ago when she'd first come upon them, Wawa had seemed disturbed and a plan had hatched in her mind immediately.

She'd use the bones if she ever had to defend her territory.

Because this was her territory now.

It was her and Wawa's home.

She wasn't going to let those green orcs take it away from her.

Taking a wide arc, she dropped the bones in random places, partially covering some with dirt and fallen leaves so it looked natural and not like she'd just put them there.

On her shoulder, Wawa watched her with interest, but he didn't seem alert to any danger.

Still, she hurried.

If this plan didn't work...if the alien didn't see the bones and assume some dangerous beast lived on the mountain, then she'd have to get rid of him somehow while he rested.

Cleo gulped.

She really hoped it didn't get to that.

She wasn't sure she could kill someone and live with her conscience.

As she set down the last bone, she didn't dare to even wait to catch a breath.

Hurrying back to where she had even more bones stashed, she grabbed what was left and began distributing them.

She was almost done when, suddenly, Wawa had stiffened on her shoulder, his gaze focused on the bushes ahead of them.

A cold chill went down Cleo's spine.

She didn't question it; she just moved in the opposite direction, heading for a foliage-covered ledge that overlooked this section of jungle.

That ledge was the one spot before the intruder came too close to her home and she prayed he'd turn back before then.

Running as quickly as her legs could take her, she dashed through the undergrowth.

Her bare feet moved over the uneven ground with ease, having had many months for the soles of her feet to harden. She didn't pause to take a breath before she climbed atop the ledge, crawling on her belly as she settled herself.

And she was glad she didn't falter because her gaze soon caught blue.

The frickin' alien was heading her way.

4

THE SCENT OF THE CREATURE WAS GROWING STRONGER AND SOHUT stopped to inhale deeply.

Now that the scent was stronger, he could definitely say it wasn't anything he'd ever smelled before.

Pausing, his ears perked as he scanned the area again.

Something white against the mud-orange earth caught his eyes and his gaze zoomed to the piece of bone protruding from the ground.

Moving over to the animal's remains, he crouched and ran a finger against the whitened bone.

It was old and judging from the part of skull he could see, it was the bone of a great tym.

This tym died a long, long time ago.

But that wasn't the problem.

The problem was that the only thing that could kill a tym in this jungle was a spined creature.

Pulling on the bone, it dislodged from the earth easily, a little too easily, and he turned it over in his hands.

The tell-tale teeth indentations left by when the spined creature buried its maw into the tym's head were still there.

Frowning, Sohut paused to study the bushes around him.

He hadn't scented any spined creatures. At least, not since he'd crossed that invisible barrier days ago.

If there was one, it had to be higher up on the mountain.

Setting the bone down, he stood, his tail swishing low on the ground behind him.

This was the point when many trackers would turn around and leave.

A spined creature wasn't something to play around with and he would gladly live his life without ever encountering one.

Still...

Taking a deep breath, he sniffed the air again.

The alien creature's scent was still there.

How could something frail coexist on the mountain with a spined creature close by?

He felt like continuing if only he could answer that question alone.

Readjusting his satchel, his ears perked as he continued on his way.

He was walking for a few more meters when he spotted another bone.

This one looked like a thigh bone and it was cracked in several places.

Possibly, it was another victim of the spined creature or the same one. He wasn't sure.

Frowning down at the bone, he touched the earth beside it.

It was soft. Soft enough to make him believe the bone had been buried and that made him frown.

Tuli sometimes buried animal bones, so he didn't know why this occurrence particularly struck him as strange.

Still frowning, his gaze searched the canopy above.

He was either walking into a spined creature's territory or something else was amiss.

For a few moments, he considered turning back.

He could tell the Gori they'd lost their creature. He could even bring one of the tym bones as proof; they wouldn't know the difference.

If it was any other hunter, that's what they would do.

But...he wasn't any other hunter...and that was the difference.

There was a thrill building inside him, a sort of dangerous excitement, and the farther he walked, the more it grew.

He was either going to discover something big or he was going to pay with his own blood.

The latter option should worry him more—only, it didn't.

5

SHE WAS FLAT ON HER STOMACH AND COVERED WITH SO MANY VINES AND leaves, she could feel their weight on her back.

She'd been the one to string the vines and leaves together to resemble a ghillie suit—only, it was more like a blanket. It'd been part of her preparations should a situation like this ever occur and boy was she happy she'd gone through the trouble to do it now.

Fully covered by vines and leaves, she was sure she was as camouflaged as an anaconda in a marsh.

Heart beating hard in her chest, Cleo watched as the alien moved slowly through the undergrowth.

It was like the motherfucker knew exactly where she was.

He was heading right in her direction.

Lying flat on a ledge a few levels above the jungle floor, her eyes tracked the blue alien as he headed up the mountain.

Through the leaves, she spotted something in his hands.

A bone, one that looked suspiciously similar to the bones she'd scattered.

Obviously, her warning didn't work.

Motherfucker.

Who would willingly walk farther into a place that was littered with bones?

She knew she sure as hell wouldn't, but maybe this idiot was a psycho and she'd judged him wrong.

Goddamnit.

Shit.

She was running out of options.

On her shoulder, Wawa stiffened, his eyes on the spots of blue peeking out from behind the leaves as the alien moved through the undergrowth.

To her horror, Wawa began moving forward.

Jerking him back, she stared at Wawa in dismay, shaking her head as viciously as she could manage without rustling the bushes.

It was a silent "what-the-fuck-are-you-thinking-sit-yo-ass-down" sort of look.

Wawa paused and blinked at her before settling against her again.

It seemed he understood 'wide-eye speak' and Cleo released the breath she'd been holding as smoothly as she could.

Turning her gaze back to the trees below, she looked for the alien again.

For a few seconds, her heart stopped beating when she couldn't see any blue.

Fuck.

She'd lost him.

Biting her lip, she searched the undergrowth below with frantic movements of her eyes and when she finally spotted the alien male, a lump formed in her throat.

He was closer now.

She could mostly see the top of his dark head as he moved, and she soon realized he was heading in the direction of a particularly dangerous tree.

And she called it dangerous for one reason.

There was a feisty bird that lived in that tree and she only knew because she'd made the mistake of venturing near one too many times.

It was a huge yellow thing that reminded her of Big Bird from Sesame Street. Only, it wasn't as nice.

It was more of a bitch bird than Big Bird.

The first time she'd made the mistake of going near its tree, the bird had shit on her head. And it wasn't like normal bird poop. This bird had the ass of a grown man.

It had taken her weeks to get the scent out of her hair.

The second time she'd walked too close, the bird had chased her. And it was HUGE. It almost clawed off her scalp as she ran away.

There hadn't been a third time.

She'd gotten the point and made sure she never walked close to its home ever again.

Now, the alien neared it and she lost sight of him again, just when he reached near the tree.

Perking her ears, she stopped breathing completely as she listened.

Then she heard a loud screech as the entire tree shook.

A grin split her face.

Maybe she didn't have to worry about getting rid of the alien herself. Maybe nature would do it for her.

There was another loud screech and the undeniable sound of huge wings flapping.

Then something else happened.

Far, far in the distance, was one of those terrible roars she often heard.

Wawa stiffened.

This time, he didn't wait. He darted off in the direction of the roar and she had to bite back a shout.

The fuck was happening?

There was thrashing and a chorus of birds squawking as they took flight from the nearby trees. She wasn't sure if it was because of the roar she'd just heard in the distance or because bitch-bird was currently having blue alien for dinner.

Frozen and unsure what to do, she was sure she heard a shout then a groan.

Both were low, because it was far away, but she was sure that's what she heard.

Cleo's eyes widened.

She'd have to find Wawa later.

Hopefully, he hadn't run toward the sound of that creature and he'd just scented some of the jungle-penguins they both ate for food.

Now, she had bigger things on her plate.

Still, she remained frozen, not daring to move. But as the minutes ticked by and there was no sign of the alien, her confidence grew.

Had...had it worked?

Had the bird really taken the alien down?

Forcing herself to stand, she did what her legs felt suddenly too weak to do.

She crept from the ledge and headed toward the scene of what might well be death by bird.

She'd just have to risk poop falling on her head again just to find out.

CREEPING through the bushes as silently as she could, Cleo made her way from the ledge toward bitch-bird's tree.

She stopped when she was a few meters away from it.

She didn't want to go closer.

Everything in her body was rebelling, but she had to know if the alien was dead.

Her survival depended on it.

As she peeked through the bushes at the tree, she frowned.

She couldn't see much but...there was no one there.

Shit.

She'd have to go closer.

Taking a deep breath, she pulled up her invisible big girl pants and crept closer through the bushes.

The blue alien was missing and there was no bird.

Panic flooded her immediately and she wished Wawa was close so she could use his unique senses to tell if anyone was around.

That's when she heard another groan.

Taking a deep breath, she ventured closer.

Peeking through the leaves, she spotted what she was looking for.

Blue skin contrasted with orange flora and on top of the alien was the huge yellow bird.

The bird seemed to be struggling and flapping its wings, trying to rise. In the process, it was battering the alien beneath it.

For a few moments, she wasn't sure what she was seeing.

She wasn't sure if the alien was dead but then he groaned again. The sound only seemed to incite the bird even more as it flapped its wings harder.

She was also pretty sure it'd dug a claw into the alien's skull.

In the next moment, the bird seemed to shake itself free and took flight, rising into the air and leaving the alien behind.

Cleo's eyes widened.

The alien lay motionless, his eyes closed and a bloody wound was on his forehead.

Her pulse hammered in her ears.

Was he dead? Dying?

Her question was soon answered when the alien groaned and sat up, his hand going to the wound on his head.

Cleo stiffened, moving behind the leaves even more as she watched him.

She was close. Probably too close.

Close enough for her to notice the alien's broad shoulders and the fact he was obviously lean.

The simple white shirt he wore was thin. Thin enough for her to see the definition through it and her eyes widened a little bit more.

As her eyes moved up his body, the lump in her throat grew to golf-ball size and she fought to swallow it down.

The alien had a strong, defined jaw and even as she watched him now, she could see the muscles ticking there.

He was agitated?

Well, welcome to the club.

His brows were furrowed and she couldn't see his eyes but he was scowling at the blood now on his hands.

His nose was a little wider than a human's, the bridge appearing flatter than normal, and every now and again, it twitched, giving the impression he was sniffing.

His head of dark hair, black like oil, was tied on top of his head and out of the way but that only brought attention to his surprisingly handsome face.

Of all the things she'd anticipated, she hadn't expected that the hunter would be attractive.

Not that it mattered.

She still had to get rid of him, or away from him, before he got rid of her.

With one startling movement, the alien yanked at his shirt, ripping a part of it away.

Staring as if mesmerized, she watched as he reached into his bag for a tube and squeezed some of the contents on the wound. Then, he bandaged it.

A sinking feeling developed in her chest.

He wasn't leaving.

This wasn't enough to make him leave.

As anxiety began to build within her once more, the alien stood and turned slightly to retrieve his bag.

Behind him, something swished.

He...he had a tail.

A furless tail except for a patch of dark hair at the end—much like a lion's tail was.

Forcing herself low in the bushes, she held her breath as the alien began moving once more.

His steps were light, almost as if he was floating across the ground, and if she wasn't looking directly at him, she wouldn't have known he was there.

Not even a twig snapped with each step he took, and the leaves hardly moved as he brushed past them—even the air seemed undisturbed.

Like the reaper, he was. Coming for her silently.

The last thing she'd expected was that she'd find the reaper that came for her attractive.

Frowning at herself for noticing his looks instead of focusing on the fact that he had come to frickin' catch or kill her, Cleo grit her teeth.

He was heading in the opposite direction, so at least that was good.

It would buy her some time so she could find a way to save herself.

She was thinking about this when the alien stopped walking suddenly and sniffed the air.

At the same time, the bushes rustled to the alien's right and some of the little jungle-penguins she used for food walked out in front of him.

They stopped to look up at him in much the same way they'd stopped in front of her the first time she'd met their kind.

They were such innocent animals, and for that, she hated having to use them for food.

Only, she didn't have a choice.

She couldn't exactly live on the flora of the jungle.

She wasn't stupid enough to try.

That would have been the fastest way for her to get poisoned and die.

Number one rule of living in the wilderness: Never try the plants unless you know them.

Wawa was content with eating the little birds too, so it worked out for both of them.

Now, the family of jungle-penguins stood in front of the alien and Cleo found she was holding her breath as her eyes moved back to him, wondering what he was going to do.

Only, his gaze wasn't on the little birds.

As a matter of fact, it didn't seem as if he even saw the animals.

Something about the way he was standing, unmoving, made every hair on the back of her neck grow legs and stand up to look at him too.

That was all the warning she got before he spun and looked right in her direction.

What the actual fu—

Even from so far away, she could see his eyes were a brilliant, captivating green.

Fuck.

44

She was far enough away that he shouldn't be able to see her.

Yet, there was not a doubt in her mind that he wasn't looking directly at the clump of

bushes in which she hid.

The alien's eyes widened perceptibly and for a second, she didn't dare to move.

She saw his lips move as he murmured something she couldn't hear and then he took a step forward.

Her heart stopped.

FUCK!

She moved so fast, she didn't wait to see if he was in pursuit or not.

Ducking behind the bushes, she ran.

Shit.

Heart in her throat, she backtracked as fast as she could.

This wasn't going to plan.

This wasn't going to plan at all.

She couldn't allow herself to get caught.

As she ran, it felt as if her world was imploding.

Suddenly, everything seemed temporary. Too temporary.

Her life...her existence.

Problem was, for the first time in a long while, she didn't know what the fuck she was going to do.

She was out of plans and now she had to rely entirely on what fate had in store.

6

THE TERU BIRD HAD CAUGHT HIM COMPLETELY OFF GUARD.

He'd smelled the thing, but he hadn't expected it to go into a rage and attack him.

They were usually peaceful creatures that kept to the trees and often they went on long migratory flights across the continent.

He should have known something was wrong with this one when he'd seen the state of the tree it lived in.

The entire tree had been covered in excrement, as if the bird had been there for a long, long time.

As soon as he'd ventured close enough, the thing had attacked.

It had been vicious, enraged, but only because it was in pain.

He'd realized shortly after wrestling it to the ground that there was a sharp object stuck in one of its wings.

That's why it had dwelled so long in one spot. It couldn't fly away.

It'd been injured.

And its attitude was because it was in pain.

He'd had to wrestle the object out even as the stupid animal clawed at him, almost pulling his face off, and it had been enough to distract him.

That was, until the alien creature's scent wafted into his nose.

The creature he'd been tracking had ventured close.

Close enough that when he'd turned, he was sure he'd looked straight at the spot in which it hid.

And something had struck him immobile.

Something that caused him not to chase after the thing.

He heard the bushes rustle in the creature's wake as it ran away. Still, he didn't move.

Blinking, he stared at the spot in which he was sure the creature had been. Several unnerving thoughts blossomed in his head.

The creature had been watching him...scoping him out.

The only reason for an animal to do something like that was if it didn't want to make its presence

known.

Only something that harbored some intelligence would do such a thing.

Phek.

This wasn't like the usual hunt.

This animal was different, able to override its base instincts to flee, hide, or attack. It could think...and possibly scheme.

He'd never hunted a creature that watched him like that before without trying to attack, and for that reason, he was hesitant. His usual hunting instinct was giving way to curiosity.

It was a timid creature. He could tell.

Otherwise, it would have attacked him already to stake its claim over its territory.

An elusive, long-legged, pale, hairy-headed creature with a flat face...

It would be a pleasure to finally capture it.

Walking slowly through the undergrowth, Sohut stepped over twisting vines, shrubs, and small fallen trees that blocked his path.

His movements were automatic.

He didn't even see the flora he was traversing over.

All he could think about was the creature.

Sniffing the air again, he caught the faint scent of spring water, and an idea immediately formed in his head.

The best way to capture elusive creatures was not to actively go after them.

He needed to cut off something the creature couldn't do without...

There was water nearby and he'd bet his gonads that that's where the creature quenched its thirst.

If it was going to hide from him, he bet he could coax it out of its hiding spot by cutting off the one thing that it definitely needed: life fluid.

～

HE FOLLOWED HIS SNIFFER, and sure enough, it took him to a spring gushing from the side of the mountain.

It was set in a small clearing, with thick vines running over hard rock.

Years and years of the water beating against the rock carved a narrow pool that filtered through the rock and allowed the water to carry on down the mountain.

Crouching, his fingers brushed over the vines on the floor.

There was a faint indentation there, like a path of some sort. The more he looked at it, the more he could see there were several of these indentations—almost as if the animal took different paths to access the water.

Sohut blinked, his brows furrowing.

He was right about the animal being intelligent.

It didn't want to leave visible tracks.

Sohut's brows dived deeper as he ran his fingers over one of the slight indentations.

To the Gori and many other beings, the vines running across the floor would look completely natural—untouched.

But his eyes were trained to see beyond what appeared to be natural.

Tracking elusive creatures was his forte and though the ground looked undisturbed, he could see the signs of regular wear.

The almost imperceptible flattening of the vines in certain parts...

The sprouts growing only in certain areas...

As he surveyed the area, he knew he was right about one thing.

Whatever the creature was, it needed watering regularly and if he stayed by the water hole, the animal was bound to come to him sooner or later.

Pure thirst would drive it to reveal itself.

Standing so he could stretch, Sohut turned his eyes upward.

Visibility was getting low.

Above, the sky was slowly turning to a deep purple and he could see the outline of Hudo III's double moons as the planet entered the dark cycle.

The good thing about Hudo III was that the nights weren't too cold. He could sleep outside without shelter. It wouldn't be the most comfortable, but it would do.

Getting his light-disk from his satchel, Sohut engaged the device and set it in the center of the little clearing.

A dull orange glow lit up the area.

It was enough light for him to see but not too much to disturb the critters in the bushes around him.

With another sniff of the air, he settled in.

The creature's scent was mostly faded.

Wherever it had gone, it hadn't run towards the water.

Still, he was betting that it would turn up.

Something told him he was pretty right about that.

7

FOR THE ENTIRE NIGHT, CLEO SAT WITH THE SPIKES SHE'D SHARPENED, waiting by the mouth of her cave...waiting for the alien to appear.

As morning rose, she still gripped them tight.

She had enough spikes to kill the whole coven in Twilight, and even as the sun rose, she gripped the two she was holding.

Unmoving, she remained vigilant behind the curtain of leaves at the entrance of the cave.

Logically, he shouldn't be able to reach her cave, but still...

He'd come too close to seeing her.

If he found her cave, she would do him worse than bitch-bird did.

A breath shuddered through her as the sun rose farther into the sky, lightening the dark purple to a soft pink hue.

Her eyes were tired but she didn't dare close them.

The moment she closed them, she'd be ambushed. She was sure.

Glancing behind her, she spotted the tuft of grass that was Wawa's bedding.

He hadn't returned yet and she was beginning to fear for his life.

It wasn't the first time he'd left for a few days, but she couldn't help feeling that the blue alien had something to do with her pet's disappearance.

What if more blue aliens were roaming the jungle, looking for her? She shuddered at the thought.

There was a possibility this was true. She hadn't had the chance to do her daily perimeter check.

It was a possibility she didn't want to face.

Swallowing hard, Cleo glanced at the makeshift bowl in which she kept her drinking water.

She needed to refill it.

She'd do it now because it seemed she'd have to spend a few days hiding so she didn't get caught.

She only had one dried morsel left too, so she'd have to ration.

Good grief...

But she could do this.

Exhausted, she stood on shaky legs before casting a glance back at Wawa's bed.

She wished he was with her.

Not having him around now made her realize just how accustomed to each other and codependent they'd become.

Where she helped him by removing burs and insects from his coat, he traveled on her shoulder and alerted her whenever danger was close.

Where she made sure he had enough water in his bowl and a warm place to sleep, he would be the one to help scare the little jungle penguins from their hiding places when it was time to hunt for food.

She missed Wawa.

With a huge sigh, she gripped her water bowl, grabbed a few spikes she'd sharpened, and took a step forward.

God help her, she'd go alone and hope she was smart enough to not get caught.

CLOSE BY, the sound of the running spring cascading over the rocky mountainside filled the air. Hidden, Cleo paused in the bushes.

And it was a good thing she'd paused.

The entire trek to the water, she'd crept through the undergrowth as if she was scared of her own shadow.

She didn't want to miss anything or end up walking right into the hunter.

Luckily, she'd made it without any incidents but now she was faced with another dilemma because, not far from the water, there he frickin' was.

Of all the places, she hadn't expected him to dwell at the water hole.

How he'd found it, she had no idea, and the fact that he'd found it so easily only caused her anxiety to rise.

But it made sense.

He must drink water like every other thing that was alive.

Bright sunlight hit blue alien skin as the tall alien inclined his head a little.

He paused, and she saw his nostrils move.

He was sniffing.

Motherfucker.

As he glanced around, she could feel the hairs at the back of her neck rise, their pitchforks raised.

She didn't know how to describe it, but it felt as if he *knew* she was there.

She was crouching low, so low she was flat on her stomach, her chin pressed into the ground below.

Alarm bells began ringing as the alien turned his nose to the air, this time inhaling deeply.

A chill traveled down her spine like a train on a track even as the golf ball bobbed up to her throat once more.

She hadn't considered it before now. But...what if he could smell her?

He looked so...human-like, she hadn't even thought about it before now.

Fuckity fuck fuck.

As the alien exhaled slowly, a rumble echoed through the air, loud enough to catch her ear.

... and it'd come from him.

She didn't know what that sound meant, but she'd been wrong about forgetting he wasn't human.

That sound was anything but human.

Suddenly she felt like making a run for it.

Forget the water. She'd die of thirst.

The alien inhaled and groaned again, but this time, it sounded like a groan of annoyance and frustration.

Fuck.

Had he scented her?

Despite the cover of leaves she was hiding under, she'd daubed a fresh layer of mud over every inch of her skin. It was in her hair, caking it so much it felt like she was carrying a heavy hat on her head, and on every visible inch of her body.

She'd put extra under her arms as well.

The only place there was no mud was over her naked private parts because, well, her alien captors hadn't got the memo that bulk panties were cheap—so she had none.

Surely, he couldn't sniff her when she was covered from head to toe with that metallic dirt caked to her skin.

...Unless he was smelling the one place there was no mud.

The gold ball that formed in her throat forced its way down.

He couldn't be.

Sheesh. She didn't have soap to wash with, but she kept down there relatively clean.

If he could smell her most private of spaces...

She could feel her cheeks grow warm at the thought even as she bit hard into her lip.

As her insides cracked into several pieces by the weight of this new anxiety, the blue male stood and moved to the water.

She watched him move closer and it took everything within her not to retreat. If she moved now, he'd definitely hear her in her haste.

The alien moved close enough to where she was for her to see his face and Cleo had to blink several times, her mouth falling open as she stared at him.

He was even more good-looking than she'd realized.

He was definitely not a hunter. Which hunter looked like that?

It would also explain why he hadn't chased after her after she'd bolted.

She'd run so fast, she hadn't even stopped when her lungs had threatened to collapse.

But she hadn't been chased.

The alien hadn't come after her.

Still studying him, she noted the dissimilarities she could see.

Down his septum ran a series of raised bumps, the same of which ran from his bottom lip down his chin like a midline down his face.

His hands flexed absently at his side and she counted not five but four fingers on each hand. Behind him, his tail swished in the air slowly.

Frowning in his direction, she watched him look around the clearing, his gaze scanning everything.

Maybe the orc aliens had thought sending a model to get into her panties was the best way to recapture her?

Well, the joke was on them.

She wasn't wearing any panties.

As the alien dipped his face into the rock pool before lifting his head again, Cleo lay mesmerized by the rivulets of water sliding down his skin.

The alien turned his head slightly in her direction and sniffed again.

That movement sent a barrage of thoughts and feelings through her that tugged in two separate directions.

Yea...about what she'd said earlier...she was going to die of thirst.

Creeping as silently as she could away from the water hole, Cleo backtracked to her cave.

8

THREE MORE DAYS PASSED.

The alien was still by the water hole.

She was out of water and food now, plus Wawa was still missing.

To add, for the past two nights, she'd heard more distant roars echoing through the jungle and she could only hope it didn't mean the animals making the terrible sounds weren't migrating to the mountain.

If that was the case, this was surely like the apocalypse.

She didn't know what to do.

She couldn't even focus. Her mind was constantly on the intruder who seemed to be making a home in the most inconvenient of places: right by her water source!

He was like a lion walking into meerkat territory only to take a nap. And who was she but not the confused meerkat poking her head up from her hidey-hole wondering just *what the fuck is wrong with this lion*?

The last time she ventured to spy on him, he'd been resting in a spot where the sun hit the bushes, his eyes closed as if he was sunning himself.

As she'd come close, she'd heard him sniff, and that one reaction had her retreating.

Withdrawing to her cave for the third night in a row, Cleo paced the floor of her cave in the darkness.

She was tired, hungry, thirsty...she was slowly dying.

Fuck.

And what's worse, she felt alone.

For the entire time she'd been a fugitive, she hadn't felt more on her own.

With a sigh, she stared up into the darkness above her. Somewhere out there, she hoped Wawa was okay.

She didn't imagine it would be this way when she finally went.

There was an enemy on her doorstep, she was slowly starving, and dangerous animals were roaming the woods.

Even as she thought about it, she was sure she heard a roar in the distance.

Pausing, Cleo stared out through the cave entrance at the night sky.

It was coming to an end, wasn't it?

A deep feeling of sadness overcame her.

She didn't want to leave the cave.

This was home.

Before she could talk herself out of it, she exited the cave and slid down the vine hanging over the edge of the cliff. Swinging onto the landing on the side of the mountain below the cave, she stopped to take a breath.

With light footsteps, she padded through the undergrowth in the direction of the water hole.

She knew where to go, even in the darkness, having walked the way many, many times before.

As she approached, the dim glow of light caught her eyes and made her spine stiffen.

He was still there.

Creeping closer, Cleo peeked through the bushes, careful to be silent.

That light source that lit up the small clearing seemed to be coming from a gadget set in the center of the clearing on the ground.

It almost felt strange looking at artificial light again. The glow reminded her of the fluorescent bulbs that used to hang in her apartment back in California.

Back then, life had been simpler in her regular bartender job.

Those days, living hand-to-mouth hadn't quite taken the same meaning as it did now in this new life.

With the light source illuminating the area, it wasn't hard to spot the blue intruder and her eyes fell on his broad back.

He was there.

Awake.

And as she stared at him, she realized she'd been holding her breath the entire time since she'd reached the edge of the clearing.

He was still frickin' there.

And drinking her water.

The alien was crouched near the rock pool, droplets of water running down his face and dampening his shirt.

A few feet behind him, against the wall, rested his bag with things. She could see a few items, gadgets she didn't know the purpose of, brimming from the top.

It probably had tools too and other useful items.

Things like a firelighter, maybe a knife...a gun possibly?

Even his little light gadget was enviable.

She bet he had things in that bag that she could use. Things that would make living in the wilderness so much easier—that is, if she somehow managed to survive this.

Over the past few months, she'd used all the knowledge her father had passed down to her to craft as many items as she had the skill to craft.

She still had the piece of metal, which served as her trusty blade now. She could make a fire using a board, some kindling, and a swindle. She'd used vines and some of the large leaves to fashion things she needed to live like her mattress and pillow. There were even some husks from some huge nuts that fell within the jungle that she used for bowls too, whenever she managed to find them.

If he had a knife though, a real one, it would make life so much easier for her. And a lighter? What she wouldn't do for something that could make a fire easily and on the go.

Cleo bit her bottom lip, her gaze shifting back to the alien. He hadn't moved.

Looking right at his back, it took her a few moments to realize that something was off.

He...he wasn't moving.

He was frozen in a sort of non-movement you'd see an animal do when it was hyperaware.

Every nerve ending in her body sent an alarm straight to her brain.

Shit.

Like before, she had the feeling he knew she was there.

Swallowing hard, she watched as the alien's back moved as he inhaled deeply, his shoulders rising and falling before he went completely rigid.

The air suddenly felt chilly as she froze in the cover of the bushes, not daring to even breathe.

Ever so slightly, she watched as the alien turned his head, right in her direction.

Fight or flight.

It was a command in her brain, as if her body could tell just what was about to happen next.

The alien was going to pounce.

Immediately, adrenaline pounded in her veins, making her heart press against her chest in thunderous beats she was sure the alien could hear because it was deafening in her ears.

Without waiting another second, she clambered through the bushes, wincing inwardly as a twig snapped underneath her feet.

Run, Cleo.

Fucking run!

Instead of heading towards her den, she went in the opposite direction.

Curse the darkness, for it was not her ally.

She stubbed her toe and almost fell over the many obstacles on the ground but she kept running, not daring to even pause for a second.

Her breath came hot and hard through her nose, making the sensitive skin inside her nostrils burn but she didn't dare to even stop.

And then she heard it.

The unmistakable sound of bushes rustling behind her.

He was coming for her...

...and she had a sinking feeling she was going to get caught.

THE ANIMAL TURNED and darted away, rushing through the under-growth and something clicked inside Sohut immediately, fueling his Merssi instinct of old.

Hunt.

It was instinctive from the days his ancestors used to hunt to survive.

Forgetting his initial plan, Sohut raced forward, cutting through the undergrowth with ease.

He could hear the bushes rustling far ahead of him as the creature tried to put distance between them but he didn't need to hear the she-animal to be able to track her.

He'd caught on to her scent now, locked on to it, and following her across the jungle would be easy.

Hopping easily over fallen trees and huge roots, he gave chase and it brought back a memory.

One of him and his brother running after they'd escaped the mines. The wind had been in their faces, freedom in front of them... and terror behind them.

Only this time, *he* was the terror and the creature running in front of him was the one dashing away to freedom.

Deep within him, adrenaline pumped in his veins, pushing him forward and it didn't take him long to notice the animal wasn't running in a straight line.

Instead of darting straight forward through the undergrowth, the creature shifted direction every now and then as if trying to lose or confuse him.

He'd been right about it being intelligent.

Eyes ahead of him, he entered a particularly sparse section of the undergrowth and that's when he caught sight of the creature for the first time.

His vision wasn't the best in the dark, but still he could see better than most and what he saw almost made him stumble.

The creature looked nothing like he thought it would and, for a second, he contemplated whether he was tracking the wrong thing.

He'd have thought so if the creature running in front of him wasn't obviously a non-native species to this jungle.

It was obviously the alien creature he'd been sent to find—only, it *wasn't* at the same time.

The animal in front of him was...bipedal.

Confusion mixed in with the thrill of the chase as he surged forward.

Ducking under hanging branches and thick vines, Sohut closed the distance between him and the creature, reaching out as soon as he was within arm's reach to grab hold of the animal.

For a moment, he didn't know what part of the creature he'd caught hold of but his confusion was only compounded when the creature let out the most feminine of sounds as they both went tumbling into the bushes.

It was a high-pitched shriek that had his ears ringing and the animals around them running back to their dens.

He didn't know what he'd expected when they tumbled into the bushes, but the first kick caught him right in the midsection.

The animal was screeching and bucking, trying to wring itself from his grasp and the second kick landed squarely in his gonads.

Phekking draxx...

He released the thing momentarily as pain surged in his groin and the creature tried to scramble away.

Grabbing what he supposed was one of the creature's legs, he pulled the animal back toward him.

More struggling ensued as the other leg kicked back, trying to find a mark.

It was like trying to keep a chid in a tantrum steady.

As he launched himself on top of the bucking creature, just so he could hold it steady, he felt another pain, this time in his arm. But that sharp pain was quickly dismissed as more prominent thoughts forced forward in his mind.

Holding the creature steady enough so he could look at it, shock rendered him motionless.

This was no animal.

Despite the darkness that surrounded them, he could see enough to tell that this...this *creature* wasn't what he'd thought it was at all.

9

<small>THE CREATURE WAS A BIPEDAL FEMALE.</small>

Not Merssi for she had no horns...unless the Gori had dehorned her—the mere thought of which sent a surge of anger through him.

If she wasn't struggling so much, he'd take the time to feel for frilli running down her septum and chin.

But she couldn't be Merssi.

The Gori would have been mad to send him after a Merssi female and expect him to capture and take her to them.

Confused, he stared down at the alien beneath him.

All this time...he'd been tracking a bipedal female.

The female grunted and struggled against him again, bringing him out of his thoughts.

She was feral, he was sure.

He'd probably have to restrain her and bring her back to the water hole where he could think clearly without fear of her running away.

Realizing he must be crushing her small frame with his weight, Sohut eased up a little but that only renewed the female's efforts to kick him in the gonads and he wasn't ready to relive that pain.

"Stop. Don't fight," he growled, his voice a little more hostile than he'd intended as he pressed down against her again.

Could she understand him?

He didn't know.

"Leht mee goh!" she screamed, struggling against him still.

He had no idea what she just said but it sounded like a language he'd heard before.

Where? He couldn't be quite sure.

Her struggling continued as she let out a pained sound—one of mental anguish.

She wasn't going to calm down. She was too frightened. Panicky.

She was livid and out of her mind.

He didn't want to restrain her but did he have a choice? He doubted she'd listen to him if he tried to calm her down.

Adrenaline was pumping within her, coursing through her veins, telling her to do whatever she could to survive.

He knew this too well— the feeling of complete madness that can overwhelm the body when it felt like all was lost.

He'd experienced it before.

Sighing, he reached for the roll of cord in his pocket.

He had to restrain her and he had to be quick about it.

He'd heard noises in the jungle over the past few days and he didn't want to be caught without his blade in the middle of the undergrowth.

Stupidly, he'd run after her without retrieving it from his satchel.

Pinning the female's arms above her head with one hand caused her efforts to double.

She had skinny arms and even though she was putting up a fight, it wasn't nearly enough to cause him to release her.

That fact was evident. Still, she struggled.

There was something sharp in her hand too, and he couldn't wrestle it away from her, so he wrapped both of her hands entirely, rendering her weapon useless.

Even as he held her legs down so he could tie her ankles together, she grunted and resisted.

It took a few minutes but, finally succeeding, he eased up from over the female, taking a deep breath as he did.

Her eyes were not luminescent in the dark but he could feel that she was glaring at him, and she had a right to be upset.

This whole situation just got a lot more complicated than he'd expected.

Crouching, he swooped the female's body into his arms and threw her over his shoulder with ease.

A series of sharp words left her mouth as she yelped and proceeded to hammer his back with her bound wrists.

This continued for most of the trek back to the water hole, till she hung limp against him. Only her chest moving against his shoulder and back told him she was still alive.

Light from his light-disk greeted him as he neared the water hole.

Stepping into the small clearing, he set the female down into a nest of vines.

Livid pale eyes stared up into his and Sohut froze in shock, his gaze running over the female's face.

With the light now illuminating her features, he could see her clearly.

The Goris had said the creature had long red fur on its head and down its back.

The female in front of him had no red hair whatsoever; there was a dark, stiff-looking crown on her head instead.

The Goris had also said the creature was pale all over but the female in front of him had a dark coat.

They'd also said it had long spindly legs, translucent eyes, and a flat face.

The female had a delicate nose set in the middle of a face with soft angles.

The more he stared, the more speechless he became.

This was definitely no animal.

And that dark coat...it wasn't a coat at all.

It was mud.

Realization dawned.

He'd been right about hearing her language before, because he had!

Back at the Sanctuary, before he left, there'd been a female there called Larn. She'd been a refugee of sorts who'd been cast in the care of his brother.

He wasn't positive, but the female in front of him looked a helluva lot like she was the same species.

The more he stared at her, the more he was convinced.

This female in front of him a *dirty*—no, a *filthy*—Larn!

As he eased up from over the female to stand, Sohut took a step back.

There was that sharp pain in his arm again and it took a few moments before his gaze moved to the area.

Deep in his flesh was a gash and Sohut blinked as he watched his blood spill and run down his arm.

He didn't remember getting injured by anything sharp as he ran.

When he glanced back at the female, she was staring at his arm too and memory of the weapon she was clutching in her hand came back to him.

She'd...she'd wounded him.

"You stabbed me." Even to himself, his voice sounded disbelieving.

There was a pause and he was surprised when she answered.

"Phuk wit mee anhd ai-will doo iht ah-gen." Her voice was strong, not betraying the fear in her eyes.

It sounded like she'd understood what he'd said.

Larn back at the Sanctuary had been able to understand him too, though he hadn't been able to understand her.

Whoever had taken Larn from her home planet had also installed a language chip in her brain. That's why, before coming on this mission, he'd gone to the exchange to get the language files for Larn's planet—just in case Riv didn't get rid of her before he returned.

Always interested in new worlds, he'd wanted to learn more about where she came from and the best bet had been to ask her the questions directly.

Staring at the female in front of him, he was nonplussed.

How did she survive out here all alone?

The female bared her teeth again, snarling at him, and he didn't spot any fangs.

Maybe she *was* feral.

That partly explained why she'd managed to survive so long on her own.

It also explained why she looked like she hadn't taken a bath the entire time she'd been in the jungle.

"Leht. Mee. Goh." She was speaking through her flat, clenched teeth and it definitely sounded like the same language as Larn's. The more he heard it, the surer he became. "Waht arr yoo go-win too doo too mee?"

Her gaze flicked from him to the jungle as if she was considering wriggling away in her restrained state.

"Don't bother. Even if you did get away, you'd still need me to remove those restraints," he noted.

Cold, gray eyes met his and the look she gave him could kill a family of mogs with one glance.

She hated him.

Even restrained, she was defiant.

He knew it wasn't the smoothest of introductions.

It probably looked like he was capturing her to keep her prisoner but he'd had no choice but to tie her arms and legs as he led her to a safer location.

They'd been in the open and, granted that he hadn't met any spined creatures since passing that invisible scent barrier, he still needed to focus on his surroundings without worrying about her trying to escape.

There was also still the scent of slizz. It was even mixed into her scent, and that was confusing.

Larn hadn't smelled like slizz at all, so he was sure it wasn't a similar scent gland her species used.

Unless the female before him was a variation of the same species.

That was something to consider.

Phek.

66

He suddenly had a lot of things to consider and phek him but he didn't nearly have enough time.

The Gori would be expecting his return soon.

They'd trusted that he would catch their creature and that he did.

The more he thought about it, the more pissed he became.

10

SHE'D FUCKED UP.

Royally.

Cleo couldn't even face herself or the situation she'd fallen into.

It wasn't lost on her that she'd been trained for this moment from her very early years.

In primary school, her teachers had been horrified when she'd mentioned the week she'd spent in the wilderness alone.

Which parent would have been mad enough to leave their eight-year-old all alone in the wild?

Thomas Barlow. That's who.

Staring into the dark sky, her brows hurt from the severe frown on her face.

Each morning she woke had been another day added to her freedom and she'd relished it.

This new life had taken some getting used to but she was darned proud of herself.

To let it slip away so easily...

She had to find a way out of this.

She wasn't dead yet.

In front of her, the blue alien was standing a few meters away.

Right now, he stood scowling at her, unblinking.

And the more time passed, the angrier he seemed to get.

Fuck.

Was he disappointed in his catch or something?

She was pretty sure he was going to walk over and snap her neck at any moment. For that reason, she tried to make herself look as nonthreatening as possible.

It felt like an hour passed and he was still studying her.

What's worse, Wawa was nowhere to be seen.

He still hadn't returned.

She could only hope that he wasn't dead.

Movement in her peripheral vision had her snapping her head toward the alien.

Fear spiked within her immediately.

"Please..." She tried to shuffle backward but that was difficult seeing as he'd put her down on a section of uneven vines. "Whatever you're going to do, don't do it."

The alien paused in front of her.

He was huge; his mere presence was overpowering.

She could still remember the feel of him pressed against her too. Her fucking confused mind didn't know if it should be enraged or happy that someone had been touching her.

It'd been so, so long since she'd felt the touch of another person.

Even in her panic, the feel of his soft velvety skin had been a little...jarring.

Trying to move back a little more, she raised her bound hands. "If you're going to kill me, just..." she swallowed.

Just what?

Don't do it?

Well, that goes without saying...

The alien paused over her.

"Whatever you're saying, I can't understand you," he finally said.

Of course, he couldn't.

She should have expected as much.

It wasn't like there were ESL teachers on whatever planet this was.

As he crouched in front of her, she eased away from him a little bit more.

"I was sent here to catch you for the Goris," he continued. "That was the plan, before I realized you were...*this*." He motioned to her body, his anger seething.

This what?

The fact he'd gestured to her body only made her warier. His anger didn't help either.

She hadn't forgotten what the orc aliens had been suggesting that time long ago.

She knew enough to know what most aliens did with females that were weaker than they were.

She shuddered to think that her fate was either to be in his bed or dead.

"What am I going to do with you?" the alien mused.

"Cut these ropes, let me go...forget we ever met?" She met his gaze but he couldn't understand her. Not that she thought it would make a difference anyway.

He was her enemy. He wasn't going to let her go.

Deep inside, a sense of danger was settling. It was a sort of caution that was there before but now she was looking right at the cause of it.

At best, this guy was only a little psychopathic...

At worst...

Fucking hell...

HE REALLY DIDN'T KNOW what he was going to do with the female.

Sohut spent the greater part of the next few hours deliberating this sudden problem he'd been thrust into.

This wasn't a situation he'd even considered before embarking on the mission.

He had never thought the creature from a Class Four planet would have been a sentient being.

Once again, he felt a surge of anger and disgust from the fact that the Goris had expected him to overlook that very important detail.

They saw the female before him as an animal.

He knew exactly what that felt like—being seen as even lesser than a person.

His own mor hadn't even thought he'd been worthy of the gift of life.

If she'd known he'd have come out ill...weak...she would have snuffed out his life while he was still growing within her.

But she'd lost that opportunity and so she'd sold him and his brother when they were only chids.

Life only got worse from there.

Working in the Tasqal mines as a chid, he and his brother were seen as barely having a consciousness...

They were used as machines, their only purpose to dig the rare talix metal from the rock.

They'd been beaten, starved, punished...abused...

Treated as animals.

His anger surged.

That's what the Gori saw this delicate being in front of him as.

No.

Correction.

They *didn't* see her.

When they looked at her they saw *nothing* and that was the problem.

He didn't need to get to know her to see the flaw in their reasoning.

Eyeing her now, the glow of the light disc highlighting her features, Sohut stopped pacing to study her.

For the entire time, she'd sat still, her body curled into a ball. Now and then, her gaze searched the bushes.

In some moments, she'd worry her bottom lip, her face becoming distressed but whenever she realized he was watching her, she would go emotionless.

She was small.

Bigger than Larn but still small compared to him.

She didn't have much weight on her either and he wasn't sure if that was because she'd been living in the wild on her own for over an entire orbit or if that was just what she'd been like before.

An alien creature lost in the Koznia Jungle.

It was amazing she'd survived.

"Just how did you survive this long?" There was annoyance in his tone, lingering from his thoughts, and he tried to keep it at bay. "This world is...new to you. Dangerous."

She didn't respond but her eyes darted to his.

She wasn't smiling, wasn't snarling...nothing. She seemed alert, guarded, as if she was waiting on him to make some mistake so she could escape.

"Tell me," he took a step forward and crossed his arms. "How did you survive?"

"Yoo cahnt uhn-der-stahnd mee enny-way." She met his gaze. "Ai dohnt noh wat yoo wahnt."

There was strength in her eyes.

Despite her circumstances, she was looking at him as if she wasn't ready to give up just yet.

He respected that.

"Iht dohzn maht-er wat ai tehl yoo."

Her language was enticing. So many soft syllables. It made it difficult to determine if she was saying she wanted to cut his gonads off or if she wanted to give him an embrace.

Moving to his satchel, he took out the language up loader he'd bought so he could understand Larn.

He'd gotten the three most popular languages mined from data retrieved from Larn's planet. He'd have to install each separately and hope that the female in his midst spoke at least one of them.

Popping out the device, Sohut eyed the female as he selected the first language file.

It was the most popular language on her planet. Something called Shai-neez.

She was looking at the device as if it was some weapon to use against her.

Pointing the device at the back of his ear, he depressed the button and what felt like an electric shock passed through his brain. He had to squeeze his eyes shut for a few moments.

"—Dah hell iz he doowin..." he heard the female whisper.

Nope, not her language.

Sighing, he selected the second most popular language.

Spah-neesh.

The second upload made him feel like he was going to pass out.

It wasn't usual to upload so much data in such short intervals. It was like smoking a whole carton of woogli smoke in one hour—completely unhealthy.

But he didn't have time to wait the recommended intervals.

It took him a little longer to recover from the second upload and when he opened his eyes to look at the female, her widened gray pools were staring at him with a mixture of confusion and wariness.

"Yoor doowin sum-thin reely freeki uhnd ai dohnt laik freeki raiht nohw."

Phek.

Not her language.

He closed his eyes again.

Looking at the language uploader, he grit his teeth.

This third language better be it.

Een-gleesh.

As the language uploaded, his consciousness waned in and out and he was vaguely aware that he'd fallen to his knees as the brain fog overtook him.

"Fucking hell, dohnt tell mee you're doing dhrugs ohr something."

He understood most of that. Triumph made him smile a little.

"Please don't tell me the alien that captured me is taking drugs. Like..." She trailed off and huffed out a breath. "I can't believe I let a druggy psychopathic hunter capture me."

What?

He wasn't a—

He opened his mouth to answer her and then stopped.

She obviously didn't know he could understand her yet.

Maybe he'd keep it that way for a bit.

Resting into a sitting position, he blinked at her as his vision cleared.

"Should have stayed hidden in my cave. Might have probably starved to death but at least I'd have died free," she murmured, her voice so low he was glad he had her language upload so he could understand what she was saying.

And being able to understand her brought a whole new level to their current predicament.

She was an intelligent being—a being whose language he now understood as well as he understood his own.

She wasn't something belonging behind a barrier in a zoo—or worse yet, as a prisoner in some mine.

Surely, the Goris knew this. Why had they sent him to capture a being that should have a life of freedom just as he and they deserved?

He couldn't take her back to them. That was clear.

Not after what he'd had to endure as a chid. Not after the life he'd have to live in captivity.

"There must be a way to get out of this." He heard her murmur again and the illumination from the light disk caught a glassy sheen in her pale eyes.

He didn't realize he'd been moving closer to her till she winced, her wide eyes turning on him, as she tried to shuffle away.

Her reaction wounded him a little.

He wasn't the monster she obviously thought he was.

Outstretching his arms, palms down, he tried to communicate to her that he wasn't going to harm her.

"I'm not going to hurt you."

She was looking at him as if she expected him to continue...as if she was waiting for the word "yet" and that alone strengthened his resolve to prove her wrong.

He was nothing like the monsters that roamed this galaxy.

Nothing like them.

"We're on the same side."

An expression he didn't understand passed over the female's face.

"Sure looks like we're on the same side." She shook her wrists, which were restrained. "I also tie up people I mean no harm."

Sohut fought to keep his face straight.

Reaching for her legs, he saw her eyes widen as she pulled them back toward herself.

"I'm not going to hurt you." He tried to keep his voice calm but deep down, her fear of him was rubbing against him. He hated the way she was looking at him.

It reminded him of too much.

When he'd been a chid, he'd had that look too many times as he'd gazed on the degenerates in the mines that he'd feared.

It was a look that should break the life-organ of any sane being... but most beings in the mines had evolved into the mindless animals the Tasqals had seen them as.

"I'm going to release your legs..." he said and waited.

The female's eyes lit up a little as she stared at him, hope flaring inside their pale depths.

Reaching for her legs again, this time she let him take them.

His eyes met hers as he released the restraints around her ankles.

"I know you can understand me. Whoever took you to this world put a translator in your head." He paused and touched the back of his ear then pointed to hers. "If you run, I will chase you...and I *will* catch you."

Her eyes darted to the bushes and he could almost see the calculations in her head.

He didn't want her running for more than one reason.

First, there was a spined creature somewhere on the mountain, and second, if he lost her, the Gori would no doubt send another tracker after her.

He needed to keep her with him in order to get them both out of this predicament.

Releasing her legs, he watched her with a wary gaze.

Her throat moved and she pulled her legs toward her again, but she didn't try to run off.

Satisfied, Sohut settled back on his haunches, his gaze still on the female.

"I was sent here to retrieve you but..." his gaze moved over her face, "they didn't tell me you were an intelligent being." He paused, still studying her. "I have to decide what I'm going to do with you."

Something akin to panic passed over her face so quickly, he almost missed it.

She was trying to hide her true emotions, probably so he didn't know what she was thinking.

Smart.

She obviously didn't trust him yet.

Her voice was soft and low when she spoke, almost stroking against his ear and it caused them to perk from the sides of his head.

"I wish you'd leave me alone and pretend you never saw me here. I wish you'd go back to those green orcs and tell them I'm dead," she said. "But even if you could understand me, I doubt you'd do me that favor. You don't owe me anything."

Her words tugged at something inside him and he fought to seem unaffected.

Pretending he didn't comprehend a word she said, he tapped his hand against his chest, catching her attention.

"Sohut. My name is Sohut." He stretched one of his hands toward her and she leaned away.

"South?" Humor sprung into her eyes and that one emotion transformed her face for the few seconds that it was there. "South? Don't tell me. You're a spawn of the Kardashians."

What?

The Ka'rdshin were a species that lived on Mexcla VII. He didn't look anything like a Ka'rdshin. How did she even know about them?

And she'd butchered his name in the process too.

"Sohut." He stressed his name.

"South. Your name is South."

Frowning, he hit his chest with his palm. "So...hut."

"Sowut? Kinda like shout?" She paused. "Grout?" A slight chuckle left her lips and despite that it was at his expense, he could feel himself relax a little.

When he nodded, she scrunched up her nostrils. "Nice to meet you, Grout."

The female had the audacity to snicker at her own silly, silly joke.

"Not like it matters anyway. I don't know why you're introducing yourself to me when you're my enemy."

He opened his mouth to correct her, but didn't.

For a few moments, she refused to meet his gaze, then she finally looked at him and rolled her eyes.

"Fine. My name is Cleo." She paused then brought her wrists to her chest. "Cleo."

Clee-yo.

It was a beautiful name. A sort of sound that made a smile spring behind his eyes when he repeated it in his mind.

It sounded like the name of a beautiful blossom.

"Cluu." He repeated, purposely mispronouncing the syllables.

Cluu was old Merssian for "wild thing."

Funny, it fit the female perfectly.

"Clee-yo." It was her turn to frown at him. "Clee," she paused, "oh. Cleo."

"Cluu." He nodded and turned away from her before she saw the smile twisting his lips.

As he stood, her sound of exasperation almost made his shoulders shake in a silent laugh.

Regardless that she'd tried to murder him earlier, he might like this Clee-yo.

It was good he'd been the one to take this job. If the Goris had gotten other hunters, there's a chance she'd have been in a cage heading to Kezna Zoo by now.

At that, his gaze fell to the signaling device the Gori's had given him.

The same device that held her DNA, activated with just the press of a button to lock on to her until they removed it.

She had no idea it was resting in his satchel.

She'd been lucky the Gori hadn't caught her before.

He guessed she hadn't approached them as closely as she had approached him.

Grabbing his satchel, he settled beside Clee-yo and pulled out one of his food packets.

He could feel her gaze on him as he took a bite and chewed purposely slowly, watching her reaction.

Her mouth curled in disgust as she watched him and he almost choked.

"You can have some." He outstretched the packet to her, close enough for her to reach it. All she had to do was lean in and take a bite.

He knew she wanted it.

There's no way she wasn't hungry.

If she'd gone hunting since he'd entered the jungle, he was sure he'd have found out.

Her eyes narrowed on him.

"I don't want your food."

The little wild thing was a liar.

Her gaze wandered and fell on the food packet.

She wanted it.

"Take some."

Pale eyes blinked at him and he shoved the food toward her once more. He could see the mental battle in her eyes.

Leaning forward slightly, she took a begrudging bite of the sluu dough and chewed.

Her lips moved so delicately as she chewed that he sat staring at her for far too long.

It wasn't only her scent that was captivating.

Regardless of her efforts to make herself invisible, she was catching his attention at every turn.

She seemed to notice his gaze and her frown returned as she jerked away.

"I know you can't understand me, but this doesn't make us friends."

No, it didn't; but it was a great phekking start.

11

THE BLUE GUY WAS SLEEPING.

Or maybe he was pretending to sleep.

Studying him now, his back turned toward her, she glanced at the jungle beyond.

She could shuffle away but glancing at her hands, she gulped.

That would be stupid.

Plus, he hadn't hurt her yet.

He'd been...kind so far.

If she escaped now, she wouldn't have use of her hands till she managed to get this alien rope off. It wasn't like normal rope at all and she was sure rubbing the bands against a sharp rock wouldn't break them.

Maybe that's why the blue guy, Grout, had fallen asleep.

He was sure she wasn't going to be stupid enough to run off.

It wasn't the first time aliens had thought she wasn't stupid enough to do something...only, this time, this alien might just be right.

Sighing, she settled her back against the vines running upward against the rock.

Her belly wasn't empty, thanks to the food he'd shared, but she was thirsty.

She'd been hesitant at first but his food was like cake, only doughier.

After a year of eating meat, having a pastry had been like having a piece of heaven.

Licking her lips at the thought of the food, she eyed the rock pool in front of them.

The reflection of the light on the water reminded her of that time her father had left her in the wilderness alone.

She'd found a small stream and had stayed by it on the second night. It'd just been her, the silence of the forest, and the reflection of the moonlight against the flowing water.

It'd been such a serene feeling back then, just her and nature.

She didn't feel so serene now.

There was discomfort, anxiety, distrust, and a myriad of other feelings circling within her but no serenity.

The alien seemed nice. She wanted to trust him but dropping her guard so soon could lead to her detriment.

Eyeing the water, she tried to stand but all she could manage was a shuffle.

She guessed it would do. She wasn't going far anyway.

She could shuffle to the pool edge and dip her head in to get a drink.

Luckily, it was moving water, so she didn't have to worry about it being dirty.

That meant she could even bathe in the rock pool and the water would be clean again not long after she stepped out of it.

Shuffling forward, Cleo cursed underneath her breath.

She was definitely going to rip the few threads still holding her clothing together.

She'd tried to fashion clothes from the leaves in the jungle but she'd yet to find something that didn't itch to high heaven and which lasted more than a week.

She'd actually found a plant that molded itself like cotton and she'd thought she'd found her solution, only to wake the next morning with a rash over her entire body.

Even in space, she wasn't safe from allergies.

The rash had only lasted a few days but in that time she'd almost torn her skin off just to stop the itching and resultant burning.

From then, she'd been careful to leave the plants mostly alone.

Who knew what else she was allergic to? She didn't need to die of poison, an allergic reaction, or stupidity.

Cleo snorted to herself.

One could argue she was going to die of the last one anyway, judging from her actions over the last day.

Finally reaching the water's edge, Cleo took a moment to catch her breath.

She'd made it.

Dipping her head over the water, her lips touched the cool liquid and she took in a huge gulp.

As she raised her neck to swallow the liquid, she choked.

There was little warning.

All she felt was a huge thump as her heart flipped in her chest when a shadow blocked the light. It moved so quickly, she hardly had time to react.

As strong arms grasped her shoulders, Cleo bucked, her fight or flight response activating immediately as her heart lodged in her throat.

She barely heard a grunt as her feet connected with the attacker and, in a second, she realized it was the blue alien that had come at her.

Grout.

But it was too late to stop what was already happening.

Frickin' Grout was attacking her.

Her body was off-balance, his weight on hers pushing her over and she was falling.

Wide eyes met green ones as they both crashed into the rock pool. They went under, sinking quicker than her mind could keep up and understand what was happening.

The water she'd been swallowing was stuck in her throat and she hadn't been able to take a breath before going under. Not to mention that he was still holding on to her.

Was he trying to drown her?

Thrash as she might, she couldn't release the strong arms around her and terror filled her as the glow of the alien lamp grew dimmer, its glow fading the deeper they went.

The rock pool was deep. She'd only dived in it once, but she knew that there was no way she was reaching the surface if he didn't let her go.

Who knew, maybe he could frickin' breathe underwater and knew she couldn't.

Not her enemy, her ass.

This was why she didn't trust aliens. Even the ones that seem good and feed you can turn on you in a second.

Using both legs like a mermaid would, Cleo kicked, aiming for his balls and hoping he had two big ones so she could hurt him really good.

But it didn't help.

She was losing energy and her lungs were bursting.

She needed air.

As a last resort, she did the only thing she could think of doing as they went deeper.

Burying her face against the alien's shoulder, she opened her mouth and clamped down, sinking her teeth into the bastard's skin.

There was no response apart from him tensing and it took her a few moments, as her energy left her, for her to realize they were rising again.

As they broke the surface, she inhaled air like a junkie sniffing coke and her lungs thanked her for it.

The alien's chest was heaving too. She could feel it for she was plastered against him, his strong arms surrounding her as he treaded the water.

"What the phek were you thinking?!"

The tone of his voice caught her off guard.

Blinking away the water from her eyes, she was about to unleash a whole string of colorful words when she focused on him.

Those words died on her lips.

The pure anger mixed with utter concern etched into Grout's handsome features stopped her instead.

Now, what the fuck did he have to be angry about? He'd almost drowned her!

"I knew you were wild but to try to kill yourself?!"

What?

Cleo's mouth opened then closed then opened again as she pulled in huge breaths through her nose.

"I wasn't trying to kill myself, you idiot! I was drinking water!" She tried to push him away, but he was holding her too tightly and she only stopped struggling at the thought that if he *did* let her go she'd probably sink because her hands were still restrained.

He was staring at her as if she'd gone mad and she surprised herself when a half-chuckle left her lips.

He'd been trying to prevent her from offing herself? What an odd way to go about it.

They both almost died.

Chuckling, she looked up at him and it suddenly occurred to her that they were close. Very close.

That she could feel every cord of muscle underneath his clothing.

That every breath he took, his body moved against hers and that, for some insane reason, he felt...good.

Brilliant green eyes stared down at her with a look that had none of the anger and concern she'd seen etched on his face earlier.

Now, he was looking at her like a man stunned and for a reason she couldn't determine, warmth flooded her cheeks slowly.

"What is it?"

She searched his face tentatively. It felt wrong, inappropriate, to let her eyes travel over his features as she was doing and she swallowed back the lump that began to grow in her throat.

He was frickin' handsome.

Why did he have to be handsome?

And he was looking at her like...like she was something to be awed at.

"What is it?!" Minor irritation was present in her voice now as she blinked, trying to make sense of his sudden lack of response. "Oh, I forgot you can't understand me." She paused. "You're looking at me like..."

Like I'm beautiful.

But she didn't finish.

For a few long seconds, the alien did nothing...and then she felt it.

As he blinked, as if coming out of a stupor, she frickin' *felt* it.

Against her legs. Something that hadn't been there before was there now.

Growing. Hardening. Pressing against her.

The green-eyed alien blinked again as Cleo looked down at the water, before turning her wide eyes back to him.

"You're..."

Fucking turned on.

Why did that make her...not grossed out?

Because, Cleo, her mind helpfully answered, *your vagina has had a year-long no-dickfest.*

Now it wanted backstage tickets to meet the lead and his two drummers.

She was sure of it.

His hard cock was pressing into her and they both knew she could feel it because his expression suddenly turned sheepish.

Even in the cool water, it felt warm against her and something deep inside her ached.

She opened her mouth to say something. Words along the appropriate lines communicating disgust at the literal alien dick pressing into her and of how wrong it was for him to have it against her...but no words came.

She could only open her mouth and close it again.

Without a word, Sohut...*Grout* treaded to the edge of the pool, lifted her, and set her down on the ground.

Water sluiced off him as he exited the rock pool to stand beside her and Cleo kept her gaze averted, refusing to look at what she *knew* was there.

When strong hands surrounded her and lifted her once more, a yelp left her lips.

"What are you do—" But he only set her back against the rock wall where she'd been sitting before.

Fuck.

She should be annoyed. Angry. Livid.

Yet, none of those emotions were there.

All she could feel was a tingling in her lady parts and an excitement building in her chest that she hadn't felt in a long, long time.

He was male.

So male.

And now, because of the ache building in her core, she was painfully aware of it.

She watched as he stretched and took off his wet shirt, hanging it over a bunch of vines in the corner, and a shiver went down her body.

His attention turned to her and she averted her gaze again, her eyes falling to her legs and that made her inhale a sharp gasp.

The mud...

Her camouflage.

It was gone.

Thin streaks of dirt were now on her skin, which had just been fully hidden by a healthy covering of mud.

Raising her arms, her eyes widened.

It was all gone.

When her wide gaze fell on the alien, she found he was still looking at her in that strange way he had been in the water.

Fuck.

He could see her.

Like *see* her.

Her camouflage had washed away in the water and now she felt...open.

The funny thing was, the only thought in her head at that moment was the fact that she must look hideous.

Hiding behind the dirt and mud had been easy but now he could see exactly what she looked like...and, well, no one had seen her in over a year—especially not a hot male that her lady parts were, admittedly, too excited to see.

He was probably thinking she was a strange-looking creature now with all the mud washed off...

But when her gaze met his, she didn't see any of that.

The look in his eyes was the exact opposite.

And it shouldn't...but it made an electric thrill shoot straight into her stomach and erupt like a firework in her belly.

12

SHE WAS THE MOST BEAUTIFUL CREATURE THAT HAD EVER WALKED ON Hudo III.

Larn, female of her species who had turned up at the Sanctuary had been beautiful too...but Cluu...Clee-yo was...

Sohut turned from her and stuck his hand in his satchel, focusing on it instead as he searched for nothing in particular.

He'd first noticed that the mud she'd plastered over herself had washed away while they were still in the water and even now he couldn't stop himself from staring.

She was pale, as the Goris had described, and that paleness contrasted against her eyes and hair.

Her hair was the color of zimsu flowers and her lips...delicate arches like the flower's petals turned into a thin line when she'd realized he was staring.

Swallowing hard, he took a deep breath.

Mistake, for the scent of her filled his nose.

For a long time, he hadn't had such a strong urge to indulge in his carnal desires.

Now, however...

Through the corner of his eye, he noticed Clee-yo shivered.

The water had been cool and with Hudo III's star on the other side of the horizon, the warmth in the air wasn't as strong as it usually was.

And her skin looked thin...

Without the mud covering it, he could see her life-blood in the vessels underneath—a concerning matter seeing that she'd been in the jungle alone.

"What is it? Why are you looking at me like that?" Her voice reached his ear and he realized he'd been staring at her exposed arm, frowning.

Blinking, he met her gaze.

What sort of destiny had led him here?

The more he stayed in the jungle, the more she became something that he hadn't expected to encounter.

Clee-yo shivered again and that knocked him out of his ruminations.

"You need warmth."

She seemed to stiffen, her neck stretching back a little as she eyed him and she looked so strange doing it that his eyes crinkled at the corners in amusement.

"We're not sharing body heat..." Then her eyes widened. "Is that why you took your shirt off? ... Shit, I forgot you can't understand me."

Her eyes widened some more. "Which girl that's been alone for a whole year wouldn't want a hot hunk plastered against them? I mean, thanks for the sentiment and all. But I don't know you."

Sohut had to look away so she couldn't see the humor in his eyes.

He hadn't been suggesting they share "body heat." He had no idea what she meant by that anyway. There was no way to transfer heat of one's body to another...at least not in his species. But now he was intrigued.

And she thought he was attractive? He'd return the compliment but that would give away the fact that he *could* understand her.

Fetching one of the sluu doughs from the satchel, he moved over to her, noticing her eyes were plastered on his chest before her cheeks took on a strange hue and she looked away, instead choosing to focus on the food in his hand.

"Do you want this?" He shook the sluu dough in his hand.

Her eyes narrowed immediately as if she was contemplating saying no. "Yes." She nodded.

Unpacking the food slowly, she watched every move of his fingers.

"You only have four fingers..." she murmured, as if awed. "Four long, thick fingers..."

Her cheeks took on that funny hue again and she closed her eyes for a second, murmuring something about having no tact.

He had no idea what his fingers had to do with her tact, but something inside him was liking this little exchange between them.

Finally pulling the sluu dough from the packet, he moved close to her and her eyes grew wide, her gaze searching his face in alarm.

"Eat," he pressed the sluu dough to her lips and for a second, she did nothing.

He knew she wanted to take a bite. Her throat was working.

She reminded him of his brother's tevsi named Grot. As a pup, Grot had always been suspicious when anyone tried to feed him.

The similarity made him want to laugh.

Instead, he repeated, "Eat."

Delicate zimsu-hued lips opened as the female bit into the sluu dough, wary eyes on him.

"I don't like you," she said as she chewed and his gaze met hers. "I don't like you and your handsome face."

A bubble of a chuckle lodged in his throat.

Begrudgingly, she took another bite. "I don't like your stupidly good tasting food either."

Holding the laughter back was hard, especially when her small pink tongue darted out to lick her lips as she took another bite of the same food she was saying she hated.

"I don't like that you're here." She took another bite, her eyes rolling back a little as she chewed, the pure taste giving her such pleasure he could see it on her face. "Why did they have to send you, huh? I thought they'd given up trying to catch me."

She took another bite. "God, this tastes so good." She chewed.

"Like, I was happy on my own, you know. But I guess they knew the weakness I didn't even know I had. Turns out, it's you."

Her eyes narrowed on him again. "I couldn't have fucking prepared for you."

As she took the last bite, her lips brushed against his fingers and Sohut bit inside his cheek at the unexpected pleasure of that touch.

"If you're poisoning me right now, I'm such an idiot for eating this." She swallowed her last mouthful and attempted to glare at him. But her glare held no substance. Deep in her eyes, he knew she didn't *really* hate him.

She was all talk and no bite.

Smiling at her, his gaze dropped to her hands.

"I'm going to remove the restraints now."

The female licked her lips slowly as she watched him with suspicion in her eyes.

Reaching for her wrists, he paused.

"I'm going to release you now but if you try to wound me with that crude weapon I know you're still holding," he said, "I'll have to restrain you again."

He paused, making sure his words sunk in.

"When I release you," he continued, "you need to take me to your nest."

She blinked at him, her brows furrowing.

"My what?" She blinked again. Then, realization dawned. "You mean my *cave*." Her eyes nictated some more. "My cave," she murmured, her gaze falling as if she was contemplating something.

"There's no way I can bring you to my cave."

Sohut raised an eyebrow but luckily she wasn't looking at him to see.

"I can't bring you to my cave..." her voice was almost a whisper now.

When she looked at him again, there was worry hiding behind her eyes.

As he removed the restraints, Sohut's muscles primed, ready to grab her arms if she decided to try and stab him again.

But she didn't.

As a matter of fact, she did nothing.

There was a twinkle in her eyes as she watched him now, almost as if she'd come up with some plan, and he wondered exactly what she was thinking.

Something told him he'd find out soon enough.

13

THE LIGHT-CYCLE WAS COMING IN AS HE CROUCHED, STILL STARING AT the female.

She was rubbing her wrists as if the restraints had irritated them.

He'd taken care not to place them tightly but her skin looked so... delicate. There was still a good chance the restraints had irritated her.

Grabbing his satchel, he stood and put it over his back.

"Let's go."

Pale eyes looked up at him.

"Ok," she smiled and beckoned to him. "Follow me."

As Clee-yo stood and began walking to the undergrowth, he was sure she would suddenly make a mad dash for cover to get rid of him.

But she didn't.

With him walking behind her, her steps were hesitant, but she didn't run.

Instead, she walked as if she wasn't quite sure where she was going and his previous thought that she was hatching some sort of plan returned.

As they got into the cover of the bushes, the warmth of the undergrowth was welcoming. In front of him, the female bat away stray vines that hung in their path, and now and again, she'd glance behind her as if she was checking whether he was still there.

"I don't know how you manage to walk so quietly in a place like this," he heard her murmur as she swat at an insect that decided to land on her shoulder.

The question was, how did *she* manage to walk so noisily in a place like this?

Gaze falling to her feet, he recognized why.

Her feet were flat like his but unlike his four-toed feet, she had five bony toes and it didn't look like she had any footpads.

Again, he wondered how she'd survived this long in the jungle all alone.

His gaze rose slowly, moving up her naked legs to stop at the piece of fabric covering her buttocks.

It was ripped and torn in many places but it still covered enough that she was modest. He couldn't see anything and he realized belatedly that he was staring as if mesmerized at the sway of her hips as she walked.

As if she could read his thoughts, she turned and looked back at him, her gaze lingering on his chest a little too long before she suddenly stopped walking.

Where she'd stopped was at the edge of a cliff.

Frowning, Sohut walked close to the edge and looked over.

It was a sharp drop. All he could see were the tops of trees below.

When he turned his confused stare to the female, the mischief in her eyes was unsettling.

Hatching a plan, she was.

He'd told her to bring him to her hideout.

This definitely was not it.

"Your camp? Where is it?" he asked, his eyes narrowing as a smirk appeared on her face.

Beautiful little trickster.

In the light of Hudo III's star as it rose, she was even more striking than he'd thought before. The female was standing before him, her palms clenching and unclenching and her shoulders were set in the way he'd seen the long-legged grazing animals of the north stand before they would spring into action and dart off into the high fields.

Everything about her stance, from the way she was standing to

the look in her eyes spelled that she was about to do something...
something to *him*.

Yet, for the life of him, he couldn't find the propensity to care. All
he could feel was intrigue.

Instead of trying to stop her scheme, he was curious to find out
what she was planning.

He must have inhaled an atri insect that'd made him go stupid.

Glancing over the edge of the cliff once more, Sohut narrowed his
eyes.

Was she planning on trying to push him off?

He doubted she could but, just in case, he planted his feet firmly
on the ground.

If that was her plan, he'd like to see her try.

"This isn't your camp." He cast his gaze to hers, still reading the
deception simmering underneath her skin.

Her eyes twinkled as she raised an eyebrow and pointed upward.

Sohut's frown deepened.

Up?

Stepping dangerously close to the edge of the cliff, he leaned out
just enough to see above.

Sure enough, there was a small hole in the rock wall there. So
small, it was almost imperceptible among the vines and hanging
branches.

"You live there?" He pointed up before turning his surprised gaze
her way.

The female smiled—one of triumph and pride.

No wonder the Gori's hadn't been able to locate her.

It was a cave and it was high enough for the tracker they'd given
him to not work. Even if they'd come to stand directly below her nest,
the tracker wouldn't have been able to send a signal through the rock
to so far above where they currently stood.

And if that was really her nest, she was smart to have found it.

It was the perfect hideout. The only thing was, it was right beside
a treacherous fall.

"How do you get up there?"

There was that twinkle again before she moved toward the side where the rock wall met the level they were standing on. There were some thick vines there, and she took hold of one.

Jumping, the female hung onto the vine with both hands and began to shimmy upward as he looked at her in awe.

So *that* was how she made it up there.

Of course.

She was a few meters up when she looked down at him.

Right, he had to follow her.

As he did the same thing, hanging on to the vine, the weight of the both of them made the thing swing from side to side and Sohut realized, when he looked down, that they were hanging over the edge.

If the vine broke, they'd both go tumbling down, and he had no idea what was at the bottom of the cliff.

She did this every day?

Turning his gaze upward, his eyes widened as he blinked and looked away.

There was nothing underneath her flimsy covering.

Nothing but pale rounded buttocks.

Phek.

And now he was growing hard.

"...have to hurry."

Caught up in his head, he hadn't realized that as they shimmied upward to her den, the female had been muttering to herself.

"...feels like it's going to break."

What was going to break?

Frowning, he was tempted to look upward again but it was already hard trying to climb with his own cock impeding his hold on the only thing keeping you from falling to his death.

Still, risking a glance upward, he realized she was much quicker than he'd expected.

She was already on the landing above and she was crouching over the edge, looking down at him.

There was worry in her eyes

It made him pause and suddenly he was aware of his surroundings again.

Something glinted in the light and he realized it was the crude weapon she'd stabbed him with.

Sohut stiffened, his gaze moving to the vine.

Sure enough, where the vine connected with the rock was growing thin.

Phek.

His gaze flashed back to hers, not believing what he was seeing.

She'd cut the vine?

His body jerked as he dropped a little, some tendons of the vine breaking underneath his weight.

There was no way he was going to reach the top before the vine broke.

There was no other warning. With a snap, the vine lost tension completely.

Wide, pale eyes locked with his as he fell—horror filling her gaze.

He stared into those eyes till he couldn't see them anymore.

Till he all he could feel was gravity pulling him down and the ground approaching fast.

Staring up at the cliff where he knew she was, his body went numb.

It brought back memories.

It wasn't the first time a female had tried to get rid of him using excessive means.

His own mor had been the first to do so, selling him and his brother to the known enemy as a chid.

That hurt had been a surprise, coming from his mor, but even though Clee-yo had reason to do away with him, his life-organ still froze up and became solid at the fact that she'd actually carried through.

Numb.

So numb that when he hit the vegetation below, he felt nothing.

14

CLEO STARED OVER THE CLIFF, LEANING OVER AS FAR AS SHE COULD.

She didn't dare to breathe, the horror of the situation too much to digest.

The drop down the mountain was a long one and she'd watched the alien free fall till he hit the undergrowth like a brick that landed smack into her stomach.

And all she could do was stare.

She'd always checked the vines' integrity periodically and for the whole time she'd used them to climb up to the cave, she'd never worried about them snapping or tearing.

Staring at the part of vine that was left behind, her hand shuddered as she touched it.

She hadn't expected his weight to have such a huge effect on the plants. Otherwise, she'd have probably tried to explain there was no way he could reach the cave.

As the horrific event replayed in her mind, she stayed at the cliff edge, her entire body shivering.

Shit.

He was probably dead.

A sick feeling filled her stomach.

She'd been so worried about taking him to her cave, worried

about her future, worried about him turning on her that she should be happy now that he was potentially gone.

But happiness wasn't what she was feeling.

He was probably ok, right? Cleo bit what was left of her fingernail and started on what was left of another one.

It was just like her to feel sorry for the one person who could put her back into a cage.

He'd said he was on her side, but she didn't really know anything about him.

He could have been lying...

A sinking feeling entered her chest.

He was probably dead.

He was probably dead and that meant she was probably free—at least for now.

Even if he wasn't dead, she reckoned it would take him three days or so to make it back to where she was.

If he wasn't dead...

She kept her eyes peeled on the jungle below, searching for a sign of blue.

There was none.

She didn't know how long she laid there, frantically searching for a sign the alien was alive, but the sun was high in the sky when she finally crept away from the cliff edge.

He was gone.

He was gone and now she was definitely alone.

Wawa was still missing and it felt like the world she knew was being turned upside down.

Plopping onto her bed, she took a deep breath.

She just watched a man die.

Fuck.

She'd been living in the jungle for a year but that didn't mean she was *wild*. It didn't mean she'd lost her humanity!

For a split second, she thought about taking the long trek around the mountain to get down to where he'd fallen, just to see if he was all right.

But that would mean putting herself in more danger.

She hadn't heard more roars over the last few hours but that didn't mean the dangerous animals weren't out there.

And so she was stuck in limbo.

It was a worrisome place to be.

CLEO'S EYES FLUTTERED OPEN.

Anxiety and panic from the last few hours came rushing back to her and she took a few moments to breathe.

Shit.

This had to be one of the toughest of situations she'd ever faced in her life.

Blinking up into the darkness, she had the distinct feeling she'd been asleep for quite a few hours.

The stress of the last few days seemed to have caught up with her.

Groaning, she glanced over to where Wawa usually slept.

Even in the dark, she knew he wasn't there.

That brought back the fact that all was not right in the world.

She'd just witnessed a death.

The horror of it came back to her and she sat upright immediately.

As she stared into the darkness though, a chill ran down her spine, causing her to stiffen.

It was pitch black in the cave because she'd never made a fire but even with the lack of light, she had the distinct feeling she wasn't alone.

The air—*the darkness*—felt thick.

Swallowing hard, her wide eyes searched the dark cave but picked up nothing.

Maybe she was just imagining things?

"Wawa?" She dared to whisper. IT HAD TO BE WAWA.

There was no sound.

Nothing moved, not even the air. Cleo's shoulders sagged a little.

It was the stress of everything she'd been through.

Squeezing her eyes shut, she flopped back against the bed.

For a few seconds, she kept her eyes shut, a sob lodging in her throat.

He'd seemed like a good guy, the blue alien. He'd been the kindest alien she'd met since she'd been taken away.

To see his life be snuffed out right in front of her was...traumatizing.

Sniffing, she swallowed hard and that's when she *felt* it. A slight shift in the air against her skin. And when she opened her eyes, a gasp caught in her throat.

The blue alien.

He was in her cave.

Even in the darkness, she *knew* it was him.

Corrosive green eyes glared down at her, shining in the darkness almost like a cat's would.

He was so close. So close she could smell him.

It was a mix of the smell of metallic soil and wet vegetation.

Her eyes widened in their sockets as she froze.

It was like seeing a ghost.

As her lungs remembered to operate and her breaths came hurrying in and out of her chest, the alien held her gaze and she was vaguely aware of him launching himself on top of her, his two arms enclosing her on each side.

"You're—" she began, but her words were cut off as the alien roared—and, it was quite literally a roar—in her face.

Fangs.

He had fangs.

How the fuck had she not noticed that before?!

He had fangs. Sharp, sharp fangs that glistened even in the darkness.

And this very angry fanged male was right above her, ready to rip her apart.

Why?

Why was he acting so...differently?

"You," he snarled and Cleo swallowed hard.

Something had definitely changed inside him. Maybe she *was* seeing a ghost.

Even after he'd caught her in those first few moments, she hadn't experienced this ferocity from him.

Frantic, she tried getting from within the cage he'd made with his body but she couldn't even move from underneath him.

There was nowhere to run.

"H-how? How did you survive?"

Something sharp ran against her cheek and her eyes widened even more when she realized it wasn't a knife but one of his fingers.

He had claws.

Sharp claws; it felt as if, should he put any pressure on his finger, her skin would break and she would bleed.

"You," he repeated, his voice so deep and threatening she could feel the fear settle deep into her bones. "You cut the vine."

Cleo swallowed hard, fear vibrating within her before his words connected in her mind.

"What? No! I didn't cut the vine."

"You did." He said it so calmly, the fact his fangs were still right above her almost seemed out of place.

Wait.

Cleo blinked.

He could understand her?

He could understand her!

"I saw you there with your blade," he came closer, moving his head to the side so he was speaking directly into her ear, his voice lowering to a whisper. "You cut it." His warm breath brushed over her skin as he continued. "And now, I'm very, very angry."

He leaned in then and Cleo stiffened, her hands flattening against his chest as she tried to push him away.

"I didn't cut the vine. It snapped!"

"I might have to punish you."

Cleo gulped.

She couldn't imagine what he had in mind.

All she knew was that he wasn't in his right mind because he didn't seem to be listening to her.

He was running his nose against her neck and she didn't dare to move, lest he bury his fangs into her skin.

But he didn't bite her. Instead, he buried his nose even deeper into her neck and did the strangest thing.

He inhaled so deeply, it was like he was trying to pull her skin up through his nose.

"Phek," she heard him mutter.

His hands moved down to grip her by the hips as he inhaled again, this time his mouth opening to the point she felt his fangs as he pulled them across the delicate flesh on her neck.

Something deep in her caused her core to throb.

Something deep, meaning that whore called Libido who didn't realize this was the worst moment to be turned on.

The alien nibbled her neck. Nibbled it! And a deep groan rumbled through his chest.

If this was his idea of punishment, despite that she did nothing wrong, she may...like it?

As the alien held her waist tighter, he nibbled her neck again before running his fangs to the center of her throat and instead of filling her with terror, her nonexistent panties were getting wet.

She felt it then, the first throb of his response, and Cleo blinked.

That hard thing nestled against her wasn't his frickin' leg.

"Umm..." She began and the alien froze.

He lifted his head and looked down at her, his green eyes shining in the darkness.

As if realizing what he was doing or what he'd almost done, he rolled off her suddenly and Cleo was left staring at what she assumed was his back.

He was on the side where she'd placed her piece of trusty shrapnel and her gaze fell to the spot at just the thought of it.

"Don't you even dare."

How the hell did he know?

"I wasn't..."

He turned and looked at her then, his gaze traveling down her body and she realized he could see much better than she could in the dark.

She still couldn't make him out properly but it was clear he wasn't having any trouble seeing her with the lack of light.

"You cut the vine," he repeated when his eyes met hers again and Cleo swallowed once more.

"I didn't."

"You *phekking* cut the vine." A sound like a huff of a laugh caught her ear and she'd have thought she was mistaken if the alien didn't lean his head back and actually laugh.

He was laughing?

"You cut the vine," he repeated. "I really didn't think you would do something like that." He paused, looked away, and she couldn't see his eyes anymore.

"I didn't cut the vine."

"Why are you lying? I saw you with your blade."

Cleo opened her mouth and paused. "I always have my blade. It's the one thing that got me out of trouble in the first place. I don't let it out of my sight." She paused again. "Ever."

The alien grunted.

"I'm being honest. I think...I think the vine broke because you were too heavy for it. Or maybe it was a combination of both our weights."

When he said nothing, she continued.

"I'm sorry you fell."

"You should be," he glared at her then. "I fell *hard*."

The way he said it made her want to chuckle and she chalked that up to the village idiot living within her.

She didn't dare to laugh.

This was serious.

"I saw you fall. I thought you were..." She trailed off. "I want my life to return to what it was before, but I didn't cut the vine. I really didn't."

She couldn't really tell what mood he was in or if he believed her.

One moment he seemed like he was trying to hump her and now he was laughing at what happened to him as if it hadn't been serious.

"And it took *phekking* long to find my way back here." He turned to her fully then. "But you know what annoyed me the most?"

Should she answer that? It sounded like a trick question.

"What phekked me off the most was that I had to climb this Raxu-forsaken rock with my bare. Phekking. Hands."

She had the feeling he was showing her his hands. Maybe he didn't realize she couldn't see shit with this lack of light.

Even with her eyes adjusted to the darkness, she could hardly make out any shapes.

Wait. His words hit her. *He what?*

No one could do that. That's why her cave was such a great hiding spot.

Muttering something she didn't catch, she felt him move off the bed and then she heard the tinkle of metal.

In a short moment, the cave was filled with light from his light disk thing and Cleo audibly gasped.

He looked *terrible*.

There were bits of twigs and leaves stuck in his hair, his hard previously-unmarred chest had all sorts of scrapes and cuts and when he turned to rummage in his satchel, a whole host of what looked like brown sea urchins were stuck in his flesh.

Ouch!

Her face must have been scrunched up at the sight because when he turned and looked at her, his green eyes bore into hers like *yes, this is your fault.*

Obviously, he still believed she'd cut the vine on him.

Ignoring her, he continued searching in his satchel.

"Only a few things didn't fall out," he muttered. "The phekking tracker is still here but all my sluu dough is gone." He turned his accusatory eyes on her. "I shouldn't have fed you any."

Cleo flattened her lips and averted her gaze from his.

The food he'd fed her had been delicious. She too felt loss at the thought of them being lost.

As the blue alien moved, his tail swung lazily behind him and it too was filled with the urchin-like burs.

They looked like they hurt. But he didn't seem nearly as angry at her as he should be. Well, he had been angry at first but not nearly enough and she didn't know how to process that.

As he moved over and grabbed his blade from his satchel, he made it a point to look at her sharply as he took up the weapon.

"Like the handiwork of your evil scheme?" he asked before moving to a space near the entrance of the cave.

Cleo huffed out a breath. "For the last time, I didn't cut the vine. And you can understand me. How?"

"I installed your language while you were restrained."

Cleo let that information sink in.

He could understand her all that time?

Frowning, she tried to remember if she'd said anything that she didn't want him to know.

It was only then that she noticed he was crouching slightly. He was too big for her small living space and that made her realize that he seemed to fill the entire small cavity.

"Why did you come back?" She spoke to his back.

He'd been far away and he was injured. Instead of finding help for himself, he'd returned.

"And leave you here? So the Gori can send some other idiot to find you? They'd torture you."

He must have seen the blood drain from her face because his gaze softened a little.

"So, you came back so they wouldn't torture me?"

"Yes," he said, "I came back so they wouldn't torture you. I'm much too kind to allow that to happen."

She should feel relief at those words. Instead, there was a sort of dread as if there was something she was missing.

"So you came back because you want to...*save* me?"

The alien's eyes met hers again and something passed behind them—something that reminded her of the few moments before when he was pressing against her with his body.

"Oh, Cluu," he used the name he'd given her and she was surprised he'd remembered it. "Do I have to spell it out for you?" His face became serious. "I came back because I have plans for you myself."

15

FUCKING.

Grout.

After dropping that line that she was currently tiptoeing around, trying not to detonate, the grout in the cave began to stoically ignore her.

It was as if she wasn't even there.

Instead, he stared out the small hole that formed the cave entrance and was doing something with his hands.

Now and then, he'd grunt and she couldn't help but draw closer to see what he was doing.

Standing as far as she could manage while still being able to look over his shoulder, Cleo's eyes widened.

He was using his blade to pry the jungle urchins from his skin and it looked painful.

Blood oozed from every spot where he managed to remove one of the things.

Guilt flooded through her as she watched him work.

When he finished prying the ones he could see from his arms, shoulders, and tail, he began reaching behind him to try to get the ones at his back.

Cleo squeezed her eyes shut for a second before her mouth moved.

"Let me help you..." She stepped forward before he could reply and closed her hand around the blade.

Rather, she closed her hand around his, for he was holding the blade.

It was the first time she'd willfully touched him and her heart sped up a bit.

Grout studied her face. "Help me? I'd be a mad jerkal to let you get your hand on my blade. You like to cut things."

Cleo clenched her teeth to stop herself from retorting.

"I only want to help you. I'm being honest when I say I didn't cut the vine. Now shut up and give me the knife."

He studied her some more. "I sense no deception."

"That's because *I'm telling the truth*."

For a few seconds, he just stared at her before his gaze moved to her hand still placed over his.

Slowly, beneath her fingers, she felt his hand loosen and soon the blade was in her hands.

Wordlessly, Cleo pressed her lips into a thin line as she took a deep breath.

Place the edge of the blade under one of the urchins, she tried to pry the thing out of his skin, but it was in deeper than she'd realized.

She'd have to touch him again to get some leverage to remove the darn thing.

Biting her lip, she rested her free hand on his shoulder and she was sure she felt the muscle underneath her hand go taut as if he was as painfully aware of her touch as she was aware of placing her hand there.

His skin felt warm, smooth, and not at all like human skin. It was firmer, yet didn't feel hard, and she found she wanted to run her fingers along his shoulder just out of pure curiosity.

Touching him felt...nice.

She hadn't had the pleasure of touching anyone else in so, so long. Even back on Earth, she'd been single for a long time.

Intimate touches that had been desired had been...scarce.

Uninvited intimate touches had been abundant.

Being a bartender had come with its downfalls.

Not that she was being intimate at the moment...

Shaking away her wandering thoughts, Cleo took a deep breath and positioned the knife beneath the urchin she was targeting once more.

"Here goes," she murmured, and the alien grunted that he understood.

Pressing the blade against his back, she tried to pry free the thing embedded in his skin but it didn't budge.

"Shit, it's really in there, isn't it. I don't want to cut you."

"You've stabbed me before... This would be a flesh wound," the alien murmured and Cleo sighed.

"It wasn't because I *wanted* to stab you. Plus, I was protecting myself. This is different."

The alien grunted again, his gaze focused outside the cave.

Finally able to hook the edge of the blade into the thing, a sharp pull had the urchin dislodging and it fell to the cave floor as blood rose from the wound it left behind.

Cleo swallowed hard.

Despair flooded through her.

"I'm sorry," she finally said and she was sure of it this time—he stiffened underneath her hand.

"Sorry for what?"

"I'm sorry you're hurt like this. I thought worse had happened but this is still very terrible." She pried out another one of the things and blood rushed to the surface of his skin.

It must hurt so bad.

"Really sorry," she whispered as she got to work on another one.

At her words, the alien turned to regard her, his green eyes narrowing.

She couldn't read what he was thinking but when he didn't say anything else, she accepted the silence and continued working on him.

◇

THE SEA URCHINS took a long time to dislodge and by the time she was finished, her own arms and shoulders were aching.

She'd ended up kneeling behind him to get the worst of them out and now, after she pried the last one out, she settled back on her haunches, a heavy sigh leaving her frame.

Her gaze traveled over the absolute carnage that was his back.

There was blood everywhere and it was a good thing she wasn't squeamish.

"That's all of them," she breathed, her voice soft as she rolled her shoulders.

The alien turned and looked at her, his gaze moving over her face.

"What's that on your face, *Cluu*?"

Her aching shoulders stiffened immediately and to her dismay, the little dots that ran down the alien's nose seemed to scrunch up a bit.

Was he making fun of her? In his state?

"There's nothing on my face." There wasn't, was there? She resisted the urge to brush her hand over her cheek. Her hands were stained with his blood and she'd only make a mess.

"Hmm," the alien said, "thought I saw regret. Must have been mistaken."

Cleo released an exasperated sound and the alien chuckled. "*I didn't cut the vine.*"

His gaze softened as he looked at her. Reaching for his satchel, he pulled out that thing he'd put on the first wound she'd dealt him in the arm.

"Wait, your back is filled with blood. Let me wash it first," she said, standing and moving away from him to where the last of her water was.

Or where it should have been...

She forgot she was out of water. She'd have to fetch some when it was morning.

As she turned and moved back over to the alien, she realized he was looking at her with a funny look in his eyes...watching her... studying her.

"I have life fluid," he said, pulling a small bottle from his satchel.

He handed it to her and she emptied the water into her bowl.

Moving behind him, she dipped her hand in the bowl and hesitated.

Prying the urchins from his back had been one thing. Now she'd be rubbing her hands all over his back.

For a moment, she planted her gaze at the back of his dark head of hair. He was looking straight ahead, his shoulders rigid, as if he was trying to steel himself against something.

Her touch maybe.

She hadn't thought about that.

Maybe him making light of the situation was his way of not focusing on her alien hand on his skin.

Her skin must feel weird to him.

Sighing, she shut down the thoughts in her head and began to wash away the blood on his back. At the first touch of her fingers against his skin, he stiffened some more.

She'd hurry then.

Luckily, it only took all of his water to wash his back and no more. As she stood to put the bowl down, she heard him mutter a thank you.

When she returned to stand beside him, he was trying to put on the ointment on the wounds and she reached for it.

The alien lifted a thick eyebrow but didn't resist, handing her the ointment so she could lather it over his wounds.

As she tended to the last wound, she was surprised to see that the ones she'd tended to first were already beginning to close up.

Either it was some miracle ointment or it was black magic.

Shit. The things doctors on Earth would do for miracle salve like this.

She was caught up in her thoughts, staring at the wounds healing in front of her eyes when the alien turned suddenly, his hand closing around her raised wrist.

Her first thought was to fight back and it took her a second to realize he wasn't being aggressive.

As he turned fully, she had no option but to lean back as he suddenly invaded her space.

He leaned over her, his gaze traveling over her face before it landed on her neck and the memory of his fangs running across her skin came back immediately.

Cleo gulped and his eyes fastened on the movement of her throat.

"What are you doing?" Why did she whisper it?

His gaze moved to her lips and he took a few moments to reply. "I don't know." He paused. "I was supposed to capture you, take you to the Goris..."

Cleo swallowed hard again. "I know. I mean...what are you doing right now?"

His gaze snapped to hers then and something inside her jumped and exploded into a million butterflies in her chest.

This wasn't logical, was it?

She didn't *like* him...did she?

The alien licked his lips, his tongue moving slowly and as the air thickened between them, that bitch Libido woke up like a demon summoned.

It was when she looked at him in the eyes that she realized he'd been staring at her, watching her as her gaze followed the movement of his tongue.

She was going to do it, wasn't she.

Moving toward him slowly, she paused just as their noses touched.

His eyes were still locked with hers and his breathing was coming a little bit faster, matching hers.

As she touched her lips lightly against his, his green gaze widened on hers and she almost pulled away, only, she found she couldn't.

His arms encircled her, pulling her against him so hard, her mouth crashed against his.

They stayed like that for a little, lips unmoving.

He wasn't kissing her.

Cleo blinked as the alien just stared back at her and it dawned on her that, possibly, he didn't know *how* to kiss.

Fuck her.

What the fuck was she doing?

But the need growing between her thighs demanded that she continue.

Opening her mouth slightly, she touched her tongue against his lips and he stiffened against her, inhaling deeply.

His lips felt divine against hers and the kiss deepened on its own accord. He opened his mouth matching her movements and when their tongues met, he pulled her against him fully, groaning into her mouth.

One hand moved to cradle the back of her neck as he pushed her head back, the play of their lips making her breathless.

When he finally released her and they both took heaving breaths, she looked into those green eyes of his, a sort of fear growing in the pit of her stomach.

She had no idea what just happened or what it meant.

And what was more fearful was the look in his eyes...

There was a growing possessiveness there—the look you get when you discover something you had to have.

Only, he was looking at *her*.

16

THE REST OF THE NIGHT, SHE COULDN'T SLEEP.

Not with him there and not after that kiss.

And despite that he should be completely exhausted from all that happened, he was wide awake.

As a matter of fact, he seemed to be completely revived and full of energy since their kiss.

For the remainder of the night, he watched her as she moved, tending to things within the cave.

He'd walked around touching everything, things she'd crafted like her food bowls and her fire pit, her roll of straw that was her mattress, her straw hat...

He seemed interested in everything she had, asking her how she'd crafted it, how she knew how to craft it, and other questions.

It was all so alien to him and the way he oohed and aahed was filling her with pride.

She'd done all this...survived in an alien wild place all on her own.

"And these?" He asked as the first light of morning began filling the sky. "How did you know how to do this?"

He was holding her fire board and spindle as if they were two parts of a puzzle he didn't understand.

"My father taught me," she answered as she used her finger to detangle a knot in her hair. She was pretty sure her hair was wrecked beyond repair but with most of the mud gone, it was easier to get the strands free from the tangles.

A strange look came over the alien...*Sohut*'s face. He wasn't exactly like she thought he'd be.

He was...softer...nicer?

Don't get her wrong, he was all hard edges. But his personality... he was surprising her with every second that she was in his presence.

When she'd seen him hop from the orcs' vehicle and head into the jungle, she hadn't expected him to be like this.

He was so...different.

The muscles in his arms flexed even with him just turning the spindle in his hands.

"Your *daran*..." he said. The word didn't translate in her head.

"Daran?" she asked.

"Yes. The male who begot you."

"Oh, my dad. Yea. He used to take me camping all the time." She paused, memories of time spent with her father resurfacing. What she wouldn't do to see him again.

"He was all I had. My mother never wanted me. She threatened to throw me away." She huffed out a laugh. Funny she could talk about it so easily now. As a child, she'd felt like a reject because of that one fact. And that's why her father, the great Thomas Barlow, had worked so hard to make her tough.

She wasn't a victim.

She was a survivor.

"Dad taught me everything he knew." She fingered another knot in her hair, working her way through the strands till they were straight again. "He taught me how to make a shelter, taught me how to find food, taught me how to make a fire from nothing. He taught me everything I needed to know to survive."

As if he knew he'd leave me one day and I'd need them in this exact situation.

She didn't say the last sentence but when the faraway look left her eyes, when the glaze of unexpected tears drained away from her vision, she realized the alien was looking at her with a strange look in his luminous green eyes.

"He was everything a child like me needed," she finished.

A sort of wry smile twisted the alien's lips. "Must be nice," he said.

The words sounded bitter despite that his facial muscles displayed no emotion.

As a matter of fact, it was almost as if he had completely closed off suddenly.

For a beat, he just stared at her, his eyes having a faraway look—the kind you got when you were looking at something that wasn't there...*remembering* something.

And then he sniffed.

Whatever he smelled pulled him straight from wherever he'd gone and his eyes widened slightly.

With a deliberate pull of his nostrils, so hard the little bumps that ran down his septum bunched up a little, he inhaled again.

"Slizz," he said, his shoulders stiffening.

Then she heard it—the sound of his claws protracting.

It happened so fast. One second, there was movement at the mouth of the cave and then something flew in so fast she had little time to jump to her feet.

A screech caught in the air as the blur materialized into Wawa.

Wawa!

His claws dug into Sohut's back, into the wounds there that hadn't fully healed yet and Sohut grunted in pain as he reached back, his entire palm closing around Wawa's small body.

Wawa screeched again—a sound she'd never heard him make before—and dug his claws deeper, his mouth opening to show a terror she never knew he even had.

Rows upon rows of sharp teeth were exposed to the morning light.

Cleo's heart lodged into her throat as her brain caught up with what was happening.

"Wawa!" she shouted, advancing toward them, but Sohut stumbled back instead, out of her reach.

Slamming his back into the cave wall, he tried to put Wawa out of business and Cleo realized at that moment that she was feeling two things.

1. She didn't want Wawa to hurt the alien who'd appeared in her solitary life like a whirlwind.

2. She didn't want Sohut to hurt Wawa either.

"Stop!" she shouted to Sohut. "He thinks you're an intruder. I'll get him off you."

The alien looked at her as if she belonged in an asylum. His eyes were the widest she'd ever seen them before.

"It's a phekking *slizz*. I knew I smelled it but I hadn't been sure." He grunted as Wawa kept harming him and Cleo gulped, the thought of those teeth she'd seen sinking in the alien's back making her rush toward them.

But the alien moved out of the way again, keeping his back away from her as he tried to dislodge Wawa from his skin.

She saw enough to tell he had one hand around Wawa's skinny body and the other squeezing Wawa's neck but Wawa's claws were dug into his back, not letting go.

One of them was going to win and the other was going to be badly hurt if she didn't intervene.

She advanced again and the alien took another step backward. They were walking in circles. Every time she moved forward, he'd go around her.

"This creature is dangerous. More dangerous than you realize. Stay away. One bite and it will kill you with its venom. You'll die in seconds."

Wawa?

The same sweet animal she'd slept beside for over a year?

No way he was as dangerous as Sohut thought...but then again, she'd never seen Wawa act like he was now...and she'd never seen those teeth.

It was as if the teeth had been hidden until he'd needed them just now.

"Wawa," she cooed mid-Wawa-screech and the screech seemed to die a little at the end. He was listening to her.

"Wawa...let the nice alien go. He won't hurt you." She said the last

116

four words while looking at Sohut but he was still looking at her as if she was insane.

"You *named* it?" He almost spat the words. "You *named* this...this little murderer? You think it's your *friend*?"

"It—*he is* my friend. He's been my only friend for over a year. If—"

"Phek me..." Then his nose scrunched up. "Raxu knows, it phekking stinks!"

The way he said it, she'd have laughed if he didn't have an animal intent on ripping him apart fastened to his back.

Cooing, she stepped to the side so she could make eye contact with Wawa.

"Wawa," she cooed, and the animal looked at her.

Cleo's hand flew to cover her mouth in shock.

Wawa's big brown eyes were completely and utterly black.

"Wawa?" The animal blinked at her and his eyes turned to brown.

"It's a slizz, not a pet, I doubt—"

At the sound of the alien's voice, Wawa screeched again, his eyes bleeding to black in an instant as he twisted his neck in Sohut's hand, trying to sink his teeth into the alien's flesh.

"Wawa!" It took her a moment to realize the authoritative voice was her own. "Stop this instant!"

Wawa's eyes turned to brown again and he blinked at her...but his teeth, wherever they'd come from, didn't retract.

"This man is my..." *Friend*? He wasn't her friend. But he didn't seem like her enemy either. Enemies didn't give you their sharp blade and turn their backs to you while you pulled thorns from their flesh, knowing very well you could slit their throat if you wanted to.

Wawa had stopped screeching, but he wasn't letting go and Sohut was looking at her with a mix of horror and disbelief—the same look you'd probably give someone who could burp the alphabet and the Star Wars theme without effort.

"Let. Him. Go."

Wawa and the alien blinked at her before Wawa's teeth...disappeared.

Where they went in his head, she didn't know. But his mouth closed, and he retracted his claws from Sohut's back.

Before she could tell the animal "good job", Wawa was a blur as Sohut threw him across the room. Her body jerked as he pushed her behind him and she got a view of his bleeding back again.

"Stay behind me," he said, his muscles tensed.

A chuckle rose in her throat.

"I'm the one that just rescued *you*. I don't need protection from Wawa."

As she looked around him though, the sight of Wawa made the hairs on her neck rise a little.

He didn't look like the normal cute little animal she was used to.

He looked terrifying.

He was kind of like an otter.

Cute, but deadly.

Just like the alien guarding her, Wawa was tense. His teeth were out again, and he was ready to pounce should Sohut make a wrong move.

Wawa's eyes darted from the alien to her and back but he stood still.

"Wawa," Cleo stepped from behind Sohut and he made a noise of disapproval as she reached out to Wawa. "Come, bubba. He's ok. He won't hurt you."

She shot a look behind her at the bewildered alien.

Wawa came forward slowly and crawled up her hand to sit on her shoulder at his usual spot, his tail swishing lazily on her back.

He was giving the alien the stink eye and it was strange to recognize that on an alien creature's face. So strange, she had to hold back a laugh.

Sohut was still looking at her like she was insane then his claws retracted slowly.

She actually heard them go back in. They sounded frickin' sharp and she was happy he hadn't decided to use them on her.

"That's a slizz..." he repeated, ignoring the fact there was blood dripping to the cave floor from his back.

"I don't know what you mean. I don't know what a slizz is," she said, moving to her water bowl but the water was finished, all used when she'd cleaned his wounds earlier.

"That thing on your phekking shoulder!" An accusatory finger was pointed in her direction. "That slizz...*likes* you." He said it, his face contorting into an expression she'd never seen on his face before. He looked utterly perplexed.

He inhaled again, his face contorting some more, before he raised a hand to cover his nose.

"It really *stinks*."

Wawa looked at him with hate in his eyes and she couldn't help but chuckle.

Wawa smelled fine to her.

"I knew I smelled slizz. Just...a slizz shouldn't be in this jungle." He paused, his eyes widening some more. "That explains everything."

"What do you mean?" Cleo's arms fell to her side as she glanced around her little cave. Despite all the things she'd gathered to survive, she didn't have much. With Sohut in the cave, it only seemed smaller and not suitable to live in.

"I don't have any more water to wash your wounds."

"It explains why you haven't been attacked by any spined beasts..."

That made her stiffen. "What?"

"This is their territory, but they are natural enemies to the slizz." He stared at Wawa in horror. "Little phekker must have been destroying their population...while protecting you."

"What?" she repeated, her eyes widening as she turned to look at Wawa, who blinked innocent brown eyes at her. She couldn't imagine it.

"Slizz are untamable little maniacs." He moved to his bag and took out that tube she'd used on his wounds earlier. "That's why they're banned and their population controlled. I haven't seen a slizz since..." he stopped to think "...forever. Whoever let it go out here was smuggling."

Cleo swallowed, her eyes still on Wawa. "Are you really what he says you are?"

"Slizz don't speak."

Cleo rolled her eyes at Sohut and chuckled. "I know that but he's my pet. You talk to your pets, don't you?"

"I don't have any pets," Sohut said, his eyes flicking to hers then back to his healing tube as he rubbed the solution into his back. "There are animals at the Sanctuary but none of them are my *pets*."

"Really? Every good person deserves a pet." She stroked Wawa's back and he rubbed his head against the side of her face.

"I'm not a good person."

17

HE COULDN'T BELIEVE THIS SMALL LITTLE FEMALE WAS HARBORING A slizz of all beasts. The thing had almost ripped his skin apart. If he'd been too weak to fight it off, he'd probably be lying stiff on the floor.

Vile, vile beasts they were.

He eyed the two now, how she cooed and purred to it, her soft lips curving into a circle as she made soft sounds to the little maniac.

Of all the beasts to bond with...

Clee-yo stroked the slizz softly, her hand running down the thing's back and he watched her hand move.

All he could think of was the feel of her touch as she'd tended to his wounds.

The last time he'd had someone touch him...care about him like that...he couldn't remember when that was.

Watching her pet the slizz, an unsettling feeling developed at the pit of his stomach.

Sohut blinked and turned away to look out the cave hole.

He wasn't...*jealous*, was he? Of a slizz? Impossible.

Yet, when he glanced behind him to look at them once more, the little beast was giving him a look as if it owned the female and that thought...*unnerved* him a little.

"I smelled his scent marking before I came up the mountain," he said, still looking out the cave entrance.

"His what?" He could hear her bare feet pad against the grass on the floor as she approached him.

"Your slizz created a warning around this mountain, to warn the spined creatures off."

There was silence and when he turned to look at her, Clee-yo was looking at the slizz confused.

"He what?"

"He's been protecting you." He eyed the creature. "It...*likes* you."

He still couldn't believe it. To his knowledge, slizz only had the propensity to hate and kill.

Clee-yo hugged the animal to her chest and he tried to keep his alarm at bay.

"You did that?" she cooed at it. "You've been protecting me?"

The slizz shot him a hateful glance before snuggling against her.

Fine. He didn't want to be friends with it either.

"We have to go," he said and that caught her attention.

"Go?" There was panic in her eyes.

"We can't stay here. We have to go farther into the jungle, head to the Torian camp there, and then from there to the Sanctuary. The Gori will be wondering why I haven't contacted them to pick you up yet. They will send someone to check."

He could almost see the alarm travel through Clee-yo's frame.

"Sanctuary?" she asked.

He nodded. "My home."

That made her eyes widen. "You're taking me to your home? Why?"

He found himself smiling. "Where else would I take you?"

Clee-yo's mouth opened and closed.

"Get ready. Let's go."

THEY HAD TO BE QUICK.

With most of his sluu dough lost when he fell, he'd have to hunt

122

on the way to the Torian camp. If not, they would starve if they didn't find anything to eat.

Sohut watched as Clee-yo put a few things into a large slemma leaf and strapped it to herself, ready to go. He had everything he needed in his satchel...what was left of his gadgets, that is.

"Ready?" he asked.

Pale eyes met his and Clee-yo smiled a little. "Ready."

With that, he slipped through the opening and launched himself off the edge, his claws protracting as he grabbed unto the rock at the last moment to swing himself unto the landing under the cave.

He just about heard her gasp of surprise.

"What the fuck?" There was a pause. "Shit, did he fall off again?"

There was worry in her voice and that made him feel a little bit... good. She cared enough about him to worry.

"Uh, Grout?" She called. "Sohut?!"

She used his name. He knew she had it in her.

"I'm fine. Jump," he called. "I will catch you."

"You must be fucking out of your mind." Her response made him chuckle.

She cursed underneath her breath and he heard something along the lines of him almost giving her a heart attack. "Get out of the way, I'm coming down."

Shortly after, a long twisted thing came falling from above. He'd hardly call it a rope, but it was close enough. It looked like she'd spent quite a long time twining various vines together to make something strong enough to hold her weight.

So she'd made precautions a long time ago in case her vine broke. Impressive.

Looking up, his next view was that of two long legs shimmying down and he had to look away quickly when she came down farther.

He'd be looking right up under her skirt and he didn't even have to see anything, the thought alone had him throbbing in his pants so quickly he had to turn away.

He heard when her unpadded feet hit the landing and was sure she was completely off the vine because the scent of slizz was unbearable again.

"Are you ok? You just launched off the cliff like you were on a suicide mission," she said.

"Killing myself would be too easy." He gave her a wry smile and he could tell she was trying to decipher his words, understand them.

She never would.

"Let's go," he said, turning from her and adjusting his satchel where it wouldn't rub the new wounds her *pet* had inflicted on him.

"This way," she said, stepping off into the brush in a direction he hadn't thought she'd take. "I need water first."

Walking behind her was a nice view, except for the ugly slizz glaring at him from her shoulder.

Even in the brambles and vines, she moved with grace and caution.

Her ears were flat against her head, and unlike his, it didn't seem she could perk them, yet he had the distinct impression that she was doing just that.

She was listening for any unnatural sounds.

She had the strange piece of warped metal clutched in her hand as she made her way through.

He wasn't even looking where she was headed. Watching her was far more interesting.

There was a soft wind blowing through the trees and if he could delete the smell of the slizz, he would be able to fully enjoy her scent and her scent alone.

The phekking slizz really needed a bath.

As if it could read his thoughts, the slizz protracted its teeth a little and bared them at him.

His fangs responded instinctively.

Ignoring the annoying beast, he turned his attention back to watching Clee-yo's hips sway underneath her worn attire. He was so mesmerized, he almost tripped over a root on the ground and then Clee-yo turned to glare at him, her strange metal thing pointed in his direction.

Her face softened immediately, as if she'd been so engrossed in walking through the undergrowth that she'd forgotten that he was there.

"You're so quiet usually, I thought it was something else." Her eyes darted to the undergrowth again. "I'm hunting some food as we go. I'm hungry. I'm pretty sure you are too."

Hunting?

He stared at her as she turned and continued walking again.

Everything about her made him curious. She walked through the undergrowth as if she'd been born on this planet.

The way she'd adjusted was...extraordinary, and he felt a level of respect growing within him.

"What are you hunting?"

"Jungle penguins," she whispered.

Sohut blinked. "I do not comprehend. Jungle what?"

"They're getting smarter and learning to hide from me now, the fat little things."

Fat little things?

She had to be referring to the senseless mogs.

"Stop," he said. "If it's mogs you want, I'll call them for you."

Clee-yo stopped to look back at him, ducking under a hanging vine as she did.

Putting both hands to his mouth he whistled. It was a high sound the mogs were attracted to and he was sure they would come waddling through the bushes directly to where they were standing.

The fact he could do this, help her, made a feeling of unexpected pride surge through him.

No doubt, she'd find it impressive. It wasn't a whistle many beings could do.

But when he glanced back at the female, she was looking at him weirdly, her nose scrunched up, her upper lip curled as she stared at him.

"What the hell are you doing?"

Sohut blinked, glancing away for just a second. "Whistling."

"With no sound?"

Now it was his turn to look at her strangely. "You can't hear it?"

It was high, but even *his* ears could pick it up.

"You mean you're actually making a sound?" Her eyes bugged out a little.

Moving closer to her, he whistled again but she only blinked at him. That prompted him to lean down to look at her ears.

So different from his. Hers did not rise to a point and her pinna seemed much less pronounced than his.

He was about to reach out and touch her skin when his hand was swatted away—and not by the female, no less.

It took him a second to realize that the darn slizz had leaned across her back to attack him.

Opening his mouth to curse the thing, he stopped, his breath catching in his throat as Clee-yo's laughter reached his ears.

"I guess he's a bit protective of me," he assumed she said, for he couldn't hear her words, all he could see was her lips move and all he could remember was the fact those same lips had been on his not long ago.

A sort of mouth phekking.

They'd mouth phekked.

And it had been glorious.

Cleo cleared her throat and movement behind him caused him to glance that way.

A family of six mogs waddled from the bushes to stop in front of them. The mogs' expectant eyes moved to their party of two—fine, three, if he was going to count the unlikable animal on Clee-yo's shoulder.

"How did you do that?" Cleo moved to stand beside him. "They hide from me."

"And that has nothing to do with you munching on them."

A slap on his arm made him wince out of pure surprise and Clee-yo's eyes grew large. "Oh my god, I'm sorry. Did I hurt you?"

Not enough, he wanted to say.

"Of course, not."

Crouching, he beckoned to one of the little animals and whistled as he did.

The mogs obliged, moving closer. Close enough for him to grab two of the fattest ones.

"And that's how you catch a mog," he said, standing with two hardly-struggling mogs in his hands. Raxu knows, they should be extinct for their stupidity.

But Clee-yo didn't move. She didn't even say anything. She just stood looking at the four remaining mogs, bewilderment on her face.

"What is it?" he had to ask. He'd never seen anyone look at their food with such pity before.

"It's different when you catch them. Seems more...heartless. They trust you."

"Which is why they're going to be eaten. Just because something is nice to you that doesn't mean it's your ally."

For a second, she didn't reply, then a look came over her face that made him instantly regret what he said.

Clee-yo's shoulders stiffened and she adjusted her gaze toward the bushes.

He could almost see his words repeating in her head and realization came too late.

He hadn't been referring to himself but that's obviously where her mind was going.

"You're absolutely right," she finally said.

18

CLEO STRUGGLED WITH HER SPINDLE AND FIRE BOARD. ACROSS FROM her, Sohut sat cross-legged beside the two mogs waiting to be prepared.

He'd attempted to eat them raw, much to her horror.

Now he sat watching her with interest.

His presence was...soothing and as she worked to get a fire going, she thought about that.

But his words from earlier kept repeating in her mind.

Just because something is nice to you that doesn't mean it's your ally.

He was right.

It was something she needed to remember.

A sigh made her shoulders rise and fall as her fire caught and she fed it slowly.

Here, underneath the canopy, the smoke wouldn't rise too high.

Her gaze was focused on the fire, but her mind was on other things.

She'd kissed him and that kiss meant nothing.

She didn't know what she'd been doing or why she'd done it in the first place and that was a shock.

Sohut had no stakes in this. Her survival depended on *her*.

The fire caught and she cooked the meat with motions that were more ingrained than conscious.

As they ate in silence, she could feel Sohut's eyes on her, but she kept her gaze averted as she considered things.

How did she even know he was taking her somewhere safe?

She didn't. She was just blindly following him along.

Her instincts told her she could trust him, but logic told her to be cautious.

As they finished the meal, stood, and headed to the water hole, she led the way.

She couldn't hear him behind her.

She was sure he was still there though; he just walked through the jungle as if he was a black panther.

He was silent.

Gorgeous.

Deadly.

And that's why she should get her mind centered and control herself.

He wasn't human.

He wasn't her friend.

She had no friends.

She only had Cleo.

Pushing the thoughts back, she sighed as she reached the clearing for the water hole.

"I'll leave you here," Sohut suddenly spoke behind her.

"Leave?" Why did that make her panicky?

"I'm going to scout the perimeter," he said.

Wawa lifted his head on her shoulder.

Nodding, she put down her makeshift bag on some dry vines running along the floor.

Sohut paused for a second and then he disappeared into the brush.

Glancing at Wawa, she smiled at the animal.

"Just me and you again," she murmured. But Wawa hopped from her shoulder, gave her a glance, and went in the opposite direction to the alien.

Now that she knew what he went off to do, she wondered if he sensed danger close.

She'd had no idea her little innocent pet had been working so hard to keep them both safe.

She was indebted to him.

Dropping against the rock wall, Cleo looked around the small clearing.

She couldn't believe she was going to leave this place.

It had become her home—the only place she knew on this god-forsaken planet.

She'd always known the day would come. Still, she wasn't prepared for it.

Another sigh lifted her shoulders, as she turned to the rock pool.

Sohut said he knew how to get them from the jungle and to the Torian camp. From there, they'd travel to his brother's location—a sanctuary of some sort. She could only hope he wasn't about to bring her right to the aliens she was running away from.

Stripping off her clothing, Cleo stood naked in front of the rock pool, looking down into the clear water.

It was so pristine, she could see right to the bottom of it.

It would be the last time she took a bath in this water—the very last time she'd sink beneath its cool surface.

For that reason, she moved slower, intent on soaking up every bit of the experience.

The sun's rays hit the yellow-orange leaves around her in such a way that the entire little clearing looked like a scene she'd expect to see on a map of a fairy kingdom.

Not only that, but the air was so fresh, so clear, so unpolluted, that each deep breath she took felt like she was purifying herself from within.

It really was the perfect spot she'd found and as she stepped into the pool, her body going below the surface, she allowed her shoulders to sag with relief.

It was perfect for the time she'd spent in the area, but her leaving was inevitable.

She had to go.

There was no way, realistically, for her to live out in the jungle indefinitely.

The change was one she was going to take in stride and try as much as she could to embrace.

And Sohut...

Something inside her fluttered at the thought of him.

As her head broke the surface and she gasped for breath, Cleo blinked, treading the water as she wiped it from her eyes.

There was no soap so she had to make do.

She'd found some berries in the jungle that made her smell good and she'd always left a few close to the water's edge so she could retrieve them while washing herself.

The animals didn't seem to trouble them so that was good.

Reaching for a few now, she crushed them between her fingers and began lathering her hair and sensitive areas.

As soon as she dipped beneath the water again to wash the residue of the berries out, she already felt clean.

She didn't know where it came from, but a smile graced her lips then.

She was about to leave and it wasn't going to be so bad. She could feel it in her heart that everything was going to be okay.

ZIMSU BERRIES...

The smell was faint but he caught it in the air anyway.

Sohut paused at the edge of the clearing and his life-organ in his chest ceased beating.

Clee-yo was like a piece of life he didn't know he'd been missing till now.

Her head broke the water's surface, and the star's rays played on her tresses making their hue seem even richer.

Small rivulets of water were running down her pale skin and for the first time, he was jealous of something so simple.

The urge to follow the path of the water droplets down her skin was so strong, it's almost as if it pulled him from the cover of the bushes into the clearing.

She looked up then, alarm making her features a little larger.

And then, as if she realized the water was no cover at all, she moved toward the edge, pressing the front of her body against the rock and essentially blocking his view as a curious hue colored her cheeks.

"You're back," she breathed, her cheeks were still that warm color and he realized she was looking everywhere except for *at* him.

"Did you find anything?"

He didn't trust himself to answer.

He didn't know if he was capable of speech.

It felt as if he would groan if he opened his mouth.

Clee-yo looked like a trimslar gem on display and all he wanted to do was to touch her.

"Nothing," he managed to croak.

The urge to touch her was one problem. The other was already stretching the crotch of his trousers.

Turning from her, he dropped his satchel beside her pack that she'd set to the side and began sliding out of his trousers. He was sure he heard a sharp exhale behind him.

"Wh-what are you doing?"

Sohut turned, his cock bobbing slightly as he did. "I will wash with you."

For a second she said nothing. Her mouth was the shape of a circle as she stared at him, or rather his cock, and that hue in her cheeks took on such ferocious intensity, he worried slightly that she was becoming ill.

"Clee-yo?"

Clee-yo's mouth opened and closed like a kuruga's and she blinked a few times before she sputtered, "You can't bring that in here!" The color of her cheeks deepened further, if that was even possible.

"I—I mean, *you* can't come in here. It's hardly enough space for the two of us."

She swallowed hard and tore her gaze away, choosing to focus somewhere on his chest instead.

Sohut looked down at himself.

Was his member not impressive?

He blinked at it, a new feeling he'd never experienced before reaching him.

What if she didn't like what she saw?

"Is there something wrong with my cock?"

"Oh God..." she groaned in a low voice, sinking a little in the water. "What's not right with it?"

His cock throbbed, jerking a little.

"What's that?" He'd heard her fine, but he wanted to hear her say it again.

"I said 'I'll come out so you can have a bath.' Turn around."

That made him want to chuckle.

Stepping forward, he slid into the pool in one smooth movement causing water to slosh over the edge and onto the surrounding rock.

Wide pale eyes stared at him in shock but she had nowhere to go. And, unlike the first time they'd been in the pool together, this time was different.

This time it felt as if the pool had shrunk by epic proportions. There was hardly any room.

"I should get out. The pool is too small." She wasn't looking at him now and her tiny hands gripped the edge of the pool as if she was ready to hoist herself out.

"Stay. There's not another one of these pools until we get to the Torian camp. Enjoy it."

She muttered something underneath her breath before the color in her cheeks grew warm again and he felt his lips twitch into a smile.

He didn't need to know what she'd just said; whatever it was, it must have been delicious.

Dipping his head underneath the water, he let the fluid flow through his hair and gave it a wash. The knot he'd put the tendrils in on top of his head came loose as he did and when he resurfaced his hair hung over his shoulders and down his back.

Pale eyes were staring at him again and she muttered something else underneath her breath, squeezing her eyes and shaking her head.

"What is it, Clee-yo?"

She glanced at him. "When did I stop being Cluu to you?"

To be honest, she'd never been Cluu. He'd just been saying it to spite her.

"I don't know," he said instead, his eyes taking her in.

Such a pale, beautiful creature.

How could he have even thought she was a feral thing the first time he'd seen her?

"Sohut?" She gulped and he realized he'd treaded the water in the little space between them. He was now so close she was face-to-face with him.

His gaze fell to her lips, and he watched them quiver a little.

When their eyes met again, there was only one thing to do.

The touch of her lips against his sent a jolt of pleasure through him.

How? How had he lived all his life without experiencing something like this?

Whoever invented mouth phekking in her culture was an icon that should be celebrated.

Clee-yo groaned into him, her arms moving to circle his neck as their bodies pressed together and he suddenly knew for a fact there was no way he was in the position to let her out of his presence. Not now...or ever again.

Clee-yo," he moaned her name as they broke for air. Hands circling her hips he lifted her in the water so she was straddling him.

The mounds on her chest popped free of the water to press against him and a groan rumbled in his chest.

She was so soft all over.

Feeling her like this against him.

He couldn't let her go.

And maybe she was feeling the same?

As his chest heaved, he searched her eyes.

It was suddenly important to him, that one question.

And though he didn't ask it, he knew he *needed* her to feel the same.

"Sohut," his name was almost a whimper on her lips and he realized her chest was heaving just as much as his was.

For a few moments, she said nothing. She just looked at him and if time stood still, he'd be lost in those pale eyes of hers.

He could hardly breathe but he could *feel*.

He could feel every bit of her body against him and he didn't want this moment to end.

"I need you to do something for me," she said.

"Anything."

"Fuck me."

19

HE TOOK THEM FROM THE WATER AND SHE DIDN'T EVEN KNOW HOW HE managed to do it with one hand for his other hand held her firmly in place against him.

"Clee-yo," he breathed, his green eyes holding hers with such intensity that every nerve ending within her felt charged with electricity.

Every movement, every touch of his body against hers as he walked across the clearing, sent tingles straight down to her toes.

He came to a stop and set her down gently against some vines on the ground.

There was a set of thick hanging vines that cascaded down the edge of the clearing and he moved to those.

With strong hands, his muscles bunched as he pulled them upward and set them horizontally and she realized he was making a place for them to rest.

A place for them to rest...

For she'd just asked him to fuck her!

Out loud!

She'd said it out loud.

Her gray eyes nictated as she took a deep breath, her gaze moving down his midsection straight to his crotch as he worked.

He was still hard.

So damn hard and just the sight of him had her clenching her thighs.

When he turned around and caught her staring, she couldn't look away, her cheeks burning red.

Fuck.

This wasn't a big deal.

It was just sex.

But when Sohut moved over to her, crouched over her and caught her mouth in a kiss once more, she found herself moaning and melting against him.

This wasn't just sex.

This was going to be so much more.

She felt gravity shift as she was lifted and she didn't care to look where he was taking her. All she could feel were his deeply sensual lips as his tongue pushed into her mouth to rub against hers.

As he set her down on the bedding of soft leaves and vines he'd prepared, Sohut crouched over her, his mouth still joined with hers.

One hand was on the smooth curve of her hips, the other pressed down in the leaves by her head.

"Sohut," she breathed, her hand moving up to rake through his hair, cradling his head as their kiss deepened.

He groaned as he left her lips to run his tongue down her neck, sucking on her skin in a path that ran down her collarbone and stopped right above her nipple.

There he paused and she opened her eyes, never realizing she'd shut them in the first place.

When she focused on him, he was staring down at her nipples and she wasn't sure what was crossing through his mind because she couldn't see his eyes.

Glancing down at herself, it suddenly occurred to her that the women of his kind must have different bodies from hers.

"It's not what you're used to, I guess?"

Sohut raised his gaze to hers and the look of absolute awe in his eyes was remarkable.

"I have the urge," he said, "to run my tongue all over these." As he spoke, he used his hand to knead her other breast and Cleo gasped, her back arching into him once more.

As his tongue stroked her nipple, Cleo resisted the urge to cry out.

His tongue was wider, flatter, a little rougher than a human's and it felt absolutely divine against her nipple.

It made her wonder what it would feel like to have his tongue there, between her legs, where the ache for him was slowly growing stronger.

As Sohut pulled his tongue from her nipple, he buried his face into her skin, inhaling deeply as he ran his nose down her midline and straight to her pelvis.

A groan rumbled through him when he stopped right above the V between her legs.

"Clee-yo," he groaned and when his eyes met hers, the look he gave her made her clench.

"Yes?" The word hardly made a sound as it came from her lips.

"I want you in my mouth."

His words made her eyelids flutter.

"Please." It was a plea that drifted away with the wind as her eyes rolled back into her head with that first touch of warmth and wetness.

Sohut flattened his tongue over her center, the tip landing right at her entrance and the feel of it made Cleo moan.

That one move alone almost brought her to climax and she had to squeeze her eyes shut tight to ride through the surge of emotion that ran through her.

With a deft upward movement, his tongue flicked over her, driving between her lips and over her clit in a wet slurp as he tasted her.

This time, a moan rumbled through him as he buried his tongue between her lips again, swirling it as he sought her entrance.

"Sohut," she called his name but she doubted he heard her over his own moans of pleasure. And when she felt the thick, slick tongue enter her, her cunt pulsed, an orgasm rocking through her that had her gripping the vines beneath her even as he circled her waist with his arms, holding her steady.

Her legs felt like jelly and her pussy felt like it was leaking honey.

Shudders made her body shake in the quake of the orgasm as she bit down hard on her lip.

Dots were before her eyes as she came to and when she cast her gaze to him, there was a devilish smile on his face.

His lips were wet with her juices and his eyes twinkled with pleasure.

"Mm," he whispered against her clit before he buried his face into her mat of hair, nuzzling her pussy before he darted his tongue inside her once more.

With a scream that surely sent the animals around them scampering away, Cleo arched her hips toward his mouth, grinding shamelessly against his tongue.

It felt as if he was a champion papaya eater and she was the frickin' papaya. His tongue swirled and flicked, sucked and dipped, and by the time she reached her second peak, her entire body was shaking with tremors of pleasure so much she wondered if he'd fucked her into Parkinson's.

As he lowered her hips and settled her legs around him, Cleo let out a strangled cry.

"Wait," she said. "I want to touch you too."

Sohut's throat moved, his green gaze boring into hers.

"Clee-yo," he said, "I don't think I'd be able to last if I feel your hands on me." He leaned down, his mouth closing over hers.

She could taste herself on his lips and fuck her if that didn't make a new wave of honey drip between her legs.

"I want to be inside you when I reach my peak," Sohut growled low, his lips moving to her ear. "I want to phek you."

Cleo gasped as she felt his tip line up with her entrance.

She knew he was big. She couldn't stop staring at it when he'd stripped before jumping into the water with her earlier.

Now, anticipation gripped her as she gripped him, her fingers pressing into his back as she steeled herself for his entry.

Sohut pressed his nose against hers and his green gaze found hers as his tip pressed against her slick entrance.

She could feel the muscles in his shoulders bunching underneath her hands, as if he was restraining himself.

He pressed into her gently, watching her reaction, and the feel of him sent notes of pleasure through her.

"More," she whispered and Sohut groaned against her lips.

"You're so small..." He hesitated.

"I'll tell you if it hurts. I just," her eyes rolled back as he pressed against her some more, "I need to feel you inside me."

That did it.

With a grunt, Sohut surged inside her, capturing her lips as Cleo felt her body rise against the vines. There was a moment of pain quickly followed by sweet, sweet pleasure.

He dug deeper inside her, and it felt as if cords ringed his cock at the base. Those cords were massaging her entrance the deeper he went.

As he found his rhythm, his tongue found one too, matching his thrusts as it delved into her mouth.

The combined sensation soon had her shuddering as she pulled him tighter against her.

She couldn't see.

She didn't know if her eyes were rolled back or whether something had obstructed her view.

All she could do was feel, and nothing had ever felt as good as this before.

As Sohut pistoned within her, Cleo brought her legs up around his waist pulling him deeper inside her wetness.

She was vaguely aware that his tail had moved to wrap around her leg and the feel of it, the fact he was so unlike anything she'd ever experienced before, made something ignite within her.

She would scream in delight, but she wasn't sure she had the energy to. There was something building inside her, something big and it was pulling all her energy to her core.

Sohut's lips left hers and he let out an animalistic growl that made her feel wild. And there was nothing wilder than this.

Eyes so low she could hardly see through her lashes, Cleo let her head fall back, baring her neck to him.

Sohut growled again before pushing so deep within her that she felt his balls against the curve of her ass.

Without warning, his head descended, his fangs baring as he buried them into her neck.

There was no pain, just sweet, sweet unexpected pleasure and Cleo called out his name as another orgasm rocked through her.

As her channel convulsed with the pressure of her orgasm, she felt him stiffen and his cock jerk within her, releasing streams of his spend deep inside her.

It took more than a few moments for her vision to clear and for the trembling to slow down enough for her to look at him.

There was a red streak running down his lips and she realized it had to be one thing.

Her blood.

She watched, mesmerized, as his tongue darted out to lick the blood away slowly.

Another shiver ran through her.

Sohut was watching her, his green gaze taking on a guarded, pained look.

"I'm sorry," he said, when their breaths calmed enough for them to speak. "I'm so sorry, Clee-yo." The pained look increased. "I...I lost control."

It took her a few moments to realize his gaze was locked on the spot on her neck where he'd bit her.

Releasing his shoulder, she touched the spot and looked at her fingers.

There was no blood, but there was a slight ache.

"I hurt you." He began to pull away and she tightened her legs around him.

Green, confused eyes met hers as she pulled his head towards hers, taking his lips with her own.

As their kiss deepened, she let out a groan and Sohut stiffened against her.

He broke their kiss, searching her gaze.

"I hurt you."

She couldn't help the smile that spread her lips.

"Not nearly enough," she whispered.

Confusion still flooded his gaze.

"Clee-yo? What do you mean?"

"I mean," Cleo swallowed, "I want you to hurt me some more."

Later, of course, after they got going, she thought, rocking her hips against him in a playful gesture.

Sohut's pupils dilated so quickly, his eyes almost looked completely black. At the same time, she felt him growing hard within her once more.

Her mouth fell open as the sensation overtook her.

"You're ready already?"

Sohut smiled and pressed her back into the vines below them.

"I think I'll always be ready, as long as you will have me."

With that, he captured her lips once more as he pulled out till his tip had almost exited her slick channel, only to drive home again.

20

AFTER ANOTHER TWO LOVE SESSIONS, SOHUT HAD FINALLY LOOKED UP at the sky, lamenting that the day was moving too quickly.

In other words, he wanted to make love some more.

His eagerness surprised her and planted a stupid smile on her face the entire time they waited for their clothes to dry and made plans to leave.

They would trek through the jungle, keeping to the parts with the thickest vegetation so they remained hidden.

He'd found some special leaves that he'd mashed into a poultice and rubbed over both their bodies to disguise their scents and had checked that all his gadgets he'd found after he'd fallen off the mountain were still there.

There was a little rectangular box in his satchel that he held for a few moments, his eyes moving to her with a look she couldn't read but before she could ask about it, he'd turned his nose to the air and sniffed.

The little bumps along his nose scrunched up as a look of disgust passed over his face.

"Phekking stinky rhag," he muttered.

"Rag?" she repeated and, just then, Wawa appeared at the edge of the clearing.

His eyes bled black as he looked at Sohut before he looked in her direction and they turned back to brown.

Taking a wide circle around Sohut, Wawa walked over to her.

"Rag? I thought you said he was a slizz." Cleo chuckled as Wawa hopped up on her shoulder and gave Sohut a stink eye.

"A rhag is a..." Sohut cast his eyes to the canopy as if he was thinking, "...a coddled chid."

"Chid?"

"Offspring."

Cleo chuckled. "A spoilt child? Wawa?"

Sohut turned his eyes on her and nodded in earnest. "A stinky rhag."

A brat.

He was calling Wawa a stinky brat.

She would argue with him if Wawa wasn't still giving him a stink eye at the moment while rubbing his head against her neck.

"Ready?" Sohut asked, glancing around the clearing.

Taking a deep breath, Cleo looked around the clearing for one last time.

There was still some anxiety there about the fact she was leaving.

"Ready," she said.

THE WALK through the jungle was much harder than she'd thought it was going to be.

Even with a full belly and the fact it wasn't dark yet, it went painfully slowly.

—or, maybe her legs were still weak from all the lovemaking earlier.

Staring into Sohut's back now, Cleo's cheeks grew warm at the thought.

The silly smile still hadn't left her face and whenever he turned around to check on her, she realized his eyes were twinkling and there was a silly smile on his face too.

The only person not smiling was Wawa.

Every now and again, he'd hop off her shoulder to disappear into the jungle's depths and she'd worry, much to Sohut's incredulity.

"That...*thing* could kill me, you, and every other beast in this jungle," he muttered for probably the fifth time, as he hopped over a fallen tree and stretched out his hand to help her over.

"For some reason, it likes you..." He paused. "Though, I can see why."

Cleo's eyes met his green ones and she felt the warmth there.

It only made her cheeks grow warmer.

The deeper into the jungle they went, the denser it seemed to get and she soon realized that where she'd been staying was nowhere like the rest of this Koznia Jungle, as Sohut called it.

Every now and again, she'd see bits of animals she had never seen before peeking through the undergrowth at them.

The first time she'd seen two yellow eyes staring back at them, she'd moved so close to Sohut, she'd bumped into him.

He'd assured her that he wouldn't let anything dangerous get close and that Wawa was also doing the same with his "high alarming body odor."

It didn't take her long to realize just how much she trusted him when she almost forgot there were animals around them at all, her mind instead replaying what happened at the water hole over and over again.

And he was thinking about it too.

She could see it in his eyes every time he looked back at her.

As night crept in, Sohut stopped by a humongous tree and looked up into its branches.

"We sleep here this dark-cycle," he said.

Cleo looked up into the branches high above.

She could climb trees. She was skilled at it, but this one had no notches she could get a hold of and the trunk was too big to wrap her arms and legs around. Not to mention, the lowest branches were at least thirty feet above her.

"Up there?" She gave Sohut an incredulous glance.

"Yup," he said and crouched before her. "Hop on."

"What?" She looked back at the tree. "You're going to climb that? And with me on your back?"

Sohut glanced back at her. "Why not?"

He sounded so confident in his abilities, the argument died on her lips.

Shrugging, she climbed awkwardly onto his back, feeling like a child doing so.

"Hold on," was all the warning she got before she heard his claws protract and he leapt unto the tree trunk.

Up he went, much quicker than was humanly possible, reminding her once more that he was no man.

He skipped the lowest branches and went higher before he stopped at a section where two branches crossed over each other.

"Can you climb off on your own?" he asked.

"C—can I what?" Cleo sputtered.

Sohut chuckled before turning so her ass was firmly against the junction of the tree's branch and its trunk. Then, he set her down, prying her hands from his shoulders for she'd held on to him tightly without realizing.

Looking everywhere but down, Cleo gulped.

"Why up here?"

"It's safer. This deep into the jungle, creatures will be curious. I don't want any of them dragging you away when we're sleeping."

Cleo's eyes widened a little.

"What about snakes that live in trees?"

Granted, she hadn't seen any snakes since she'd been in the jungle but that didn't mean there were none.

"Nayks? I don't know what those are."

"Long, cold-blooded, fanged beasts. Some are venomous. Some aren't. Some wrap themselves around you so tight they kill you then they eat you."

Sohut stopped searching in his satchel and gave her a funny look.

"I'm long...fanged..." His gaze fell to her lips then moved to her chest. "I want to wrap myself around you..." His gaze fell lower. "But I'd probably eat you first."

Cleo almost fell out of the tree and he had to reach for her to steady her.

A deep warmth spread over her cheeks.

"Well," she said when she found her voice. "Snakes aren't creatures to play around with."

"And you want to play around with me?" There was a heat in his gaze that made her choke on air.

No, she wanted to answer. *I don't want to play. I want you for more than that.*

That answer stunned her and they fell into silence as he searched for something in his satchel.

"How will we sleep?" She broke the silence. Glancing around, still trying not to look down, she tried to predict what he was thinking of doing. "I'm scared to close my eyes so high up and fall to my death."

Sohut chuckled again. "I wouldn't allow that to happen."

Finally, he pulled something from his bag. It looked like a carpenter's measuring tape with a cord coming from inside it.

Sohut pressed the cord onto one section of the branch and somehow it attached to the wood.

Making a wide circle over the crisscrossing branches, he stopped when the cord completed the revolution.

Then, he pressed the center of the device.

Right in front of her eyes, the device began moving across the outline of the circle, creating a pattern like a spider's web. It was absolutely fascinating to see and she couldn't take her eyes off it till it stopped working.

As Sohut grabbed the device, he smiled at her.

"You've never seen something like this before, have you?"

Cleo shook her head.

"We don't have anything like that on Earth."

Sohut studied her a bit before he set the device back into his satchel and stretched out over the "web". The web hardly reacted to his weight.

"Come. Lie with me." His eyes were on hers and they moved to her lips so slowly, she felt a slight shiver.

Sohut watched the movement of her tongue as she licked her lips and climbed hesitantly onto the web.

It felt like very strong yarn and she tested it for a few moments before putting her whole body weight on it.

Sitting beside him, she put her pack of things near her feet and looked up into the leaves above.

She could feel his eyes on her. It was a feeling like silk moving over her skin.

"Tell me about your planet. I didn't get to ask Larn about it."

"Larn?" She turned to face him.

Sohut blinked.

"There is another of your species at the Sanctuary."

The news sent a shock through her.

"What?"

"I met her before I came on the mission to find you. She is staying with my brother."

She'd always known, deep down, that there was no chance she was alone...but to hear it as a fact...

"Are you sure?"

Sohut nodded, studying her. "Does this make you...happy?"

Cleo blinked. "Yes...and no. I wouldn't wish this experience on another human. It wasn't nice being...taken."

Sohut studied her some more and his arms surrounded her, pulling her against his chest.

Cleo settled against him.

"Did you leave family there?"

"No." She shook her head, tears welling into her eyes. "I'd only had my father. He died a few years ago. I was an only child and my mother...I never met her."

"Lucky you."

The way he said it had her raising her head to look up at him to find a myriad of emotions swirling in his eyes, the one at the forefront being anger.

"What do you mean?" she asked softly.

Sohut's throat moved and it seemed he was contemplating whether he should tell her something really deep or not.

When his mouth finally opened, the pain in his eyes was clear.

"My mor gave me...*sold* me and Riv when we were chids. She sold us to a Tasqal who owns the talix mines to the north of here." He stopped and she could sense that there was more. But she wasn't going to press him about it.

She knew too well how hard it was reliving childhood trauma.

"It's ok." She settled her head against him again. "You don't need to tell me about it. I can tell it...hurt you. Deeply."

A sigh lifted his frame and when he settled again, she felt his fingers in her hair.

"I should tell you. You need to know the male you just mated with. And if you can accept me, I hope you will want to mate with me again."

Cleo felt her cheeks burn.

The word "mate" sounded so...*carnal*, dirty, and hot as hell.

When she didn't respond, he continued. "I was born weak. Ill. I came too early." He took a breath. "My daran was a toxic male piece of—" He stopped and took another breath.

"My daran disowned me, leaving my mor to care for not only a weak chid but a young one too—my brother, Riv." He continued. "Merssi females don't usually work for economic gain. That is the male's responsibility. And so, my mor was left with a choice. Work to provide for her chids or the three of us would perish. She tried for a few moons but she soon turned to woogli smoke, lamenting the days when life was easier. And it was my fault."

Cleo's eyes widened and she opened her mouth to correct him.

"My mor blamed me." He took another breath, the weight of his mother's decision still on his shoulders. "The Tasqal's mine was horrid. Riv never complained. He stuck up for me. He protected me. Yet, he was the one that got dismembered there." He paused.

"Dismembered?" Shock registered in her voice.

"The Tasqal jekin removed his tail." He paused again. "Riv is incomplete because of me. A Merssi without a tail is...not wanted." A breath shuddered through him. "The one person who has always stood beside me will never...no Merssi female will ever want him.

And all this because I didn't die in my mother's womb when I should have."

Cleo lifted her head to stare up at him.

"Don't ever say that. You were not a mistake." She placed a hand against his cheek, turning his head so he was forced to face her. "You were never a mistake. Your parents were wrong. So, so wrong. A child is a miracle. And you are not weak! You're the most respectable alien I've met and so far, I've been thinking the universe was filled with pieces of shit."

His eyes softened a little at that.

"My mother didn't want me either," she confided in him. "She wanted an abortion and only carried me to term because my father said he'd take full responsibility for me."

She sighed and settled against him again. "I never met her and while I was growing up, I hated her. Now, I don't hate her at all. She gave me life, even if she didn't want anything to do with me and at least I had one person on my side."

Strong arms circled her and pulled her closer to him.

"Clee-yo," he said and when she lifted her chin to look at him, there was a swirl of emotions in his eyes.

His hand trailed down her cheek down to her neck and over the wound of the bite he'd inflicted earlier.

The cut wasn't deep but she could still feel sensation that a wound was there even as he touched her now.

His gaze focused on the wound and he brushed his finger over it again.

"I'm not an animal. But when you bared your neck to me in that signal of complete submission...I bit you because...there was an over-whelming urge to..." He trailed off.

"To what?" Her words came out like a whisper.

Sohut hesitated, as if what he was about to say was a bit absurd and he wondered what she would think of it.

"To own you."

And maybe something was wrong with her because, instead of making her pull away from him, those three words created the oppo-site reaction.

Between her thighs, her center throbbed.

There must have been a carnal look in her eyes because Sohut's head dipped suddenly and her lips were against his.

Moaning into his mouth, her tongue met his even as he pulled her harder against him.

"I love this mouth phekking," he murmured.

"Mouth what?"

"It makes me want to do so many dirty things to you." His voice lowered so much, she felt the vibration of his words against her lips.

Sohut groaned, slipping one hand under what was left of her dress as he caressed the round curve of her buttocks.

As their kiss deepened, Cleo straddled him, her thighs settling over both of his legs and her ass against his crotch.

She could feel him pulse in his pants underneath her, and it made her moan into his mouth.

He pulsed again, hard like a rod, and Cleo ground her hips against his hardness.

Sohut ripped his mouth from hers to tilt his head back a little.

"Phek, Clee-yo."

She felt him pulse again and anticipation rose within her.

Memory of how good he felt came back into her mind and before she knew it, she was rising over him so she could pull his trousers down from over his hips.

Sohut lifted his head a little to watch her, his green gaze hypnotic.

Sliding down his body, she came face to face with his hardness and it made a gasp lodge in her throat.

Even in the dimming light, he was impressive.

As she took him by the base of his cock, Sohut jerked in her hand. She could feel those hard rings that corded around him. They were underneath his skin, and when she squeezed her hand around them gently, he jerked again.

"Clee-yo?" There was shock in his eyes as he watched her, mesmerized.

Her gaze moved to the head of his cock and there was a glimmer of clear liquid there.

It slid down the tip and toward her hand at his base, like an invitation.

As she licked her lips, she felt Sohut stiffen underneath her.

"Clee-yo?" He called her name again.

Smiling up at him, Cleo licked her lips once more before closing her mouth over his cock.

Sohut stiffened completely as she took the head of his cock into her mouth, sliding him toward her throat.

There was no way she could fit him in without gagging and when she reached her limit, she raised her eyes to his.

His green orbs were two huge pools that stared back at her in complete astonishment.

His throat moved as if he wanted to say something and she kept her eyes locked with his as she rose toward his tip again.

Sohut's eyes dilated completely and if she didn't see him do it before, she'd have been a bit alarmed.

As she worked him in her mouth, Sohut threaded his fingers in the web below them, clenching his fists tight as he fought to keep himself still.

It was almost as if he was afraid of moving lest he hurt her or scare her away.

The thought only made her go down on him harder, swirling her tongue around his shaft even as she tasted him in her mouth.

A groan made his body shudder and he finally found his voice.

"I want to be inside you, Clee-yo." He paused. "Now." His throat moved with the effort of his restraint.

She didn't need to hear him twice. She was already wet and ready just from the taste and feel of him in her mouth, his reaction to her, and the fact that he felt so good.

Rising, she watched his eyes widen again and she knelt over him.

"Like this?" he asked, his almost black eyes searching hers. "I've never done it this way before."

A thrill went through her. "Then let me show you."

Steadying him with a hand at his base, she lined up at her entrance and eased back slightly.

A moan slipped through her lips as his slick head popped in and Cleo paused, relishing the feel of him within her.

Sohut's chest was heaving as he watched her, seemingly not daring to move as she settled herself on him.

Only when she adjusted to his width within her and started finding a rhythm did his hands move to her hips.

As she moved over him, taking him as deeply as she could, Cleo's eyes moved to his.

He was looking at her as if he was seeing something...perfect.

No one had ever looked at her like that before.

Moving a hand from her hips, he pulled her toward him, grinding his hips against her pelvis as she took him while he captured her lips with his.

This wasn't just sex. This was more than sex.

The feelings blooming within her were almost overtaking her and she cried into his mouth as an orgasm hit her unexpectedly.

Sohut groaned against her lips and he held her hips steady, pistoning in and out of her for a few more strokes before he stiffened beneath her too, his cock jerking inside her as it let out streams of warm spend deep inside her.

"Sohut." Her voice quivered and Sohut pulled her closer.

"Clee-yo," he answered.

And that was all he needed to say.

She knew, because it was obvious that whatever she was feeling, he was feeling it too.

21

WAWA APPEARED SOME TIME IN THE NIGHT AND CLEO WASN'T SURE HOW he found them up in the tree but he quickly climbed up the trunk and settled between them, much to Sohut's annoyance.

Nevertheless, they got as comfortable of a sleep as they could lying on a web so high in the air.

Morning came, they hunted and ate, and set off once more.

It was a long walk and Sohut offered to carry her several times, but Cleo refused.

Instead, she tried to keep up and not slow him down, which she managed, but her entire body argued about it.

For two more days, they traveled. In the nights they rested in trees high in the canopy and in the days they took few breaks as they made their way through.

It was not until darkness began to fall on the third day that Sohut suddenly stopped walking and looked back at her.

"We're here," he said.

Cleo's gaze darted to the bushes around them. She couldn't see anything out of the ordinary.

"The camp is just beyond these trees," Sohut said. "I'll go ahead and announce our arrival. These Torians are a bit..."

"A bit what?"

Sohut smiled a little and shrugged. "You'll see."

With that, he looked at Wawa, who was at his spot on her shoulder.

"You," he said to the slizz, "don't let anything happen to her."

Wawa frowned. She was sure he did.

He locked gazes with Sohut, his eyes slowly bleeding black and she was sure he was going to attack. She reached for him, but his eyes slowly bled back to their usual brown.

Cleo's mouth fell open.

Was Wawa...was he beginning to *tolerate* Sohut?

He still didn't like the blue stranger, but he was no longer trying to kill him all the time.

Moving toward her, Sohut clasped the back of her neck and tilted her head up to him.

His kiss was sensual, slow, and Cleo's eyes fluttered as he let her go.

"I won't be long," he said. "Don't move."

Nodding, she watched him leave.

It was getting dark. Dark enough for the shadows of the trees to begin to look ominous and she hoped he wouldn't be gone too long.

Just in case, she took hold of her piece of shrapnel that hadn't failed her yet.

If anything came out of the bushes while Sohut was away, she'd have something with which to defend herself.

Settling on the stump of a fallen tree, she looked around, trying to see any signs of life.

She had no idea what the aliens they were coming upon were like, but she trusted Sohut.

She trusted him enough to believe he wouldn't willingly put them in danger.

That thought was jarring.

She'd gone from thinking he was her enemy to sleeping with him then to trusting him with her future, her life...not in that order.

The jungle here was a lot less dense than the jungle they'd been traveling through for the past few days, but she still didn't see anything out of the ordinary.

Rolling her shoulders, she released a sigh.

She was exhausted.

She hadn't mentioned it to Sohut but she hadn't known how much longer she could have gone before taking a rest.

She was nearing collapse.

Wawa stiffened on her shoulder and Cleo's senses primed immediately.

It was only when Wawa relaxed and she noticed Sohut coming back through the undergrowth that her shoulders sagged with relief.

"Is everything all right?"

He was alone. She'd expected to see aliens accompanying him.

Sohut smiled. "They are waiting to meet you." His eyes slid to Wawa. "And you. Don't attack them."

Wawa stiffened on her shoulder and cocked his head at Sohut.

It was the first time he actually tried to communicate with Sohut and that surprised Cleo.

"I think he's wondering what you mean."

"He knows exactly what I mean." Sohut crouched so he was on eye level with Wawa. "Listen you little thing. Don't attack the Torians. They won't hurt Cleo and they're the only place we can stay before we go across the arid lands to the plains. Do you understand?"

Wawa cocked his head again and Sohut frowned, turning his worried eyes to her. "I don't know if he understands me. He only listens to you."

Cleo glanced at Wawa and he bumped his head into her neck before focusing on Sohut again.

"He understands."

Sohut's frown deepened. "How do you know?"

Cleo shrugged. "I don't know. I just do."

With a huge sigh, Sohut stood, offering her his hand so she could stand too.

"Ready?" he asked.

Cleo nodded. "Ready."

As they walked in the direction in which he just came, the density of trees slowly reduced.

They were walking for what felt like roughly fifteen minutes and Cleo looked up at the alien walking in front of her.

"I thought we were going toward that alien camp."

"We are," Sohut answered.

"But we've been walking for so long now. I thought we'd have reached it already. You were gone for this long."

"That's because I used the trees. We're walking. Takes longer." Sohut looked over his shoulder to smile at her and her shocked expression only made him chuckle. "No worries my zimsu flower, we're here now."

She'd have taken the time to think about the fact he just called her something endearing if they didn't suddenly walk into a clearing.

Hanging lanterns dotted the circular expanse. One of the lanterns was close by and it looked like a paper lantern with fireflies inside.

Wawa's eyes lit up.

"My companion is here with her...slizz," Sohut said and she realized he was speaking to someone in front of them.

As she stepped so she could see around Sohut's tall frame, her entire body froze.

There were maybe seven or so short green aliens in front of them. They had huge heads with balloon-like projections at the back, much like an octopus looked. Each alien had four eyes that were focused on Sohut and now that she'd stepped slightly from behind him, they collectively gasped.

She realized then that they had spears, all pointed her way, and four arms each.

"Um, Sohut..."

"Yes, my flower..."

"Why do they look like they're going to attack us?"

Sohut paused then looked down at her.

"Not you." His gaze moved to Wawa. "Him."

"Great, Raxu. It really is a slizz," one of the aliens whispered.

"I can't see well, my eyes are dark. Is it really?" another whispered.

"That's what I just said Nupak. Are you deaf?"

"Of course, not! ... but I am a little blind. That's what I just said; I can't see!"

"It really is a slizz, but it isn't attacking us. The Merssi said it wouldn't." One more joined in.

"I don't trust it."

"You don't trust anything, Krior. But you are right, I don't trust it either."

"I really can't see. Is it moving?"

"Phekking Raxu. A guard that can't see in the dark. It's unbelievable we haven't been attacked yet."

Sohut chuckled slightly. "The slizz won't harm you. It is...*tame*."

There was silence before more whispering ensued, the spears moving as the aliens argued.

"Tame! A tame slizz? I'll give all my arms if that was possible."

"But it isn't attacking, maybe it is true."

Cleo looked up at Sohut, her anxiety slowly ebbing away. "Do they know we can hear them?"

Sohut shrugged and she could see his smile. "Welcome to the Torian camp."

Half of his face was in shadow and for a moment it struck her just handsome he was.

There was a gasp from the aliens and then more whispering.

"What is that?"

"I don't know. Looks like a Merssi female but no horns."

"Not Merssi then. How many arms?"

"Two. Disgusting."

"Hideous creature."

"Very hideous."

Cleo's mouth fell open.

The bubble-head aliens were talking about *her*.

Sohut put his arm around her, pulling her into his side. "Don't listen to them. They think anything without several limbs or arms is vile."

One of the aliens took a step forward, four of his eyes darting from Sohut to Wawa.

"You're sure it won't attack us, Merssi? I can't let you into the camp if it is even slightly aggressive."

Sohut glanced at Wawa and Wawa blinked at him.

"He won't be aggressive."

Glancing back at his companions, the alien slowly lowered his spear and the others behind him followed suit.

Cocking his head to the side, the alien peered at her.

"And you are the female the Merssi is escorting," he said.

Cleo glanced at Sohut, who nodded. Her hands flexed at her sides, still gripping her lucky piece of metal.

"I am," she said, stepping forward.

The alien's four eyes darted to Wawa and he visibly shivered.

"Welcome to our camp. You will be safe here. I am Senrit." His eyes barely moved over her face before focusing on Wawa again. He was obviously perturbed by the animal. Wawa, on the other hand, was busy rubbing his head against her cheek and ignoring the alien in front of her.

"Come," Senrit said, stepping away, and with a glance at Sohut, their little party entered the camp.

22

THE CAMP WAS MUCH LARGER THAN SHE'D INITIALLY THOUGHT AND Cleo soon realized they were walking toward what appeared to be a circle of light made by the same type of lanterns that dotted the clearing.

There was *music*—music that sounded like Irish traditional music but played from wind instruments instead, like a set of flutes.

It was such a strike to her senses that she paused a bit.

She hadn't heard music in so, so long.

There was chatter too, lots of it.

Realizing she'd stopped walking, Sohut glanced down at her.

"Is everything all right, Clee-yo?"

Cleo blinked. "I—yes. It's just..." She exhaled. "There's life out here."

Sohut studied her face a little before he pulled her closer into his side and they continued walking again.

"Maybe too much life," he said after a few moments and when she frowned up at him in question, he chuckled. "You'll see what I mean."

As they approached the circle of light, Cleo realized there were quite a few of the bubble-headed aliens there, more than she could count. Several of the aliens lifted their heads to look their way.

Most of them looked extremely sleepy, their four eyes heavy as she caught their gazes, and some had wisps of smoke drifting upward from their nostrils.

"We have visitors!" Senrit announced and that made the aliens who hadn't noticed their arrival till then turn to take a look.

"One female, a Merssi, and a...a slizz," one of the other guards said and the chatter around the circle of light suddenly hushed. Even the music stopped.

"A WHAT?!" someone in the circle exclaimed.

That exclamation was suddenly followed by a chorus of other exclamations and some of the aliens stood hurriedly, their four eyes darting to the huts at the sides as if they wanted to run to them.

"He won't hurt you," Sohut spoke up and several eyes focused on him. "The slizz is tame."

"TAME! ABSURD!"

Senrit glanced at Wawa again. "To be honest, I'm beginning to wonder if it really is a slizz. It is...*loving* to the female." The corners of Senrit's mouth turned down and Cleo almost chuckled at the absolute disgust on his face.

Wawa continued to ignore them as he rubbed his head against her neck.

"I guess it would have attacked already if it was going to kill us..." said someone. "I've never heard of a slizz waiting that long to attack anything."

There was a collective pause.

"You're right as usual...but I might have urinated a little from just looking at it," said another alien.

"Me too."

"Me too."

"Yep, me too."

Another pause.

"So, it's safe you think?" asked someone else.

"I mean...we're alive."

There was another pause and just like that, what looked like a collective shrug of the shoulders occurred before the aliens began chattering again.

"Music!" Senrit exclaimed and the music got louder. "Let us welcome our guests in true Torian fashion!"

Before she could protest, several arms circled her waist and arms and Cleo was pulled away from Sohut.

Her mouth fell open in alarm before she realized she was being carried by two of the bubble-headed aliens.

There was no malice on their faces, only stupid little smiles.

As the music flowed through the clearing, the two aliens holding her took each of her arms and began spinning her from left to right in rhythm with the music, doing the same with their own bodies.

"Dance!" someone exclaimed.

They were...*dancing* with her.

Horrified eyes found Sohut's green ones and she found him tracking her movement around the circle.

He seemed amused. Even from the distance between them now, she could see his eyes twinkle. That was, before several arms grabbed him too and he was also forced to dance with the aliens as well.

The utter mortification on his face made a bubble of laughter rise within her and Cleo chuckled. Her laughter only seemed to spur the aliens on and before she knew it, they'd let her go and she was doing their dance on her own.

She would have stopped if the entire clearing wasn't suddenly dancing too.

It felt...good.

Free.

Laughter filled her throat.

This was not what she had been expecting at all.

It was a funny sight—a crowd of green aliens dancing in the dim light, their bubble heads pulsing as they did, their eyes hooded with sleep.

As she watched Sohut, who was now across from her as the circle of dancers moved, she smiled.

He was staring at her and the light, the ambiance, the music...it all made her feel young again.

She was exhausted from their trek through the jungle, but she didn't want to take a seat on the raised surface within the circle, lest she offend her hosts.

So when the dancing finally died down and they began to sit, she was somewhat relieved.

Making her way back towards Sohut, she didn't get far when she was pulled to sit between two of the aliens.

"You are missing limbs, but you dance well," one of the aliens said and she realized it was one of the guards who'd met them by the jungle edge. "I am Krior."

"Nice to meet you, Krior." Cleo smiled.

"Don't offend the female," said the alien on her other side. His eyes darted to Wawa before he continued. "Some beings don't like it when you mention their deformities." His eyes lingered on her arms. "I'm Nupak," he finally said.

Cleo opened her mouth to correct them on the fact that having four arms would be a deformity where she came from, but she didn't bother.

That was a conversation that wouldn't lead anywhere good.

"Nice to meet you, Nupak."

"Here." Krior pushed something toward her. It looked like a piece of sugarcane.

"It's fermented rai," said Nupak. "It's delicious."

She had no idea if it was poisonous or not.

Searching for Sohut, she found his green gaze on her, as if it never left. He nodded and she took a bite of the food, not expecting much.

As she chewed, Cleo paused. It tasted like a salt and vinegar rice cake.

"Thank you," she mumbled as she took another bite and both aliens beside her smiled.

Around the circle, chatter ensued as if nothing had changed and it didn't take Cleo long to relax.

Between the rice cakes she was fed and the water to wash it down, she filled her belly while she watched the aliens inhale a strange-looking smoke from glass vases.

"Woogli smoke," Krior mentioned. "Do you wish to try it?"

As he asked this, she noticed Sohut was being offered some as well, which he promptly refused.

"I'm fine, thank you," Cleo said.

That didn't stop the two aliens from indulging themselves and soon the clearing was so thick with the smoke, she might as well have been smoking it herself.

For the next few hours, she watched the aliens smoke, drink, and tell stories and she found herself relaxing as she listened to them.

It felt strange being in society again, even if it was one as strange as this, and it made her wonder about life after they left the jungle.

Would it be like this?

She'd been on her own for so long... There were times she'd wished she had company, but she wasn't even sure she'd be able to integrate into alien society.

Her eyes found Sohut through the din and he was still looking at her.

He had a life outside of this jungle.

For some reason, she'd forgotten that.

As the aliens continued to party around them, she realized Sohut's gaze didn't leave hers.

He was speaking to the aliens who spoke to him, but his eyes never moved.

His gaze was intense and it made her feel as if he was imagining just what they'd done in the trees when the nights came in.

That thought made her forget her ruminations.

"—with Clee-yo." Her name made her blink several times. Sohut was saying something about her. "She's had it hard the last few days, trekking through Koznia."

One of the aliens, she assumed it was Senrit, stood on wobbly legs. Maybe he had sniffed too much of that smoke.

"I'll take you to your quarters," he said.

Following Sohut's lead, she stood and met him at the edge of the circle before they both walked behind a staggering Senrit.

Before long, they stopped in front of one of the huts.

"This is yours for as long as you like," Senrit said, his four eyes meeting hers. "We have no feminine products here, I'm afraid."

"Oh," Cleo smiled. "I'm—I'll be okay."

She'd lived in the jungle for a whole year. She doubted going a few more nights without shampoo was going to kill her.

As Sohut opened the door and led them in, Cleo's eyes widened.

Inside the hut, there was a huge cushion on the floor and she assumed it was the bed. Off to the side, there was another room.

Sohut gazed down at her. "After you."

Cleo stepped in and Wawa immediately hopped off her shoulder to settle in the middle of the bed.

"Hey!" Sohut frowned at him. "That's for all of us."

Wawa blinked at him before, surprisingly, he moved to settle on the side of the bed.

Cleo's eyebrows shot up. "Well, that's a first. He listened to you."

Sohut smiled, a devilish glint in his eyes as pulled her into him.

"A wash before we sleep? I know you're tired," he said.

"A bath?" What she would do for one right at that moment.

Sohut nodded before taking her hand in his and leading her to the second room in the hut.

As soon as they stepped in, he pressed her into the wall, his body holding her hostage.

"Clee-yo," he groaned, as he dipped his head to her neck. "I've missed you."

A chuckle developed within her. "What? I've been with you this whole time."

"Not close enough," he breathed down her neck, sending a shiver down her spine.

Sohut took her skin between his teeth and flicked his tongue over it, causing her to inhale deeply.

One arm pressed against the wall beside her head while his other arm moved underneath her dress to caress her leg.

"I'd rip this off you if it didn't mean you'd be walking naked..." he murmured, nibbling her skin as he did. "I don't want those Torians looking at what's mi—"

He stopped short and froze suddenly before he lifted his head to look her in the eyes.

There was shock in his as she studied him.

"What were you going to say?" Cleo wet her lips.

Sohut's throat moved as he stared into her eyes, but he didn't answer.

Instead, it was as if a switch flipped and he leaned from off the wall.

Cleo watched him move, a ball developing in her throat that prevented her from saying another word.

Because...she was pretty sure he was just about to say...that she was *his*.

23

"WE SHOULD GET YOU CLEAN AND COMFORTABLE. YOU DESERVE THE rest." Sohut stepped away from her and moved over to a circular indentation in the ground.

Confused, she watched him and for the first time, she noticed the room.

It was smaller than the room with the bed in it but large enough to hold both of them.

Off in the corner was one of those lanterns with what she was going to assume was alien fireflies. It lit the room in a warm glow.

Sohut crouched over the indentation in the ground and pulled out the stop from what looked like a wooden pipe. As soon as the stop was released, steamy water came pouring through.

"They have hot water here?!" Cleo moved forward, unable to believe what she was seeing.

She hadn't taken a hot water bath in like...forever.

Sohut smiled as he moved to another side of the room and dug his hand into a bag that was placed there.

"They have more technology here than you would think. Torians can't resist favors. If a Torian helps you, usually they ask for high-tech favors in return," he said as he threw what looked like small pellets into the bath.

As the pellets hit the water, they fizzed and produced a sweet smell.

"All ready." Sohut smiled again but the smile didn't reach his eyes.

He looked guarded...scared almost.

As he made to brush past her, she caught his shirt in her hand.

"Is everything all right?"

Sohut inhaled deeply and froze for a second. He wouldn't face her.

"Sohut?" She didn't know what to make of his sudden change in behavior. One moment he was saying he'd missed her and the next it was as if he couldn't wait to escape her presence.

At the sound of his name, Sohut inhaled deeply before tilting his head to the ceiling and groaning.

His arms wrapped around her as he pulled her against him.

"Clee-yo," he said, dipping his forehead to hers.

"Is something wrong? Are you okay?"

Sohut breathed hard before he answered. "Everything is okay."

She tried to see his eyes to garner what he was thinking but he held her head steady between his hands so she couldn't move it.

"I'm not joking when I said I missed you, Clee-yo," he murmured. "I would take you right here, right now, if I didn't know you were exhausted."

Part of her wanted to argue with him about that but he was right, she was extremely tired.

"Then why are you leaving?" The whisper came from her lips before she could stop herself.

Sohut groaned and his hands slipped under her dress again. This time, he didn't pull away.

Instead, he lifted the ragged hem of her clothing and brought the entire thing over her head.

The garment was deposited somewhere on the floor as he took her in.

Even in the warm, dim glow of the firefly-lantern, she could see the obsession in his eyes.

It melted something within her, made her a little anxious...but most of all, there was anticipation.

"You should—" his voice came out much deeper, hoarser than usual, and he cleared his throat "—you should go in the bath before the water gets cold."

He was right.

Taking a step toward the bath, she asked, "Aren't you going to join me?"

There was silence and when she glanced back at him, her breath caught in her throat.

His eyes had bled to black, his pupils completely dilated as he watched her.

Swallowing hard, she stepped into the bath as she watched him and he followed her every movement.

"So...are you?"

Sohut blinked. "Am I what?"

"Are you going to join me?"

He blinked again before moving into action.

His clothes came off easily and he followed her, sinking into the pool just as the warm water covered her body to her shoulders.

Cleo watched him, her eyes glued to his.

"You know...your eyes, when they go like that, it's a bit startling."

Sohut blinked again. "Go like how?"

"All black."

Cleo watched his throat move as he studied her, and for the first time, it dawned on her that he was really a hunter.

The way he looked right now, feral and hyperaware...it should scare her, but it didn't.

"Does it scare you?"

Cleo smiled but kept his gaze. "No."

"Good."

Without warning he was crouching over her and Cleo let out a yelp of surprise.

His arms found her legs under the water as he held them apart, enough for him to settle between them.

"Clee-yo," he groaned, before he captured her lips.

His kiss was insistent. It was the type that would probably leave a bruise.

The type that pushed her head back as he demanded her lips.

Between them, she could feel his hardness pressing against her cunt.

He was gyrating his hips, causing his dick to rub against her clit, and that made her cling to him.

Water sloshed over the side of the bath, as he ground against her, and when one of his hands cupped her breasts, she cried out against his mouth.

"Clee-yo," Sohut broke the kiss and his hot breath brushed against her ear.

His cock was insistent against her clit, those cords that ringed his dick moving over her softness as he drove himself between her inner lips.

"Clee-yo," Sohut groaned her name again before her took her earlobe into his mouth.

She was so close she wasn't sure she was going to be able to hold off before he entered her.

"Sohut—"

"I'm going to make you come. I'm going to make you come right now, like this."

His free hand gripped her ass and pulled her harder against him.

"Do you know why, Clee-yo?"

She barely had the conscious thought to answer him, but she didn't need to.

"Because you're mine, Clee-yo," he growled into her ear. "Mine."

Her orgasm crashed through her like a wrecking ball to a wall and Cleo screamed against Sohut's skin.

"Mine," he whispered.

And as the quakes of her orgasm made her shudder, the word lingered in her mind.

Mine.

How could she ever leave this jungle and think otherwise?

She didn't know when or how it'd happened but somewhere along the way, everything had changed.

Because he was right.

She *was* his.

24

THE DAYS SEEMED TO BLEED INTO EACH OTHER. SO MUCH SO THAT SHE wasn't aware how much time had passed since they'd entered the Torian camp. All she was aware of was that time was passing.

After that first night in the Torian camp, one of the lookouts had notified Sohut that they'd seen some Tasqal guards on the outskirts of the jungle.

It had caused quite a stir in the camp and because of that Sohut had thought it was best they stayed put for a while.

And so they had.

It wasn't a bad idea. Life in the camp was refreshing.

The Torians woke early and went to bed late but most days were spent singing and dancing at the center of the camp.

When they weren't dragging her towards huts to do crafts, they were meditating in the sun. Sometimes they even did a strange form of stretching that resembled yoga...only they were alarmed at her trying to do it with her lack of limbs.

It was like living in an ethnic enclave and Cleo slowly grew to appreciate and even enjoy the company of some of the aliens that lived there.

They were all still wary of Wawa and kept their distance whenever he was around. Still, they tried to make her comfortable by constantly offering her woogli smoke and more of the salt and vinegar rice cakes whenever they saw her alone in the camp—which was hardly ever.

Sohut stayed by her side, only leaving now and then to scout the perimeter.

When she wasn't caught in his arms or doing some activities with the Torians, she would head into the nearby jungle to catch mogs for dinner.

Today was one of those days. The camp was running low on food.

Sohut was just coming out of Senrit's hut when he noticed her heading into the jungle. He jogged up to her and caught her around the waist.

"Going hunting again?"

Cleo smiled and leaned into him. "They've been so nice to me, to us, it's the one way I can contribute."

Sohut glanced back at Senrit's hut before eyeing the jungle beyond the clearing.

"Where's Wawa?"

"He ran off into the woods some hours ago," she replied.

"I'm coming with you then."

Cleo nodded as they started to move toward the growth of trees.

It was usual.

If Wawa wasn't around, Sohut didn't let her enter the jungle alone.

They were her two bodyguards.

An unlikely pair, but she treasured them both anyway.

"Is Senrit still wary?"

"Yes, but there's been no sight of the Tasqal's Hedgerud fighters. I don't know why they'd been in Koznia anyway."

Cleo nodded.

If the aliens were wary, she was too.

As they made their way into the jungle, away from the camp, she kept her eyes and ears peeled.

With Sohut around, he could just whistle and the jungle-penguins would come but she knew they still had to be alert.

They were walking in silence and the undergrowth was becoming thick.

Being in the camp for the last few days made the jungle seem terrifying and if she hadn't been living in it for a year, she wasn't sure she could have gone hunting alone with only Wawa by her side.

Such were the thoughts in her head that when Sohut's heavy hand landed on her shoulder, the suddenness of it had her freezing.

Turning slightly, she cast a wide-eyed look at him.

He was holding her rigidly as he came to press his body against hers—so close she could feel the cords of his chest muscles pressing into her back.

His hot breath fanned her over her ear. "Don't. Move. Don't even breathe."

Cleo stiffened.

Something about his entire being made goosebumps rise over her skin.

He was staring straight ahead into the bushes, his green gaze cold, and every muscle in his body felt alert and ready.

A chill traveled down her spine and Cleo stiffened even farther as a strange feeling suddenly enveloped the area.

It was the sort of feeling you get when you become aware that you're in the presence of something very, very dangerous.

She was vaguely aware that Sohut was reaching into his trousers and pulling something free and a side-eye told her it was his blade.

There was something out there, something threatening, and she wondered if it was one of those guards the Torians had spotted.

The thought that there was an enemy in their midst...

For a few long seconds, nothing happened.

There wasn't even a sound.

Still, she didn't dare to move. She didn't dare to breathe, as Sohut had said, and as she held her breath, the bushes in front of them stirred.

Wawa...please let it be Wawa.

But what appeared through the bushes looked nothing like her little companion.

It was as black as night. So black that it took a few moments to realize she was looking at an animal and not into a dark void.

Even its eyes were dark.

It stood on four legs but on its back, rising into the air, were four sharp spikes that stood from its spine.

It stepped out of the bushes and paused, looking at them.

Behind her, Sohut was as hard as stone and she realized he was moving slowly to stand in front of her, blocking her from the literal nightmare in front of them.

"The fuck..." She breathed almost soundlessly. "...is that?"

"A spined creature..." Sohut was in front of her now, blocking her from the beast that stood unmoving. "Don't move."

A spined creature?

The same creature he mentioned was Wawa's prey?

How the...

Moving just slightly enough that she could see around Sohut, Cleo's eyes widened in disbelief.

No way.

That...*thing* in front of them was huge. There was no way little Wawa could take it on and survive.

Even as she looked it now and the rest of its body appeared from the bushes, she couldn't imagine Wawa taking down something that was that big.

There weren't four spikes on the thing's back. There were many. Four large ones came before the smaller ones that ran along its spine right down to its long reptilian-like tail.

"Run."

One word.

One word uttered from Sohut's mouth before there was a blur of black in front of them and a horrible, horrible growl that seemed to shake even the leaves around them.

In the panic of her mind, it took a second for the word to register and then adrenaline pumped through her so fast, she took off, heading in the direction from which they came.

As her feet beat against the jungle floor, she prayed this wasn't the time she fell over a root or vine. This was the exact time people fell in the movies—when their lives depended on them not stumbling.

Fear pushed her forward. But as she ran, her breath coming in sharp gasps, she realized something.

She was running alone.

Cleo stopped dead in her tracks, a bunch of low-hanging branches giving her a sharp slap in the face as she did.

Turning, she searched the bushes behind her for some movement, any movement.

Where the fuck was he?

In the few moments she took searching the orange bushes for some sign of blue, a gut-wrenching reality dawned on her.

Sohut wasn't coming.

He was frickin' fighting the thing.

Panic had her frozen for a few moments.

She was an idiot.

She shouldn't turn back as she was doing now.

She shouldn't run back *toward* danger.

The fuck was wrong with her?

Her lungs were about to give out, but the closer she got, the more she could hear.

It was a deep growling sound that made the air vibrate.

The creature sounded powerful, lethal, unyielding...

As she reached the spot, her gaze followed the trampled leaves and bushes that led farther into the undergrowth.

That's where the growling was coming from and her heart beat so hard, it almost broke through her ribs.

She couldn't hear Sohut, only the beast.

Shit. Shit shit shit.

He couldn't be dead.

Oh God, please don't make it so he's dead.

Then she heard it, another snarl, one that obviously came from the throat of a man, a huge dangerous man, but a man nonetheless.

The relief she felt was almost staggering, but she had no time to decipher it as she rushed closer.

For a second, she saw blue and then black.

175

They were wrestling and she didn't know who was winning.

Sharp black teeth glinted in the light as they were aimed at Sohut's throat, but he managed to hold them off, grabbing both jaws of the beast with his two hands.

The beast reared, flicking its tail in a semicircle that connected with Sohut's legs, bringing both of them down into the bushes.

It had its two front paws on Sohut now, pressing him into the ground below as its tail lashed behind it.

Dislodging her piece of shrapnel from the edge of her dress, Cleo gripped it in her hand.

She knew she had to do something.

There was a tree just behind them. If she could get there…

Her feet were moving before she could finish the thought.

Moving as fast as she could, she gripped the trunk of the tree, finding a low-hanging branch that would give her some leverage. Finding a foothold, up she went, slowly at first then her muscles remembered what they needed to do.

It was just like the time her father had left her alone in the wild, when she'd had to climb a tree at night after she'd been too afraid to sleep alone on the ground.

She could do this.

Soon, she was high enough above them to see.

There was a branch that jutted out, close to where they were and she headed for that one, hugging the branch with her legs as she moved slowly forward.

The branch was rough, and her thighs were going to hate her for this later.

But she didn't care.

The only thing in her mind was that Sohut was in danger.

He needed her help.

Sohut was on the ground, his teeth grit, his face twisted into a ferocious snarl as he wrestled to get the animal off him.

His sole focus was the beast and it seemed neither he nor the beast realized she was there for when Sohut's gaze caught movement above them and his eyes settled on her, the look in his eyes moved swiftly from ferocity to horror.

That one second of hesitation and the beast pressed into him harder, its sharp teeth moving even closer to Sohut's neck.

Cleo breathed hard.

She didn't have a plan.

She didn't have a frickin' plan!

Just then, the beast did something she didn't expect.

Its dark spines flattened against its back as its tail lashed menacingly, and she knew then exactly what she was going to do.

Gripping the piece of metal, she didn't think twice.

She let go of the branch.

It was like slow motion when she fell.

Her eyes were locked on Sohut's, on his brilliant greens as his gaze widened even more.

Gravity being her ally, Cleo aimed and when she landed, she slammed her hand as hard as she could into the beast.

The sharp pain that she felt immediately almost made her cry out.

The metal sunk deep into the creature's back, slicing her hand open in the process.

It reared back. One moment she was on its leathery back, the next she was landing in the bushes.

She barely had time to see Sohut rise with a growl she didn't know a man could produce, his blade slicing through the creature's midsection.

The sick squelch of guts spilling reached her ear.

The beasts' huge body went limp and only then did she breathe.

Her hand hurt.

Turning her palm to her face, Cleo winced.

It looked bad. Her blood was so red against the yellow-orange bushes around her that she didn't know if she should be awed or horrified that she was bleeding so much.

She was looking at her hand when a shadow fell over her.

"YOU." Sohut was glaring at her and when she looked up, she didn't know what to say.

His face was a mixture of horror, dismay, disbelief, anger, and...yearning.

Before she could protest, she was in his arms.

He pulled her from the bushes, pulling her against him as he buried his head against her neck.

"Why did you come back?"

Cleo swallowed hard.

Because I couldn't leave you to die?

"You could have found a way back to the camp. The Torians would have protected you. You could've left me..."

"*No.*" Was that her voice? That shaky thing? "I couldn't leave you."

He nuzzled her neck for a few seconds and Cleo allowed herself to relax against him.

"You could have died." His words were just a whisper.

"You too," she whispered back.

Sohut inhaled deeply and eased off her to study her face.

His eyes filled with rage by the second.

"Metal...I smell metal," he uttered, before snatching her hand.

His eyes didn't calm down when he saw the state of her palm and for the first time in her life, she wished she didn't bleed.

He bared his teeth, his fangs protruding in a snarl so ferocious she almost pulled her hand away.

As a matter of fact, she did try to pull her hand away, but he held her fast.

"*You hurt yourself.*" It was as if he was choking on the words. They came out of his mouth as if his throat was suddenly not working as it used to.

His gaze met hers.

"You hurt yourself because of me."

The look in his eyes was so tortured, she opened her mouth to tell him that she was all right and he didn't have to make such a big deal over it. But he cut her off before she was even able to mouth the words.

"*Never,* do that again."

~

SOHUT SET her down and began cleaning her wound and all she could do was blink at him.

Somewhere behind them lay a huge beast that they'd just killed, yet he was tending to her so carefully and gently that she couldn't believe it was the same person that had just sliced the beast in two.

For more than a few minutes, he crouched over her, meticulously removing every single foreign object from her wound.

Bits of leaves and sticks were removed by his dark claws one by one and never did he let her help.

He seemed adamant about doing it himself and as he worked he kept his gaze on his task, not raising his eyes to hers.

He cleaned her wound with dew from a nearby leaf and dug into his pocket for that vial of healing stuff he carried around. Still, he didn't look at her the entire time.

"Sohut?"

He didn't reply but she knew he heard her because the muscles in his shoulders stiffened slightly.

"Sohut."

He finally raised his gaze to hers, and Cleo inhaled deeply.

Did aliens cry?

Because he sure looked like he could cry.

The pain in his eyes was so real it made something within her wring into a knot.

She reached forward, cupping his face with her good hand without even thinking about it.

"You don't have to feel so bad. I've cut myself worse before," she murmured, her gaze searching his.

He didn't reply.

"Sohut?"

His gaze fell to her lips. For a moment, he just stared at them. "You say my name strangely," was what he said.

What?

Cleo paused, an unexpected chuckle bubbling inside her.

It wasn't what she'd expected him to say judging from, oh well, she didn't know—his entire demeanor!

"Am I not saying it correctly now? I don't call you 'Grout' anymore, not even in my head."

He was looking at her differently now, the sadness seeping away from his eyes as another emotion took hold. Something *else*, something intense, and her voice fell.

"You say it beautifully," he finally said and it felt like the air crackled between them.

There was no warning.

One moment he was stripping her bare with his eyes and the next he was pushing her into the soft patch of vines he'd set her on.

A moan that she thought was internal turned out to be a very verbal one as his mouth met hers...and then she couldn't breathe.

Breathing wasn't important with the feel of his lips against hers.

Suddenly she wasn't in the jungle anymore, she was somewhere else, somewhere safe and he was the reason she was there.

Wrapping an arm around his back, she pulled him closer as their kiss deepened.

This kiss was nothing like the many others they'd shared.

The way he kissed her it was as if he wanted to absorb her into himself.

Sohut groaned so deep, his entire chest vibrated against her as he pushed her head back into the leaves and, as if her body couldn't get enough of what he was inciting within her, her legs wrapped around his tapered waist, pulling him into her.

At that moment, it felt like he was everything she needed.

The world didn't matter anymore.

The jungle didn't matter.

All that mattered was the fact that he was here now and the strange thing about it...it felt like he was always meant to be there.

She was his...and he was *hers*.

She didn't know how long they'd been kissing for, only that when he finally broke away to take a breath, it felt like the sun had moved a little across the sky.

"Phek..." he muttered, taking huge gasps as he looked down at her. "Phek me."

Yes, that sounded about right.

"That's…" He began then trailed off. "You're…"

Yep, that sounded about right too.

He leaned down again to rest his forehead against hers and, this close, his green eyes were like the most brilliant demantoids she'd ever seen.

"You can't stay in this jungle," he finally said. "We can't wait around anymore. We need to go. We need to get to the Sanctuary."

Cleo nodded.

She knew staying at the camp had been temporary.

"You can't stay," Sohut gulped and continued. "They know…"

Mild confusion made her search his gaze. "They know what? They who?"

"That spined creature was hunting *me*. With Wawa around, it wouldn't have taken the chance to come close to *you*. It was after *my* scent." He paused. "It was coming after me."

Cleo blinked. Several thoughts, so many questions, rose in her mind.

In the process, she realized her legs were still wrapped around his waist, her skirt falling so her nakedness was plastered against him.

But as she tried to take her legs down, Sohut reached back and held them in place, a warning flashing through his eyes.

She could feel her cheeks warm but she didn't move.

It wasn't the worst place to have her legs.

"They know I've been…*protecting* you." He paused, waiting for her to say something before he continued. "It's not…normal for me to take this long to bring in a bounty."

Suddenly, the gravity of his words hit her full on.

He was talking about the orc aliens.

"You think they sent that thing after you?" Her gaze drifted to the dead animal not far from them.

"I don't think it. I *know* it."

Her throat suddenly felt dry. "They don't know you found me. What if you'd failed to catch me…"

"I never fail."

Cleo digested his words.

"So, you're saying they sent that…*thing* to kill you?"

Sohut didn't answer but the look in his eyes told her the affirmative.

"Shit...what does that even mean? *They hired you.*"

"It means they know I'm not bringing you in. They don't want me helping you to get out of this place."

There was a pause as she considered his words and then everything came falling down.

The hope she had for a future with him, the promise of something more than living like a fugitive...it was all falling to pieces.

"They know where you live...if you bring me there, they'll come after me...they'll come after *you.*"

Sohut didn't hesitate.

It was as if he'd considered all this before.

"I am prepared for that."

No.

The last thing she wanted was to bring trouble to him and his brother.

"I can go farther into the jungle with Wawa," she blurted, her heart rate picking up. "I can leave. And you can go back to those orcs, tell them you didn't find me. Tell them I died?"

"No." It was said so quickly and with so much conviction that something deep inside her ached.

"You expect me to leave you here after I found you, gnora?"

"Gnora?"

His eyes lit up a little as she repeated the word, but he didn't indulge her with the meaning.

"I'm not leaving you here. You're coming home with me."

Home.

A word that made an unexpected pang hurt the muscles in her belly.

"Home."

"To the Sanctuary."

Cleo blinked back what felt suspiciously like tears from her eyes.

She wasn't the emotional kind.

"I've found you, Clee-yo. I'm not letting you go. Ever."

25

SOHUT GRUNTED AS HE WALKED THROUGH THE BRUSH, SWATTING AWAY some of the long vines that hung down to brush the ground, careful that they didn't swing and hit the load on his back.

His *gnora*.

He'd called her that, but he was sure she didn't know what it meant.

It's why he'd said it.

He wasn't sure he could face her denying what he was sure was the bond in his soul.

The thought made him both nervous and elated.

He'd found the one to make him whole.

It wasn't a hunch or a presumption. It was intuition and for the past few days at the camp, he'd had to face that fact.

He'd found her.

Of all the Merssi to be blessed, he was.

"I can walk, you know." Clee-yo, *his* Clee-yo, murmured against his neck, her breath brushing against his skin to awaken something down below almost instantly.

It was hard focusing on his task when the one thing he wanted to do was stop among some of the soft vegetation and show her repeatedly just how much she made him feel.

"You hurt yourself." *In an effort to protect me.*

"My *hand*. I hurt my *hand*." The sound of her laughter was like water crystals sliding down gheuf leaves. It was a sound he was finding he could listen to till the end of time.

Holding her thighs tighter against his sides, he hurried on through the undergrowth back toward the Torian camp.

The Gori had sent a spined creature after him. Why?

He wasn't sure.

They hadn't communicated that Clee-yo was worth many credits. But the fact they'd spent an entire orbit and were still looking for her had told him that she was worth a lot to them for some reason.

So much so they were willing to kill him to get to her.

There was more to this than the Gori had communicated and there was no way he was going to let her fall into their hands.

He could no longer take any chances.

He needed to head through the other side of the jungle, through the arid lands, and toward the edge of the plains. It'd be a trek but once he got her to the Sanctuary, she'd be safe.

And she was going to be safe.

He would make sure of it.

Movement above them had him looking above and he locked eyes with Wawa.

"She's safe," he muttered and the animal blinked at him before focusing on Clee-yo.

He must have heard or smelled the spined creature and had rushed toward the sound.

"Who are you speaking to?"

"Wawa." He motioned to the slizz with his head.

"Oh." Clee-yo looked up and he could almost feel her relief. "Thank God he's okay."

She still didn't believe he was as dangerous as everyone said, apparently.

"The little rhag is sturdier than you think."

Clee-yo laughed again and her teats moved against the hardness of his back. He liked being the reason for her laughter—only, despite how good it made him feel, there was still that underlying feeling of dread.

As he headed back to the Torian camp, the smell of Clee-yo's blood slowly drifted away as his healing serum worked.

She'd gotten hurt to protect him.

Flashing images of his bloodied brother returning to the depths of the mines with his tail removed came flooding into his mind.

He wouldn't allow the people he cared about to be hurt because of him anymore.

It was the last time her blood would be spilled for him.

The last time anyone's blood would be spilled for him.

SAYING goodbye to the Torians was more emotional than she thought it would be.

"One last dance!" Senrit announced and Nupak pulled her toward the center of the camp.

Music filled the air as the celebration began, their feet moving in the soft dirt in time to the beat.

But it wasn't like the other times they'd danced.

There was a sense of uncertainty that had settled over the camp and even though the Torians pretended all was well, she could see their worried looks.

Whenever she wasn't looking directly at them, she could see their four eyes darting in her direction.

As they danced, Sohut smiled but the smile didn't reach his eyes, and when the celebration ended and they were loaded up with rice cakes, a sort of resolve had settled over his features.

Walking back into the jungle felt different this time.

She was suddenly very aware of the real danger that roamed these parts.

They traveled without speaking for the most part and it was only when they were deep in the jungle, far away from the Torian camp, that Sohut paused.

Tilting his nose to the air, he sniffed.

"Water," he said.

"You can smell it?"

Sohut glanced at her and nodded. Looking into the undergrowth around them, he sniffed again.

"Stay here." His gaze moved from her then to Wawa. "Stay here. I'll scout the area. We could rest there this dark cycle."

Glancing upward, she realized what she could see of the sky was slowly turning purple. Night was coming.

She hadn't realized they'd walked for that long.

"Okay," she nodded. "Hurry."

Sohut pulled her into him and planted a kiss on her head. "I will."

He disappeared in the bushes in the next second and Cleo stood, her eyes searching the bushes around her.

Wawa was relaxed on her shoulder so she took that as a good indication that she was safe.

In no time, the bushes rustled again and Cleo gripped her piece of metal.

When Sohut appeared, her shoulders sagged a little.

"It's safe," he said. "Come."

It was a small stream nestled in the middle of the undergrowth and Sohut took the time to fill his water bottle before passing it to her.

"I think we sleep here tonight," he said, looking around them. "We could continue pushing forward but," he glanced at her, "you should rest."

Cleo frowned.

If he was stopping because of her...

"I don't need sleep."

Her eyes fell on Wawa as he approached the stream, his tail brushing against Sohut's leg as he took a sip.

"You do." His gaze fell on Wawa too. "I'm sure he agrees."

As if Wawa understood them, he turned to blink at her before he began drinking once more.

Fine.

186

Looking upward, she realized there were no tall trees nearby.

He must have read her mind because Sohut stood suddenly and began pulling some vines together.

"We'll rest here." He glanced around again. "If anything comes near, I'll smell them before they can get close."

Swallowing the water, Cleo cast her gaze around at the darkening jungle.

She trusted Sohut.

What she didn't trust was the potential danger chasing them.

26

Cleo's eyes fluttered open and it took a few moments to focus.

She felt warm, protected...safe...and she realized the reason why immediately.

Somehow while they slept, Sohut had draped his body around hers completely.

It was like she was in her own little blue alien cocoon.

Yawning, she rubbed her eyes.

The light from his light disk made it seem as if it was already morning, but now that her eyes were open some more, she could see that the jungle beyond was still dark.

Above them, nestled in a bunch of vines, she could just about make out Wawa's white fluffy tail. He was asleep too...but *something* had woken her up.

There was a slight sound of shuffling and, with much effort because of the heavy alien stuck to her like a second skin, Cleo managed to rise on her elbows, her gaze moving near to Sohut's feet.

His satchel was moving and out of the open end poked the butt of one of the jungle-penguins.

There were three of them. The other two were standing close by, poking the satchel with their red beaks.

Yawning, Cleo shook her head.

To think they'd come this close without running away, even though she was their predator.

How they survived this long in the wild was a mystery.

The one with its head in the satchel gave a shake and some of the things in the bag went rolling out.

Groaning at the noise, Sohut lifted his head.

"Clee-yo?"

The jungle-penguin lifted its head then, with the bag still stuck over it, and began waddling away.

Cleo had to giggle.

"They're so cute. I hate having to eat them all the time," she murmured.

"Cute?" Sohut rose beside her and she felt him stiffen.

There was a tickle at her throat and she rubbed her hands there absentmindedly. It felt almost like a ring of itchy nerves was around her neck.

Sohut moved so fast, she lost her balance, and when her wide eyes reached him, her mouth fell open a little.

He was gripping one of the little birds so tightly, she was sure it risked being popped like a balloon.

For the first time since being around the animals, she saw an expression other than innocent ignorance on their faces.

The one Sohut was holding was bug-eyed as it looked at Sohut, its mouth slightly open with one of Sohut's gadgets between its beak.

The gadget was blinking and the more she looked at it the more that feeling around her neck tightened.

It took her a few moments to realize Sohut had his fangs out, snarling at the little bird before he snatched the device from its beak.

And when he turned to look at her...something deep inside her turned into cold, cold marble and fell.

Something bad was about to happen.

She knew it.

The look of absolute horror and dread in his eyes had her swallowing hard.

"Sohut?"

The feeling around her neck was tightening now and her heart was beginning to hammer against her chest.

"Sohut, what is that?" Her gaze fell to the device blinking in his hands.

But he didn't answer. The next thing she knew, she was being hoisted over his shoulder as he dashed into the bushes.

If she could see in the dark, her view would be that of the back of his legs because she was upside down.

She could feel his chest heaving, feel the fear in his bones and even though she'd consider herself a mentally sturdy gal, his response was beginning to terrify her.

"Where are you going?!" He didn't answer. He was running. Running much faster than he was supposed to be able to in the darkness in a jungle, but he was managing it anyway.

Vines and bushes slapped against them, as he all but flew through the darkness.

He was moving as if he was running away from something, and that scared her.

This was the same alien who'd told her to run while he fought the literal darkness-come-to-life.

He wasn't afraid of anything.

"Sohut! We left our stuff...and Wawa..."

She didn't understand what was happening, but whatever it was, it clearly had something to do with the device he carried in his hand.

"Wawa will find us. He knows your scent. The little phekker has bonded to you." It didn't sound like the Sohut she knew.

His voice sounded...strained.

"Sohut...talk to me..." She swallowed hard and reached up to touch her neck. There was no physical thing there, but it felt like a chain was around her neck, constricting against her vocal cords. And the more she fought it, the harder it squeezed.

"What's happening to me?" Fear was laced in her voice and at her question, it was as if his breaths started to come harder, harsher—and not because of his exertion.

It was almost as if he was hyperventilating.

She could feel the huge, hurried breaths he was taking as her upper body was pressed against his back.

But Sohut didn't stop. He kept on running.

She didn't know how he knew where he was headed in the pitch black of the jungle, but he somehow did.

She didn't hear it at first, not from the sound of her own blood beating in her ears, but as soon as she picked it up, her senses began screaming that something dangerous was happening.

There was a sound above them, like an engine of some sort and Cleo forced herself to think rationally.

She didn't just hear that.

She hadn't heard an engine in so long, the sound was...*alien*.

But it was definitely an engine.

She could hear it clearer now, as if whatever vessel it was, was lowering from the sky.

"Sohut?"

He swallowed hard. She could feel that even in his back.

"Clee-yo..." His voice was hoarse and so, so pained. "I'm sorry, Clee-yo."

Her mouth spoke the words in her mind without much input from her. She suddenly felt...numb.

"What's happening, Sohut?"

He swallowed hard again and even though he was blazing through the forest like Usain Bolt's alien brother, he didn't pause or slow down.

He was running for his life...or for hers.

"They're coming." was all he said.

She didn't need to know who *they* were.

Her whole being knew who *they* were.

Time paused and there was a sound.

A sound she'll never forget.

It was a blast so strong, it flattened everything in the surrounding area.

All the trees...the vines...every single plant lay flat on the ground and she knew this for a fact because the light that suddenly flooded around them was so bright it was as if the sun had risen in an instant.

Sohut stopped. He stopped so suddenly, it took her organs a second to fall back into her body from the sudden lack of motion.

The light.

It was so bright.

As her eyes adjusted it became clear, however, that this was no sun.

It was the light from whatever vessel was hovering above them.

She could hear the engine clearly now—a soft hum that cut through the quietness of the jungle. And even as she lifted her head, trying to see through the veil her hair had made, she saw something that cut through her senses, turning her to cold stone.

Someone, some *being*, landed behind Sohut. A leathery tail swung behind the legs.

She knew those legs...that tail...she'd seen it before.

A long, long time ago...so long ago, she'd thought the memory had been locked in the recesses of her mind, but it was right in front of her now.

Clear as day, she remembered, as if it hadn't happened over a year ago—as if no time had passed and she was back on that alien slave ship.

It was the legs of one of the guards. The same guards that had manned the ship that had taken her away from Earth.

They were here to take her away. Not the green orcs that had pulled her from the rubble to sell her to the zoo, but *them*.

She'd rather jump off a cliff than go back with them.

She couldn't breathe now, literally, and it had nothing to do with the constriction around her neck.

"Merssi...you have been foolish, keeping us waiting so long." The voice came from behind her and a chill ran down her spine.

There was more than one of them.

Sohut stiffened.

"You're not taking her." He was growling, an animalistic sound that would have scared her if she didn't know who he was, and she knew his fangs were bared.

His arm tightened around her and she heard the unmistakable sound of his claws protracting.

He was ready to fight.

So was she.

He just had to put her down. She'd claw their eyes out with her bare fingers if she had to.

Their laughter was sickening.

It was the sort of sound that seemed to clap the air, echoing into the darkness.

"Of course, we are taking her. You sent the signal, made our work easier."

The signal.

Cleo blinked, unmoving, her mind trying to make sense of their words.

Which signal?

Then it came to her.

The device that was blinking even right now in Sohut's hand.

For a moment, a little voice in her head made her doubt everything.

That device was why they were there. It had summoned them, and Sohut had possessed it all along.

He'd had the means to make them find her at any moment.

"Sohut?" Her voice cracked as she said his name and she felt him stiffen even more, his growling interrupted for a second.

The guards around them laughed again.

"Qrakking human. The Merssi has developed feelings for it, don't you see?" The guard laughed.

"Are you surprised? They are both useless beings. Excrement tends to stick to excrement."

Sohut growled, but he didn't move.

There was movement in front of her and suddenly she was face-to-face with one of the guards.

He bent so he could look into her face and Cleo stifled a gasp as the guard's alligator-like snout came far too close for comfort.

"You didn't trust him, did you, *jekin*?" The way he said the word made it sound as if he was calling her a bitch. "You thought you were free?" He laughed in her face. "The Merssi had the tracker for you the entire time. You belong to our lordships, the High Tasqals. The Merssi cares nothing about you."

They were wrong.

She knew Sohut better.

They'd made love, many, many times. She'd given herself to him. *Trusted* him.

At that moment, she knew with certainty a thought that she hadn't forced herself to acknowledge before: she'd rather die than let them hurt the man she loved.

The man she *loved*.

A ball of emotion developed in her throat, causing her to choke.

"Release the jekin," one of the guards ordered. "Her master awaits."

"NO!" For a moment, she thought the word came from Sohut—it was uttered with such ferocity, such power, such defiance—but the sudden strain on her throat made her realize the exclamation had come from her.

She felt Sohut's arms tighten around her.

"She's not going anywhere," he spoke through gritted teeth.

There was a pause and then the guards cackled. They cackled as if they'd just heard the funniest joke and their lack of concern sent a chill down her spine.

What were she and Sohut going to do?

They were outnumbered, outmatched.

She was sure they could probably outrun them and put up a fight, but she wasn't sure how she'd fare in one-and-one combat—that didn't mean she wouldn't fucking try her best.

One of the guards spoke, his words slicing through her senses, making her think she'd missed a part of the conversation.

"Qrak, we'll make you then."

Sohut stiffened even more, and he took a backward step as something zinged in the air. It sounded like an electrical current, the sort of sound you hear if you get too close to compromised power lines.

"Don't you phekking dare. You'll hurt her too!" Sohut growled.

"Does it look like we qrakking care?"

That was all the warning she got before the pain.

A searing pain that felt as if she was burning from the inside out. Her entire body shook as she lost control of her limbs and she was vaguely aware of going down...

But she wasn't the one falling. Sohut was.

He fell to his knees, his arms still locked around her as she heard him grunt and she realized that whatever the guards were doing, they were doing to him, not her. She was only receiving the second-hand effect.

As Sohut fell forward and her back hit the earth below, she was suddenly staring upward through her watery eyes into the faces of three alligator-guards.

Their cruel yellow gazes stared down at her and Sohut as the weapon in their hands glowed strangely in the light of their ship.

It looked like a power rod. A shock rod.

They'd shocked Sohut with a direct current.

A rage she didn't know she had burst within her organs and she screamed—only no sound came from her mouth. Her scream was silent as her body shook with the after-effects of the current.

She didn't have time to get to her feet. The gator-guards helped her with that as one moved forward and pulled her from Sohut's arms.

No.

"No." Sohut groaned as he tried to stand. He reached for her, but the shock rod was promptly planted into his back and another dose of the current sent through his body.

His skin was turning black.

They were killing him!

His green gaze met hers and this time the scream that ripped from her body echoed into the forest.

She tasted the blood before she realized her head snapped to the side. The pain of the slap followed but she didn't care.

She turned her burning rage on the guard that had slapped her, kicking and flailing but as her legs connected with his underbelly, he only grabbed her to stop her movement.

"I'll kill you," Sohut groaned again and began to move and something inside her crumpled and wrung. "I'm going to kill every last one of you."

He needed to stay down.

They were going to kill him if he didn't.

The guards cackled again and the world around her began to fade.

They were being beamed up into the ship above them and there was nothing she could do about it.

Her eyes locked on Sohut's, on the man that had stolen her heart without her even realizing, and the utter pain in his eyes was enough to break her heart.

"Sohut..." She gulped.

The last thing she saw, an image that would be committed to her memory forever, was Sohut reaching for her...

Her heart broke.

It broke into a million pieces because there was a distinct feeling that she'd never feel his touch ever again.

27

Sohut fell on his back, his breath coming in labored gasps.

They'd almost shocked the life out of him and he'd have let them if that had meant he could've saved her.

But he couldn't.

He'd failed.

Again he'd failed.

In the darkness of the jungle, the world never felt more alone... more desolate.

Clee-yo was gone because of him.

Once more, he was the reason the person he cared about the most was going to...

He didn't dare to say it.

He didn't even dare to think it.

The feeling of dread that he'd been harboring finally settled around him.

This was what he'd been afraid of.

This was the future he hadn't wanted to happen.

This was the reason it'd all felt too good to be true.

A pained sound left him as he tried to rise into a sitting position, propping himself up on his elbows.

In his hand, something blinked red in the darkness.

The tracker.

His life-organ skipped a beat.

He still had the tracker.

It gave him a bittersweet feeling and he gripped the device tightly.

He couldn't have destroyed it. Doing so would have activated it anyway. He'd needed to decommission it completely and the only way to do that would have been to take it back to his friend, Ka'Cit.

Ka'Cit would have had the tech to do such a thing.

Bio-trackers were finicky devices. It wasn't something he'd wanted to play around with.

So he'd kept the thing.

The very thing that had led to the Hedgeruds finding them... finding *her*.

His physical pain turned emotional, churning in his stomach and he almost doubled over.

It was like when he was a chid and his mor had decided to send him and Riv to the mines. It was the same feeling all over again.

"BUT, *momor, I don't want to go!*"

"*Shut your phekking mouth. Look at me! I cannot. No longer can I do this alone.*"

"*But momor...*"

"*This is your fault, Sohut. Remember that. I could deal with Riv alone... but not you. Not you and your weakness...*

Remember that you are the reason your mor has to beg on the streets of Dragxul because you are weak. I rue the day you fell from my body...you pest."

"*Mor...*"

"*This is your fault. It is your fault your saran left us. It's your fault you're going to the mines. You are weak. No Merssi should be as weak as you. You are a curse from my womb. A curse upon me, a curse upon your daran, and a curse upon your brother.*"

. . .

A CURSE.

A failure.

All because he'd been a sickly child.

He was the reason his mother had sent him and Riv to the mines. He was the reason his brother had had to shoulder so much.

He was the reason his brother had lost his tail.

He was the reason his brother, the only person to have loved him, had almost died.

Till this day, he hadn't told Riv about that conversation with their mor.

He couldn't.

How could he say he was the reason his brother's entire life had been upended?

He didn't have the gonads to.

And so he'd taken the field jobs. At least then, he was useful. He was of use and such jobs caused him to stay away from the Sanctuary as much as he could, just so he didn't have to face the recluse his brother had become *because of him*!

He should have run away that day after his mor had said those words.

But he didn't.

He'd been weak.

Too weak to protect Clee-yo.

As his labored breaths began to calm down he was vaguely aware of a sound at the edge of the fallen trees.

Squinting in the darkness, he caught the shape.

Wawa.

The slizz snarled at him, racing at him through the darkness. He only managed to catch Wawa mid-air.

The slizz was snarling at him, its teeth protracted, and its eyes bled to black.

It could smell that Clee-yo wasn't there anymore.

"I didn't kill her!" Sohut growled. "She was *taken*." He hated saying the words but Wawa seemed to calm down a little at the sound of his voice, so he continued.

"I didn't kill her," he murmured again. "She was taken by Hedgeruds."

The slizz made a sound in its throat as its teeth retracted.

It was a questioning sort of mewing and Sohut let out a sad huff of a laugh.

It loved her.

Wawa loved her.

Of all the creatures, his Cleo had befriended a slizz.

Of all creatures, she had befriended *him*.

"I don't know, Wawa," he finally said and he could see, even in the darkness, that Wawa's ears perked. It was the first time he'd had a proper conversation with the animal. "I don't know why the Hedgeruds..."

As Wawa wasn't trying to kill him anymore, he set the animal down and watched it as it paced in front of him, sniffing the ground as it did.

Twiddling with the tracker in his hand, Sohut frowned.

The Hedgeruds had come...not the Gori...and that spelled trouble.

The Hedgeruds only worked for the High Tasqals.

Rich, powerful and cruel, it was no secret that the High Tasqals trafficked beings from Class Four planets—mainly for their entertainment.

Their slaves never lasted long. Not with the disease the Tasqals carried. It was the same disease that was decimating the Tasqal race.

They were dying. Rotting.

And so they bred, forcefully, with beings that had no legal protection on this side of the universe.

His stomach twisted.

The thought that the Hedgeruds were taking Cleo to the High Tasqals for her to be...

He couldn't stomach the thought.

He needed to get her back.

Groaning, he stood. Every nerve in his body protested.

"We have to get her back," he muttered and at his feet, the slizz made a sound of agreement.

Taking a few steps in the direction of the stream felt like he was trying to claw his way up a mountain that had one-hundred percent more gravity than usual.

But he could make it.

He would make it and his body wouldn't hold him back.

He hadn't let it hold him back when he was in the mines, even though he was sick and close to dying most of the time. He had stayed alive for Riv because dying would have been the ultimate insult to his brother's life.

He could do that again.

He'd overcome the pain in his muscles and he'd force his limbs to move.

"Let's go get her, little one." He looked at the slizz and Wawa jumped on him, perching on his shoulders just as he did with Clee-yo.

Sohut gripped the tracker in his hand.

They could do this.

They were going to get their female back.

IT FELT like hours before he was walking back at normal pace, but he managed to retrieve the contents of his satchel that the cursed mogs had thrown all over the vines near the stream.

Grabbing everything he could see, he set off at a run, his breath coming in gasps as he pushed his body forward.

He didn't have a plan but what he was about to do was dangerous.

Nobody went against the Tasqals.

Nobody except the rebels in the Restitution and he was no rebel.

But he was in love.

Clee-yo was his gnora. His soulmate.

He could feel it.

And he wasn't going to lose her, even if it meant he had to die getting her free.

Riv. He needed to call his brother Riv.

Connecting his sat phone, he punched in his brother's code.

"Sohut?" Riv's voice sounded over the line. He sounded phekked off, but that was his brother—he was never in a good mood.

"Riv," he breathed as he ran through the darkness, trusting his instincts that he was heading the right way. "I phekked up badly, brother."

"What do you mean?" The concern in his brother's voice was immediate and it wrung his life-organ. Riv had always cared for him, like a father more than a brother.

He was so indebted to him he didn't know how he was ever going to repay him.

"There's something I have to deal with." Sohut breathed. "I don't know when I'll be coming back to the Sanctuary."

"Something like what?" Riv asked.

"Remember that exotic animal I'm here to catch?"

"Yes..."

"She's not an animal."

"*She?*"

Sohut gulped.

"*She*, brother. *She*. The same species as Larn."

"You mean La-rehn?"

"La-rehn. Yes." Why was saying this so hard? "Well, I helped capture one of her kind and..." He paused. Saying it was like admitting that he was really weak.

"...I phekked up, brother. I think I'm going to have to do something stupid," he finally said.

He could hear the silence on the other end of the line.

"Explain," Riv growled after a few moments.

"No time. I have to get to the exchange." But there was no longer the low crackle of the connection.

Glancing down at the device, he realized it was out of charge.

It seemed the phekking mogs had detached the sol battery.

Phekking little fat excrement holes.

Gritting his teeth, Sohut pushed forward.

He'd get to the exchange, get a distorter, and find Clee-yo.

As he slipped the sat phone back in his satchel, Sohut gulped.

That might be the last time he ever heard his brother's voice but now he only had one objective and she needed him.

Clee-yo.

He was going to find his Clee-yo.

28

CLEO'S EYES FLUTTERED OPEN AND FOR A SECOND, SHE DIDN'T KNOW where she was.

The lighting was different, the smells different, the sounds...all different.

Anxiety made her sit upright immediately.

She was in a...

Looking around, her eyes widened.

It was a like a magical garden for fairies.

Purple blooms that resembled sakura trees hung over her and there were actual butterflies.

Real butterflies.

She stared at them...unable to believe what she was seeing.

What were monarch butterflies doing on an alien planet?

The soft trickle of a stream caught her ear and she stood on shaky legs.

Was she dreaming?

Was she dead?

Reality slammed her like a semi out of control.

Sohut!

As she dashed from underneath the trees, her heart in her chest, she noticed two things.

One, she really was in a magical fairy land.

Two, she wasn't alone.

In front of her, huddled together, a group of aliens sat on the rocks.

Something within her chest clenched.

"She's awake," one of the aliens murmured.

As her eyes darted from one to the other, Cleo took them in.

Their features were soft, and they didn't look threatening.

Females.

They were all females, Cleo assumed.

Some had strange fleshy bits on their heads that reminded her of Medusa and others were bald-headed.

"Hey." One with the Medusa-head turned and looked her way. "Are you okay?"

Cleo just stared at them.

What in the actual fuck was happening? What the hell was this?

Something moved to her left and her head snapped that way.

There was a clear panel there.

It looked like glass and it rose against the wall, separating the magical garden from whatever was on the other side.

"Where the hell am I?" She breathed, moving toward the glass.

What she saw on the other side almost made her collapse and it was only because she pressed her hands against the glass that she didn't.

There were toads, walking toads on the other side.

Toads dressed in white robes, all walking around as if they were viewing goods...viewing *her*.

Cleo took a step back.

There was movement to her right and her instincts took over as she snatched whatever was coming toward her.

It was an arm. The arm of the female that had spoken to her, and the woman looked at her in surprise.

"It's okay. Calm down. You've been unconscious for a few days. Take it easy."

A few *days*?

Glancing at her hand holding the woman, Cleo let go and took a step back.

"Who are you? Where am I? What are you doing here?"

The woman gave a small smile. "My name is Lee-yunna. I was chosen just like you were." She motioned behind her. "Me and the others."

"Which sector did you come from?" one of the other females asked.

"Sector?" Cleo took another step back, the reality of the situation weighing on her mind.

She'd been captured...*again*.

And Sohut...he was probably dead.

The thought made her want to collapse.

"I wasn't in a sector, whatever that is," she replied, threading her hands into her hair as she stared wide-eyed at the ground. "I was free."

"I know you're probably in shock right now—"

"What is this place?" Cleo turned her wide eyes to the female in front of her. "Where am I?"

"This is our terrarium. It's where they're keeping us before the auction."

Auction?

She was in a cage.

There was that feeling around her neck again and she touched her neck as she took a step toward the transparent barrier.

She could just about see her reflection in the glass and there was a thin blue line around her neck.

It wasn't solid, but it felt like it.

It was a clasp of some kind and memory of the moments before she was taken came rushing back to her.

Sohut.

Slamming her fists against the glass, she screamed at the beings on the other side.

She wasn't an animal, goddamnit!

She wasn't going to be caged, auctioned, and bought!

She'd die first.

As the beings on the other side paused to look at her, some coming close enough she could see the sores on their bodies, she looked one of them in the eye.

On the other side of the glass, the toad-man smiled.

Lee-yunna took a step toward her, causing Cleo to step back farther.

"Stay away from me," she said, as her gaze darted around the fairy forest.

It was all for show.

There wasn't anything magical about this. That reality was making panic rise within her.

"I have to get out," Cleo murmured, her gaze still darting around.

"You've been unconscious for a few days..." Lee-yunna said. "Come sit with us. We will explain it to you."

The female smiled at her and Cleo nodded slightly before she allowed the alien to lead her over to the other females.

They were all sitting on a set of rocks out in the open and as she and Lee-yunna approached, the conversation didn't wane.

Whatever they were talking about though, Cleo didn't hear.

Her focus was on the transparent glass and the many toad aliens she'd seen on the other side.

"How long was I unconscious for?"

"We are not sure," one of the females stopped talking with the others to answer. "We are sometimes drugged after their tests. It is hard to tell the time, but the drugs don't seem to affect Lee-yunna."

Cleo's eyes moved to the female who'd spoken to her first and Lee-yunna smiled.

"It's been at least five days."

Five days?!

Alarm made Cleo rise suddenly.

Sohut.

"I need—" she stuttered. "I need to get out. There's somebody out there. Somebody I need to get back to."

"There's nobody to get back to," one of the other females said. "You will be the property of a Tasqal in a few moons. They are all."

The thought made Cleo feel sick.

As reality slowly settled within her, she frowned.

"You can understand me. How?"

"You were not awake for the tests. They update everyone's language chips. It makes the process easier, in case you are bought with another..."

She didn't say another what, but Cleo knew.

Another slave.

Lee-yunna reached a hand toward her. "There's no escaping this. We are sacrifices, given by our people for the safety of our people. It is an honored tradition. Surely, your people told you this before they sent you off."

Cleo couldn't breathe.

Sacrifices?

Her people?

When Lee-yunna smiled again, she realized she'd spoken out loud.

"Our people have given us to the Tasqals in exchange for peace." Lee-yunna's smile waned a little. "It is an honor."

No.

"Do you really believe that?" Cleo asked the female.

Lee-yunna blinked and forced her smile wider. "Yes."

Something made Cleo believe what she really wanted to say was "no."

Cleo sat because she was sure her legs were going to give out.

"What is it?" One of the other females frowned. "You seem perturbed by this."

Cleo swallowed down the lump in her throat.

"My people didn't send me here. I was taken." The females around her glanced at each other and when she met their gazes, she was sure they could see the resolve in hers. "I was taken, and I'd rather die than be a sacrifice to one of those things out there."

208

29

It'd taken him far too long to reach his destination.

Trekking through the jungle back to the road that ran through it had taken days. More days than he had the heart to count.

And the longer he was away from her, the more terrified he became.

What if he was too late?

Sohut let out a breath as he stood in front of the exchange.

Before him, hover vehicles zoomed in and out carrying shoppers, all unaware of the fact that before them was a Merssi with his world crumbling around him.

As he moved forward, there was only one thing on his mind.

It kept him focused.

Focused enough that he could walk into the exchange hardly clothed and injured.

He was drawing the attention of the beings around him.

The exchange was packed. There was hardly even space to walk.

Yet, the crowd of shoppers parted to let him through and he could feel their gazes.

Or maybe it was the fact he had an adorable slizz on his shoulder.

Either way, the beings around him were not his concern.

After buying a fresh healing serum and administering it, he'd moved through the sketchier sections of the exchange searching for a distorter to purchase.

Distorters were rare illegal tech but he was sure he could find one.

Word from some of the sellers suggested the stall he was in front of might have exactly what he needed.

Rapping on the metal window of the stall, Sohut waited.

After a few moments, a slot opened in the window and the seller spoke.

"What."

Great customer service.

"I'm looking for a distorter," Sohut spoke in a low tone.

There was a pause before, "What do you want it for?"

Sohut's jaw clenched and he resisted the urge to reach his hand through the slot and close it around the seller's throat.

"None of your business."

"Fifty teruva coins," the seller said after a few moments.

Sohut's jaw clenched again.

Nobody had fifty teruva coins just hanging about and he didn't have time to phek around.

The seller was mostly hidden and the slot that he looked through from his stall was only on the level of Sohut's chest.

"Three thousand credits." Sohut's voice was like ice. "Three thousand or I can introduce you to my little friend."

As soon as he said so, Wawa climbed down his shoulder to look straight through the slot in the stall.

There was an exclamation on the other side and the sound of things falling.

"Deal. I don't want trouble here."

Good.

As soon as the transaction was over, he stepped away from the stall, gripping the distorter in his hand.

He'd use the device to distort his image when he needed to.

That was the second part of his plan.

But right now, he was searching for one particular group of aliens.

The healing serum he'd administered must be giving him a buzz or maybe it was the pure rage at the fact that he'd lost Clee-yo. Whatever it was, he welcomed it.

All he knew for sure was that he wanted to break some necks.

Donning a white robe he bought, he slipped into a side alley and tilted his nose to the air.

His enhanced nostril sensors would do most of the work now.

He knew their scent, his prey.

They couldn't hide even if they wanted to and, as he wove through the exchange, it didn't take him long to find the Gori he was looking for.

There were two of them, the two that had hired him.

Standing with their backs turned to him, they didn't even hear him approach.

Wawa snarled at the sight of them, his teeth protracting immediately as if he knew the two males.

At the sound, one of the Gori turned, his eyes bugging out.

"A—A slizz!" The large male staggered backward, his midsection jiggling.

His companion turned with the same expression.

Sohut dropped the hood of the robe. "I think you have more than the slizz to worry about."

At the sight of them, the other shoppers in the vicinity screamed and there was a flurry of feet as they tried to get away.

"Y-you!" one of the Gori exclaimed.

"You're supposed to be dead," said the other.

With one step forward, Sohut was in front of one of the males, his fist landing a punch that sent the male crashing into a wall.

Sohut cocked his head, a sneer on his face.

If only he wasn't still healing; he'd have punched the Gori into tomorrow.

The other Gori put his hands in the air.

"H-hey. We don't want no trouble, Merssi."

"Where did they take her?" Sohut turned, raising his fist. On his shoulder, Wawa puffed up his fur, his teeth protracting even more.

"Phek," the Gori muttered, raising his hands higher as he glanced in his friend's direction.

211

"Tell me," Sohut growled, moving too fast for the male as he closed his unclenched hand around the Gori's neck. "Speak the right words or they might be your last."

The Gori tried to swallow, his eyes darting to his companion, who was still crumpled on the ground.

"You don't want to mess with the Tasqals, Merssi. It's not worth it."

"Wrong answer," Sohut growled, his fist connecting with the male's cheek. Dark-green blood spewed on the ground and even more shoppers screamed and ran away.

"I'm going to ask you again," Sohut growled as he brought his fangs close to the male's face. "Last chance." He barely was able to say the words as he grit his teeth, trying to pull back the rage pulsing through his veins. "Where. Did. They. Take. Her?"

No answer.

Pulling his fist back, he punched the male again and the Gori's head lolled a bit.

The Gori spat, some of his teeth flying. "To Sector 89. It's an underground private auction. There's no way you can get in."

That one word made his blood run cold.

Auction.

"When is this auction?" In his peripheral vision, the male he'd knocked out was rising.

Wawa growled and hopped off his shoulder to stand in front of the male, his fur bristled making him appear larger than he was and his teeth were bared.

The Gori took one look at the slizz and stopped moving.

"Two moon cycles from now," said the Gori in front of him.

Phek.

Two moon cycles to find a stronghold guarded by the secrets of the entire planet.

It wasn't nearly enough time.

CLEO SAT under the sakura-like tree, her eyes darting to look through the pink blossoms every now and then.

212

The other females were still huddled in the same spot they huddled in every day.

Between moving to get the food the guards placed in the enclosure and moving to the pool at the back to clean themselves, they always sat in the same spot, seemingly unconcerned.

It'd been days, too many days to count and the longer time passed, the more anxious she became.

Every time the guards entered the terrarium, she was sure it was time to get sold and her heart would lurch, but so far it seemed time was on her side.

She was still working on a way to escape her god-forsaken situation.

Eyeing the alien females now, Cleo pursed her lips.

They were mumbling to each other but she couldn't join them in conversation.

They all seemed to have accepted their fate.

She did not.

She *would* not.

Reaching underneath her dress, she took out her lucky piece of metal.

It was always tied there, in that spot by a ripped piece of fabric, just in case she lost it.

Turning the thing over in her hand, she glanced through the pink blossoms again.

She needed a plan and, if she was going to escape, she needed more weapons.

Today just happened to be the day luck might be on her side.

On the ground beside her, there were hardly any fallen branches, but she'd managed to find two thin ones...twigs almost—they would just have to do.

With another glance through the blossoms, Cleo got to work, filing down the twigs so they had sharp ends.

She was working for maybe thirty minutes, refining the edges when a sound caught her ear and she looked up. Lee-yunna stood there.

"Hey," Lee-yunna said.

Cleo glanced at her, before continuing to work. "Hey."

"What are you doing?" She could hear the surprise in the female's voice and it made her shoulders stiffen.

What if the woman gave her non-plan away?

But when Lee-yunna walked over, she saw that it wasn't surprise in her eyes.

It was excitement.

"Can I have one?" she lowered her voice to a whisper.

Cleo glanced at the female and back to the weapons.

She'd only have two wooden shivs and her metal blade. Not nearly enough if she was going to stab her way out of there but having an ally was probably even better.

A glance at the other females still huddled together made her press her lips into a thin line.

If they stood a chance, they'd all have to fight their way out. Each and every one of them.

"Why do you want one? I thought you were all doing this for your people."

Lee-yunna's eyes fell. "We are."

Cleo studied the female and watched her shoulders slump.

"We are, but I don't want to." Lee-yunna met her gaze. "You said you were free before...what was that like?"

It was an unexpected question and Cleo studied the female some more.

"I was living in the wilderness doing my own thing. I got up when I wanted to, hunted when I wanted to, ate when I wanted to. I had fresh air. Fresh food. A nice place to lay my head. And someone..." Her voice broke and she took a moment before going back to sharpening the shivs once more.

"Someone what?" Lee-yunna pressed.

Cleo took a moment before answering. Meeting Lee-yunna's gaze, she spoke. "Someone who loved me."

Someone who *loved* her, and she wasn't ready to let him go.

He was alive. She wouldn't believe that he'd died that night and as long as she breathed, she was going to fight to be with him.

She wasn't ready to let him go.

Not yet.

Not ever.

"I don't know what that feels like," Lee-yunna finally said.

"What?" Cleo blinked, bringing her thoughts back to the present.

"Love."

The alien female looked genuinely saddened by this and it tugged at something within her.

"Look," Cleo said, thrusting one of the wooden shivs toward Lee-yunna. "Take this. I don't know how or if you'll use it, but it's better to have it than not to."

Lee-yunna blinked at the shiv before she threw herself at Cleo, placing her hand against Cleo's forehead firmly.

Cleo blinked, wide-eyed and not sure what to make of the gesture.

"Thank you," Lee-yunna breathed. "Thank you so much."

As the female released her, Cleo nodded, looking away.

"We have to get ready soon," Lee-yunna murmured. "For the auction."

"How do you know?"

"I heard the guards murmuring when they came in to feed us. They will return today to...make us beautiful for the masters."

The words made Cleo's stomach turn and, like a bad omen, there was a sound in the terrarium and exclamations from the other women.

Hurriedly stuffing the shiv and blade behind the tree, Cleo stepped from beneath the blossoms.

It was the gator-guards.

She didn't need Lee-yunna to tell her. She knew it herself.

It was time.

30

Phek.

He was an idiot for doing what he was doing.

It could get him killed.

Sector 89 was reserved only for high-ranking beings on the top class of Hudo III's society.

The Tasqals.

Taking Wawa off his shoulder, he looked into the slizz's eyes.

They were in an alley, just before the entrance to the sector.

It had taken him what felt like forever to find intel on the stronghold and he had almost run out of days to do so.

Luckily, with Wawa by his side, threatening disreputable beings was a lot easier than if he was doing so on his own.

Still, no one wanted to cross the Tasqals.

Through extensive measures, he'd gotten enough intel that he was confident he could get into the sector and out of it alive, possibly.

He'd just have to rely on luck for that last part.

Tall, flat walls of gray rose into the air around them, telling him that he was in the right place.

It was rumored that Sector 89 went underground and that the structures on top were only for show.

Well, he was about to find out.

"You have to stay here," he whispered and Wawa gave him a dirty look. How the animal managed to do that, he didn't even know. "I can't take you in with me. You'd give away my cover immediately."

The animal made a sound in its throat while still giving him a dirty look.

"Oh, Riv is going to *love* you." Sohut smiled a little, before letting a huge sigh leave his body.

"This is it," he said more to himself than to the stinky little animal in his presence.

Stepping out of the alleyway, he pressed the distorter on his arm and felt the little zing as his image was distorted to that of the life form he chose.

A Hedgerud fighter.

Turning, he made to say goodbye to the slizz but realized Wawa was no longer there.

Cursing underneath his breath, he looked around for the little animal, but he couldn't see where it had gone.

Phek.

But now wasn't the time to try and find the thing. He might be late enough as it is.

As he headed toward the doors of the sector, he swallowed hard. This better work.

The large gray doors stood before him, dwarfing him in their magnificence.

"Fighter, state your code."

It was a crackle that came through the wall. He couldn't even see the speaker that it came from.

Sohut gulped.

He'd beat as much information as he could from the Gori's and the thought he was placing his confidence in what they'd told him was making him feel sick.

"Code 9808 under His Excellency Tormud."

All he needed was the right code and the right name.

It was lax security...but who was mad enough to do what he was doing?

No one.

No one dared to get in the way of the Tasqals.

It was a death sentence, quite literally.

There was a pause on the other side of the doors and for a second, he wondered if his plan was blown but the door began to slide open.

They were huge, yet they made no sound and soon, right in front of him was a long, brightly lit corridor.

Pristine white walls were on either side, and the lights themselves looked as if they were shining through crystals.

Sohut's life organ skipped a beat.

This was definitely Tasqal territory.

They had a strange obsession with white and crystals...an obsession with purity even though they were so filled with impurity themselves.

As he walked through the open doors, he glanced up at the Hedgerud fighter on a platform above him.

The fighter jerked his head in greeting and Sohut mimicked the movement before continuing to walk forward.

A discreet glance behind him told him the doors were closing again.

As he walked, he kept his head slightly down and his gaze forward as two more guards came up the corridor.

They were mumbling to themselves and he hoped they wouldn't speak to him. But apart from jerking their heads in his direction in greeting, they said nothing.

So far, so good.

The corridor was leading downward and he realized the rumors must be true.

Sector 89 was a stronghold built underground.

It didn't take long before the ground leveled out and Sohut found himself in front of another set of doors.

These ones opened without needing a code and as Sohut stepped through them, he shuddered.

There were Tasqals and Hedgerud fighters everywhere.

His mortal enemies.

It was a—Sohut stopped moving, not believing what he was seeing—a sort of pleasure center.

There were chained *soephrims* playing stringed instruments in different parts of the room and lounging on raised platforms were Tasqals, male and female alike, getting...pleasured.

His stomach turned at the sight and with that feeling followed a fear he never knew he could feel.

His eyes darted across the space, looking at the beings pleasuring the Tasqals...looking but not wanting to see a female with hair like zimsu flowers.

Clee-yo.

As his life organ beat in his throat, he didn't realize a Hedgerud fighter had approached him.

"You look ill, comrade. Did you eat the klee shells too?"

Sohut blinked.

Phek.

"Klee shells?"

The Hedgerud's yellow eyes narrowed, and for a second Sohut wondered if he'd just blown his cover with that simple question.

"You must be new," the Hedgerud said. "Hired for the auction later today?"

The auction.

So, he wasn't late then.

Sohut's shoulders slumped a little with relief.

"The auction," he answered. "Yes."

"That way," the Hedgerud motioned in the direction off to the side and Sohut saw a dark corridor leading from the room. "Your master will be looking for you."

Without another word, the fighter walked away and Sohut made his way in the direction that was pointed out to him.

It couldn't be this easy.

Something was bound to go terribly wrong.

Unlike the pleasure room, this corridor was dark and led even farther down into the stronghold.

It opened into a dimly lit room, so dim it took his gaze a few moments to adjust.

There were Tasqals everywhere, though these ones were clothed.

They were moving around, looking at displays set into the walls and at first, he couldn't see what was inside the displays.

It was not till one of the Tasqals moved that his eyes caught sight of a creature he'd never seen before. It was Merssi-like, except it had four arms and what looked like wings.

The auction.

These were the beings being auctioned.

Clee-yo.

Her name sounded so loud in his head, he worried that he'd said it out loud.

Moving swiftly but carefully so as not to draw attention to himself, he moved toward the displays, his eyes searching desperately for a hint of his female.

And he found her.

At least, he thought he did.

It was a display with a garden and on the other side were females that looked Merssi except for their skin coloring and heads.

There were about six of them...but no Clee-yo.

His life organ fell.

He was about to move away when his eyes caught movement underneath a large tree off to the side of the display.

Moving closer, he peered in just as a female stepped from underneath the blossoms.

She was...*gorgeous.*

Pale skin. Long legs. Hair like zimsu flowers.

This time his life organ leaped inside him.

Clee-yo.

But she looked different.

Her hair shone as if it had recently been washed with softening products and she was wearing a see-through shimmering gown that stopped mid-thigh.

His life organ crashed then beamed.

His *gnora.*

She was alive and well.

Beside him, he could hear the excited grunts of the Tasqals gathered in front of the display.

The sound of them almost had his claws protracting right there to rip their throats out.

Their attention was on his gnora. Clee-yo.

It was no wonder she'd been hiding under the tree.

She was obviously sought after by the brutes.

As she moved toward the transparent barrier, she was frowning at the Tasqals gathered at the display when her gaze fell on him.

Without realizing what he was doing, he reached out and placed his hand, now claw, against the transparent surface.

For a moment, she just stared at him before her frown became confused and she knelt before him.

She stared at him for a few moments and even though he knew that to her, he looked like the enemy, he hoped something in his eyes could let her know she was not alone.

That he was there to save her.

That he would get her out of this.

She must have seen something, because the confusion grew in her eyes before she stood again, her gaze still on him.

In the next moment, her head snapped to the side, her eyes widening before she stood and darted back under the tree.

Confused as well, it took him a moment to realize Hedgerud fighters had entered the terrarium.

They were pulling the other females not so gently toward the door they'd entered through while, on his side of the barrier, the Tasqals and their guards were moving.

Showtime.

Yet, he couldn't leave the spot till he saw that Clee-yo was okay.

In the next second, she came from underneath the blossoms, her arms folded across her chest and a glimmer in her eyes.

He knew that look.

She was planning something.

His claw pressed against the transparent barrier as she walked bravely toward the guard, not even flinching when the beast took her roughly by the shoulder.

He was going to snap that guard's arm and pull it from his body as soon as he had the chance.

Stepping into the shadows, Sohut activated the distorter on his arm once more, changing forms. Before his eyes, his arms changed to those of a Tasqal and he knew the distortion of the rest of his image was complete.

To everybody else, he would look like one of the awful elite.

This was it.

Clee-yo was ready to fight, and so was he.

31

CLEO GRIPPED HER LUCKY PIECE OF METAL AND THE SHIV UNDERNEATH each arm as she was led from the terrarium.

Her entire survival depended on what she did in the next few moments.

And she was going to survive.

She had to keep telling herself that.

Swallowing hard, she glanced back at the fairy garden before her gaze fell on the gator-guard who was still at the transparent barrier.

He was still watching her, and her heart lurched again like the first time she'd noticed him.

She didn't know what it was and she couldn't explain it, but he made her feel strange. She'd almost put her hand against his claw as it had pressed against the glass.

Apparently, she was starting to go crazy after all the many days spent in captivity.

That's why she had to keep repeating to herself that she was going to survive.

She could do it.

She had to.

It was either that, or lose her mind.

As the gator-guard pulled her roughly along, she didn't give him the satisfaction of seeing her fear, even though it was crawling all over her spine.

It also came to her that she was alone with the guard.

The other females were nowhere to be seen and soon she was pushed into a small dark room that was flooded with a red light. To her back were dark walls and to her front was another transparent wall of glass.

The room wasn't much larger than a small bathroom and she immediately began to feel claustrophobic.

To boot, the thing around her neck felt like it was squeezing her tight whenever she had any intense emotions like this.

Gulping, she turned her gaze to the front of the room and what she saw on the other side chilled her completely.

Five or maybe six of the toad-men, the Tasqals she'd come to learn they were called, were sitting there.

They all looked similar, all dressed in white robes, but the one thing that was most creepy about them was the sleazy smiles they all had on their faces.

All except one.

He was sitting at the back, and for some reason, her gaze gravitated toward him.

He wasn't smiling like the others and even though he was focused on her like all the others were, his gaze seemed different.

She wasn't sure if that was a good or bad thing yet. For all she knew, he could be the crudest of them all.

Behind her, the door to the room closed and she was left alone.

"Specimen: human," a robotic voice boomed.

Wait.

Panic flooded her.

It was starting already?

"Age: estimated at twenty and a half orbits," it continued. "Warranty: none. Estimated life cycle: thirty rotations with hard usage."

Cleo swallowed hard as the horror of the last words reached her bones.

Was it saying that if they treated her roughly, she'd only last a month?

As her gaze focused back on the beasts in front of her, it took everything within her not to take a step backward.

"Let the auction begin," the robotic voice announced.

As the beasts in front of her began raising glowing blue cards, one by one, she did take a step back.

Her breath deafened her ears with every inhale and exhale as she watched the cards move.

Bidding.

They were bidding on her life.

And she had no control over it. Gripping the weapons she still held underneath her arms, Cleo focused on controlling her breathing.

Focus.

Restraint.

She couldn't let her emotions, her fear, mess up any opportunity she had to escape this.

As she stared across the room through the transparent wall in front of her, she saw that the group of aliens bidding was becoming more frenzied.

She couldn't read the currency they were using on the cards but it was obvious tensions were getting heated as the cards were being lifted at an increasing pace, almost as if the bidding war was getting tense.

Off to the corner, that same toad-man she'd noticed before was still staring at her with the serious expression he'd had when she'd walked in...only now, his seriousness seemed to be slowly transforming into utter rage.

He must be losing then.

That made her gaze drift over the others, trying to determine which one was winning the bid.

Her gaze landed on one in the center—a huge male with a curious scar over one eye. Its other dark eye focused on hers, unblinking.

As soon as it realized she was looking at it, a slow smile spread its lips and Cleo resisted the urge to puke.

It lifted its hand slowly. There was a blue card between its fingers that suddenly turned red as he held it in the air.

Her spine froze.

Somehow she knew what that meant.

He was the winner.

And her suspicions were only confirmed when the beast's comrades rose and began filing out of the room, leaving the one with the red card in the middle.

It didn't move, it just stared at her, that disgusting smile still on its lips, and for a few moments, she wondered what it was going to do.

Then it stood, and this time, it did get a reaction from her. Cleo took another involuntary step backward.

It was huge.

She knew it was big, but when standing, it was a whole other version of giant toad.

Fuck!

She took another step backward as the Tasqal came toward the transparent barrier.

It couldn't get through, could it?

But before that thought could even leave her mind, the barrier in front of her dissolved as if it had never been there.

Swallowing hard, she took another step backward and felt as the constriction around her neck tightened a little, reminding her it was there.

It did that, she realized, whenever she had thoughts of resisting... whenever she wanted to flee...and she tried to calm her hammering heart—only, that was difficult to do with something that belonged to a swamp advancing toward her.

"Pretty...little...thing..."

The Tasqal talked.

That only made it so, so much worse.

"I finally have acquired one of your species," it said.

"What do you want?" Her voice sounded alien to her, made of steel even though her insides were turning into water that wanted to run away into the creases of the floor below her and disappear.

226

The beast's throat moved and the sound of bubbles popping filled the little room.

It was laughing.

To her horror, the beast lifted a leg onto the platform and stepped into the room, filling the space even without touching her.

This was worse than claustrophobia. There was nowhere to run. Nowhere to hide.

Squeezing the weapons still gripped and hidden underneath her arms, Cleo took another step backward, and her back bumped into the wall behind her.

Out. Of. Space.

Her next move would have to be the one that allowed her to escape this room, this situation, unharmed.

"What do I want?" The toad-man cocked his head, his one good eye studying her. "You, of course."

It didn't hesitate. In one movement, its white robe fell and it took another step toward her.

Her vision blurred with the sudden burst of adrenaline that flooded through her.

She couldn't see the creature's disgusting, diseased-looking body. She couldn't see its hand caressing it's member as it advanced on her.

All she could do was feel.

She could feel the rage flood through her, replacing the blood in her veins.

Arms unfolding, she aimed for the eyes, sinking the wooden shiv into the good eye and her lucky shrapnel in the other.

The beast howled and reached for her arms but then something she didn't understand happened.

Before he could even touch her, his body was against the other side of the wall.

Cleo's eyes widened.

It was the other toad man. The one who'd been sitting in the corner.

"Qrakking jekin!" the injured Tasqal howled. His eyes were bleeding a dark fluid and she doubted he could see. "My eye!"

"Shut the phek up," the other toad man said, and Cleo took a step back, her eyes darting from one to the other.

"What is this?" the injured toad-man said, his hands grasping the arms that held him against the wall. "What are you doing? KILL THE JEKIN who dared to harm me!"

Cleo's eyes darted to the space where she knew the door was.

Two disgusting aliens who wanted to rape her were having a spat and she was sure she shouldn't stay around to see the end of it.

But as she made to move, the words of the new Tasqal caught her ears, making her freeze in the spot.

"Don't you dare run, *Cluu*. I'm not about to lose you again."

Cluu?

She turned to stare at the beast that had spoken, her mouth falling open, her eyes wide.

CLUU.

How did he know that name?!

Sohut.

A feeling of dread filled her, she almost lost her balance.

Sohut had given her that name. The only way the toad would know that name was if he had somehow gotten to Sohut.

Somehow, her lucky metal dislodged from the other beast's eye and fell to the floor.

Snatching it quickly, she only had one second to stand before the body of the toad-man that had bought her slumped to the floor.

His throat leaked green ooze.

It's been slit.

Eyes rising slowly to her new captor, Cleo gripped her piece of metal. The end still dripped the ooze from the other Tasqal's eye.

"Clee-yo..." the toad-man said before taking a step forward but when she raised her metal, pointing it toward him, he paused, his eyes darting to the metal then back.

"It's me..." he whispered.

Her eyes narrowed some more. Somewhere inside her, hope bloomed but it must be some hope for the impossible.

This wasn't her savior. She didn't know this being.

And he was her enemy.

"Me who?" She took a step back, eyes darting to the door once more.

"It's me, Cleo. Touch me."

Her nose scrunched up.

What sort of request was that?

His voice was low as he spoke.

"Touch me and you will see. I'm using a distorter. It was the only way I could get to you and we need to hurry. Wawa has gone missing outside and I just know the little rhag is up to no good. I don't think he trusts me to get you out of this."

"Wawa?"

How did he know about Wawa? Did she dare believe him?

A beat passed before she reached out tentatively to touch the outstretched hand of the toad-man.

It felt strange. Smooth. Velvety.

Not at all like the coarse, bubbly-filled skin she was looking at.

She stifled a yelp as she was suddenly pulled forward and against the toad-man's chest.

But it didn't feel like she was embracing a Tasqal.

This body she was pressed against felt familiar.

It felt like...Sohut.

Her mind could not comprehend.

"Raxu, Cleo. I thought I lost you."

A sob caught in her throat.

"Sohut? *How*?"

"No time," he said, even as he patted her head gently. "We have to go."

Swallowing hard, she nodded as he allowed her to ease off him.

It was like a grater to her senses, looking into the huge black eyes and knowing that behind those eyes, the man she loved was looking back at her.

Sohut was moving, his hand grasping hers as he pulled her behind him gently but with urgency.

"Walk behind me, closely. Keep your head down."

Nodding, she did as she was told.

"How do you suppose we're going to get out of here?" she whispered as they headed toward the door.

"I don't phekking know, to be honest. Luck."

"Luck?" Not that she'd expected more. Luck meant there was a chance.

Sohut turned and the strange face she was seeing split into a smile.

"Don't do that," Cleo groaned.

Sohut chuckled.

"I am one lucky phekker," he said before they reached the door, where he paused.

"Let's do this," he breathed, glancing behind him to ensure she was ready before they stepped out.

32

She didn't know what she expected but it wasn't this.

There were beings, so many beings, all mixed in with the Tasqals. And they were...

Cleo swallowed the bile that rose in her throat, keeping her head down as she hoped no one could see the horror on her face.

They were *raping* them.

And the females she'd been put in the terrarium with, she could only hope Lee-yunna had found a way to escape too. She couldn't see her, although, she couldn't lift her head to search the room.

She was too terrified of blowing their cover.

If they were stopped, it wasn't just she that'd be in the shit. Sohut would be too and he'd almost been killed once already because of her.

As they reached the far side of the room and entered a corridor, Sohut picked up his pace and she all but trotted behind him like an obedient puppy.

"How do you know where you're going?" she whispered into his back.

Sohut inhaled deeply. "I can smell the fresh air outside."

Of course, his answer wouldn't be a normal one and the thought made her smile into his back.

They moved through doors that opened and closed, passed guards that stopped to salute but said nothing otherwise.

Her heart almost fell out of her chest on each occasion they had to pass one of the gator-guards but they never once questioned why one of their masters was taking one of the slaves outside of the building.

She guessed that's why Sohut had gotten the disguise of one of the bosses.

Soon, they reached a set of huge doors that looked like slate. They rose so high that she had to crane her neck to see the top.

"Master?" the voice of a gator-guard caught her ear and she realized there was a set of guards posted on a platform above them.

Beside them was a set of controls that she assumed controlled the massive doors.

Sohut stiffened as he came to a stop, his eyes on the door.

She could feel it too...freedom was beyond those doors.

"Master? You have ventured so far...*alone*?" The gator-guard glanced at his comrade, his yellow eye suspicious and she could tell they were wondering that the hell was going on.

"You dare to question me?" Sohut asked, turning his dark eyes on them and she could see them cower.

"N-no, Your Excellency," one of them sputtered.

"Open the doors," Sohut ordered and the guards glanced at each other again.

As one moved an arm toward the controls, he paused.

The two guards exchanged glances again before turning their yellow gazes on her and Sohut and when their eyes settled on her, she could feel something fall inside her.

"Phek..." she heard Sohut mutter low before sniffing the air. "I should've known this wouldn't be easy."

His eyes scanned the wall and she raised her head, trying to see what he was looking at.

It took her a while but then she saw it. A little speck of gray high up. It was moving down the wall so fast, it looked like a blur.

"Your Excellency," one of the guards continued...

Cricking the bones in his neck, Sohut ignored the guard and began undressing to her wide-eyed horror.

Thrusting the white robe he was wearing toward her, he met her eyes. "Put this on."

And then he was gone.

Her confusion was reflected on the guard's faces as Sohut scaled the wall up to the platform.

How he did it, she did not know, but it was clear to the guards that something was very wrong because they both raised their weapons ready to fire.

But they didn't get the chance to.

That gray blur moving down the wall leaped into the air, latching itself onto one of the guard's faces, its razor-sharp teeth sinking in.

It took her a moment to realize that the terror ripping the guard's face off was her beloved pet. Wawa screeched, his sound of rage echoing down the corridor.

Behind him, Sohut was making quick work of the other guard and the guard tumbled off the platform, falling not far to the ground in front of her.

Its shock rod skated across the ground to the side and the guard groaned, not dead.

Her feet moved fast, fueled by the adrenaline pumping in her veins, and she grabbed the shock rod.

There was a narrow depression on the handle and the way she held it, her palm pressed against the area. Just by chance, the rod zinged to life.

She could almost feel the power traveling up her arm.

Sohut moved quickly, activating the door just as the guard on the ground raised his hand.

She saw it at the moment. There was a square that looked like some kind of radio-device in his hand.

No.

He wasn't about to send a message and fuck everything up.

"You!" she screamed as she spun and hit the guard in the chest with the glowing end of his weapon.

The guard's body shuddered as if he was having a seizure and only the smell of burnt flesh filling the air made her stop her attack.

When she lifted the rod, the guard wasn't moving and she stared at him, her body trembling even though she felt numb.

Strong arms surrounded her waist, and she realized Sohut had swooped her up in one motion and was rushing toward the opening door.

Vaguely, she realized he grabbed the robe as he ran and that Wawa jumped from the platform, landing smoothly on his shoulder.

"They're going to know something happened. We have to get out of here."

As if she was going to resist that.

The next few moments were a dash to freedom as her heart beat in her throat.

The door didn't open fully. It paused with a gap just big enough for them to squeeze through as a shrill alarm echoed down the long corridor.

Then they were on the run.

Outside, the air was clearer and as they ran up the incline she wondered how Sohut was able to run with such speed without pausing for a breath.

He only stopped once to set her down and briskly slip the robe over her shoulders, pulling the hood over her head in the process.

At the same time, he deactivated whatever gadget he was using for his disguise.

Seeing him again, Cleo's heart skipped a beat.

Wawa made a low sound and crawled over to her, transferring himself from Sohut's shoulders to sit on her neck, under the cover of her hood.

There, he rubbed his head against the side of her face and she had just enough time to pet him before they were off again, weaving through streets she didn't know the name of, alleys she'd never remember, until they were in the middle of a throng of shopping aliens.

All the while, she felt as if there were eyes on her back, but she kept her head down, trusting the one person she could trust at that moment.

Her love.

Sohut.

Glancing up from under the hood of the robe, she caught a glimpse of Sohut's face.

If he was nervous, he didn't show it. His face was composed, unreadable, as he led them through the streets.

She had no idea where she was, but it seemed like it was a market of some sort.

There were so many aliens...so, so many and at another time, she'd have taken the opportunity to look at the many different life-forms the rest of the human race had no idea existed.

But for now, she kept her head low.

Reaching forward, she slipped her palm against Sohut's, and the only indication he felt her touch was the slight squeeze he gave her.

They were moving for a while, weaving through the throng, and now and then, he'd glance behind them, checking if they were being followed.

Then he muttered something underneath his breath.

"Geblit," he said.

She wasn't sure if it was a curse of some kind because she didn't understand the words, but then he walked up to an unsuspecting alien that was innocently buying wares.

It looked like a Torian and she didn't know how she knew it, because they mostly looked alike to her, but this Torian wasn't one she'd met before.

Sohut released her hand to pull the Torian into a choke-hold before dragging him to the alley beside the stall.

Cleo didn't know what to think.

"Let me go you ruffian!" The Torian was irate, his big balloon, octopi-like head pulsing with veins. When Sohut let the alien go so he could turn around, the alien's eyes grew into four wide bowls. "Oh no, not you."

Glancing from one to the other, she had no idea what was happening.

"Yes, me. Fancy seeing you here. I need your help," Sohut stated.

The balloon-head alien frowned, his glare directed at Sohut as he seemed to not notice her presence yet.

"Nope. Not helping," he said. "Whatever problem you have, I am not interested. Now, if you'll excuse me, my darling mate, Cargga, is waiting for her anti-mold crystals."

The alien began to walk away on limbs that looked so thin, she wondered how he was managing to lift his body weight.

The Torians in the jungle were skinny but not *that* skinny.

"Geblit." Sohut held on to the alien's arm and she realized then that "Geblit" was his name. Funny, because he looked exactly like a Geblit.

"We need to get out of here. Hide somewhere. You can help us with that, can't you?"

"We?" It was then that Geblit finally looked in her direction. Stooping a little, he moved so he could see her face underneath the large, white hood.

"Oh no, no, no, no," he began to say and at that moment, Wawa decided to pop his head out.

The green alien jumped back so fast, his limbs splayed against the alley wall. His mouth and eyes were as wide as planets in their own solar system as the color seemed to drain from his skin.

He looked petrified.

"A-A slizz!"

"Quiet!" Sohut plastered a palm over the alien's mouth but even then she could hear him screaming behind Sohut's hand.

Wawa seemed unperturbed as she pat his head and he went back into the depths of the hood.

"Listen, forget about the slizz. He's a pet. We need your help."

It felt like ages before Geblit was calm enough to speak.

When his eyes finally regained their usual size, Sohut removed his hand and a slew of words spilled from the alien's mouth immediately.

"Nope. Can't help. I am done with helping these humans and I am definitely not helping a slizz!"

Humans?

He'd helped other humans?

She opened her mouth to ask about that but Geblit was already speaking.

"And where did you find a human? To my knowledge, only the Tas—" His eyes widened again, this time in more shock than horror. "No. Tell me you didn't."

"I had no choice. You know what the Tasqals do to their slaves."

Geblit took a step back, his wide eyes on her.

"If they catch you—"

"But they won't catch us now will they. Not with your help." Sohut paused. "I'll owe you a *favor*."

The way he said the word like it was the ultimate bargaining chip made her eyes dart back to the green alien beside them.

Geblit's eyes darted from Sohut to her to Sohut then back again.

"Don't tell me you have *feelings* for this ugly thing."

Was...was he calling her ugly?

She'd have been hurt if she didn't really care. She'd gotten used to the jungle Torians insulting her looks and she just wanted to get as far away from those Tasqals and gator-guards as possible. If Sohut thought this was the way, then so be it.

"A favor," Sohut said again.

Geblit closed his eyes for a second, his shoulders slumping as he crossed his arms.

"Raxu, phekking qrakking Sohut," Geblit muttered. "This is the *last* time I help you and your brother."

Sohut smiled.

Geblit's eyes darted to her again. "Follow me."

33

GEBLIT LED THEM THROUGH THE BACK STREETS AND AS HE DID SO, SHE
had to glance at Sohut.

Laughter bubbled in her belly despite the fact they were running
for their lives.

In front of them, Geblit was leading the way and he was literally
creeping on tiptoes like he was up to no good.

Anyone looking at them would no doubt see that they were doing
something illegal.

Now and then, he'd pause, his body going still and his eyes
widening a little at whatever danger he saw, then he'd usher them
forward.

It wasn't long before they were in a tunnel and Geblit stopped in
front of a wall.

Knocking the wall with a series of raps that sounded like a code,
Geblit waited, his legs shaking.

Soon, the wall moved...or rather, the secret door in the wall
moved and a tall alien dressed in armor stood on the other side.

Gripping Sohut's hand, Cleo squeezed it a little and Sohut gave
her a reassuring squeeze back.

"Ambassador," the soldier said and for a moment she wondered
who he was talking to before Geblit spoke up.

"Y-yes," Geblit held his head high.

Oh.

She wouldn't have guessed.

"I am here on official business with—" his eyes darted to her and Sohut "—friends. Official *legal* business."

Goodness gracious.

It was so obviously a lie she felt like slapping her face into her palm.

The soldier wouldn't buy it.

But with a creak of his armor, the soldier stepped to the side and Geblit almost jumped for joy.

As a matter of fact, it was obvious he tried to hide his glee and relief because all he did was flash them a smile before rushing through the door.

He led them through a series of corridors to a small, empty office and got to work, tapping his fingers on a metal desk. In front of him, the hologram of a data screen came to life in the space.

"You want to register her, right? For protection?"

Sohut nodded.

"Register me?"

Sohut glanced down at her. "So you'll be protected by the Union." He paused. "So you'll be free."

Free.

She never thought she'd feel so much hope in just one word.

"So you will be her sponsor?" Geblit asked, his finger still tapping the desk with amazing speed.

"Sponsor? I need a sponsor?"

Sohut nodded. "Yes, I'll be her sponsor."

Geblit glanced at him momentarily, his forehead skin moving as if he was thinking "you idiot" and didn't care to hide it.

"Wait," she pulled on Sohut's arm. "What does being a sponsor mean?"

"It means he's relinquishing half of his assets to the Union in good faith that you will be an upstanding citizen." It was Geblit that answered.

Cleo's heart skipped a beat.

"What?" Her gaze searched Sohut's but he didn't respond. "Is he speaking the truth?"

"Why would I lie?" Geblit's head rose, his brow furrowed and the expression on his face was as if he was taken aback by her unsaid accusation.

"Geblit—" Sohut raised a hand, his gaze never leaving hers. "Yes, he's right."

Cleo gulped.

But why?

She didn't realize she'd asked the question until Sohut began answering.

"Because you're my *gnora*..." he said.

In the background, she was vaguely aware that Geblit was choking on air at that proclamation and Wawa took that moment to growl at him, halting the choking immediately.

Her entire focus was on Sohut.

He'd used that word again.

"What does that mean?" she asked.

Sohut didn't miss a beat. "After all this is over, I promise I'll show you."

Geblit choked again and, this time, it was Sohut that glared his way.

Clearing his throat, Geblit reached in his desk and took out a flat, clear disk.

"Deposit your fluids here."

Cleo frowned. "My what?"

"Spit on it."

Oh.

"Why?"

"The union will need your biosignature as part of the registration process," Sohut answered.

Oh.

She guessed it was a little like having her fingerprints taken.

Bending her head a little, she aimed for the disk Geblit had outstretched but his hands were shaking so much it was clear that she would surely miss.

"For phek's sake." Sohut snatched the disk from the green alien and Geblit rolled his eyes in relief.

"Thank Raxu. I did not want to risk this one's juices touching me." He wiped his hands anyway.

Ignoring him, Cleo deposited a drop of saliva on the disk and Sohut slipped it back across the table to Geblit.

A ray of green light passed over the fluid as Geblit resumed typing on his holo-computer. "Sohut U'xol Cal-Pholy..." he muttered as he typed. "Sponsor of human..." He glanced her way. "What name do you go by?"

"Cleo," she said, glancing at Sohut as she did. "Cleo Barlow."

Geblit made a sound in his throat then continued typing.

In the next few seconds, he uttered, "Done."

Before she could even breathe, she was being pressed against Sohut's chest so tightly all she could inhale was him, and he smelled like home.

His shoulders slumped as he hugged her and she could hear Geblit groan in the background, muttering something about her lack of limbs.

Sohut inhaled deeply, his head in her hair.

"Phekking, Wawa," he muttered, "I can't even have the luxury of smelling my female without your scent interfering."

His female?

A warm feeling bloomed inside her at those words.

He'd said it before but hearing him say it again after all this time they'd spent apart felt like a new proclamation.

She wanted to be his woman, now and forever.

At the sound of his name, Wawa popped his head out from under the hood and this close to Sohut, she was sure he was going to try and bite him. She was beginning to pull away to avoid that but Sohut held her closer and surprisingly, Wawa only rubbed his head against Sohut's chest.

They must have been embracing for a while because Geblit's voice broke the calmness in her mind.

"Don't mind me or the fact I just helped two beings wanted by the phekking TASQALS," he said, "but you still need to get out of here."

Sohut groaned a little as he inhaled again. "Give me the key code for your cruiser."

In her peripheral vision, a big balloon-head was shaking vehemently.

"Nope. No way. My hover car is the finest in this district. There is no way—"

～

As they sped across a plain filled with tall yellow-orange grass in a hover car that gave her the impression it was like a luxury vehicle in these parts, Cleo let the hood of the robe fall from her head.

"This is...beautiful," she breathed. Off in the distance, large animals that reminded her of cows were grazing and by the side of her face, Wawa rubbed his head appreciatively, liking the cool breeze.

"Very beautiful..."

Sohut murmured and when her gaze cut to his, he was looking at her with such heavy emotions in his eyes, it made her breath catch in her throat.

He'd come to save her. He'd *freed* her.

It was hard imagining that her life wasn't going to be living as a fugitive in an alien jungle anymore. Or that she'd narrowly escaped being raped by a giant toad.

"You came for me." A smile came over her lips as she looked at him. "You could have left me."

The hover car slowed down as Sohut decelerated.

"Of course, I came for you. After they took you, I—"

She launched herself against his side, wrapping her arms around him as something wet ran down her cheek.

"Sohut. They almost killed you."

It felt like they were no longer moving and she realized the hover car stopped, and was slowly descending to the ground below, nestling within the tall yellow-orange grass.

"And I would have died if it meant protecting you. I couldn't—" he stopped talking, the emotions on his face receding.

"You couldn't what?" Her voice sounded thick and she knew the wetness on her face was coming from her eyes.

The events of the past few weeks were all being processed at once and even though her eyes were betraying her with tears, she was slowly acknowledging that it had been a lot.

It had been a helluva lot to go through.

"I couldn't let someone else get hurt because of my failure. I—"

His gaze fell and she touched his chin lightly.

A breath shuddered through his body and she realized that he too was processing all that had happened between them recently.

"If I know anything about you, Sohut, it's that you're one of the strongest people I know."

For a moment, he didn't raise his gaze and when he finally looked at her, the glimmer of hope in his eyes almost broke her heart, right before a look of horror covered his features.

"You're leaking. From your eyes." He touched a tear. "Have I—" he eased off her, his gaze flicking over her body. "Have I hurt you?" He gulped hard. "I'm going to take you to the Sanctuary. You'll be safe there. But now that you're free...you don't have to come with me. You can go anywhere on Hudo III." He swallowed hard. "I can take you there."

The suggestion in his words cut her deep and she gripped him tighter.

Why would he say such a thing?

Didn't he know that all that time away while she'd waited in that terrarium, he'd been the only thing on her mind?

That she couldn't see herself living without him.

That she wanted to be by his side forever.

No, she realized. He didn't know because she'd never actually admitted it to him.

Still clinging to him, she opened her mouth and said it.

"I don't want to go anywhere. I want to stay with you."

Sohut stilled at her words before his finger moved to wipe away another tear.

"What are you saying, gnora?"

Cleo sniffled. "What does that word mean?"

She could swear his color changed to a darker shade.

For a few moments, he just looked at her and she thought he wasn't about to answer, when he did.

"My people, the Merssi, we believe there is one being out there that completes us...a being that fits with us like a puzzle."

"A...a soulmate?"

His color became even darker. "Yes."

"And you think I'm that...for you?" There was a note of hope in her voice that even she heard and when Sohut nodded she couldn't help but pull him down against her as she settled back on the seat of the hover vehicle.

"I want you to be mine," Sohut said. "I don't want to be without you."

"I wasn't planning on going anywhere," Cleo whispered. "I don't want to be without you either."

Sohut's head rose over hers, his green eyes piercing hers.

"You will have me?" he asked.

"Every day. Forever."

A look of complete elation passed over his features before it was promptly replaced with something more animalistic, something more carnal.

"Wawa," Sohut growled. "Leave us."

To her surprise, Wawa listened, hopping from the hover car to dart into the long grass.

"What are you doing?!" Cleo giggled as Sohut lifted the robe up over her hips, pulling it higher till she had to stretch her arms to get out of it.

"Something I'm going to do every day, forever," he said.

CLEO'S LIPS felt like little sweet buds that he wanted to devour.

As he took them between his own, he tried to slow down, tried to control the urge to pin her beneath him and bury himself deep inside her hard.

This was his gnora.

244

And no one was going to take her from him.

Protracting his claws, he used a finger to rip away the flimsy garment the Tasqals had dressed her in. He tore it away from her body, every thread of it, and threw it over the side of the vehicle.

He didn't want to see her in it, to be reminded of what had almost happened, right before his eyes.

He'd almost lost his gnora. But he had her now and she was safe.

She was safe, and she was beneath him, whispering his name as her body called out to him.

Her teats brushed against his face as he ran his fangs over them and her breath hitched in her throat.

Sohut groaned.

He loved the way she responded to him.

He wanted to hear her cry his name while she was beneath him now, needed to hear her pant as he took her, branded her...*claimed* her.

Clee-yo's neck arched as his tongue flicked over the tight little bud on her chest before he took the entire thing into his mouth.

Her small hands found his hair as she strung her fingers through the dark strands, pulling him harder into her and he indulged her.

His tongue flicked over her teat some more as his hand delved between her, seeking that warm spot between her legs.

His forefinger found the other tight little pleasure bud, the one between her thighs and she arched into him even more, her pale eyes rolling back into her head as she whispered his name.

"Sohut..."

The sound of his name on her lips made him groan.

He hadn't been kidding when he'd told her she said his name beautifully.

He wanted his name on her lips always, continually, forever. The way she said it was like a sweet caress that gave him images of pleasing her...giving her his all.

Just like he was doing now.

Licking her teat, he moved lower, his lips traveling over her pale skin down to the knot of nerves that gave her so much pleasure.

Burying his face between her legs, he inhaled deeply.

"Clee-yo," he groaned.

It was the scent that had driven him crazy when he'd entered the Koznia Jungle. The same scent that had made his body react even before he'd encountered her.

Clee-yo smelled like heaven.

Opening his lips, he took her into his mouth and she cried out against him, her hips pressing upward and into him.

He licked and suckled on her, enjoying the noises she made as her arousal dampened her sex and her scent filled his nose.

His chin was wet with her juices but he wanted more, more of his Clee-yo. He wasn't ever going to get enough.

As his tongue darted deep inside her, Clee-yo's fingers dug into his scalp.

With a scream of his name that flew away on the wind, she reached her peak.

"Sohut," she whimpered as he spun her around so she lay on her belly.

His cock was so hard, he was pretty sure it was the pure need to be buried inside his female that prevented him from coming already.

As he released his shaft, it sprung up eagerly, pressing into the delicious rump offered up to him.

Clee-yo whimpered again at the feel of his cock against her and the sound almost pushed him over the edge.

Holding her hips steady, he grit his teeth as he surged forward.

Her tightness welcomed him. It squeezed him tight as her juices coated his shaft.

His thrusts were hard, deep, as he moved in and out of her.

"You're mine, Clee-yo," he grunted.

A moan ripped from her that pushed him right over the edge.

Gripping her hips as he buried himself deep and released his spend, Sohut's entire body jerked with the force of his orgasm.

"And you're mine," he heard her whisper.

34

As the hover car lifted and began speeding across the alien savanna once more, Cleo smiled as she rested her head against Sohut's arm.

This was real.

Of all the ways she'd expected her life to turn out, she had never once imagined this. But here she was and it was real.

Back when she'd been taken from Earth, abducted and thrown into a world that was not her own, she'd thought her life had gone to shit.

But it had all been leading up to this.

Snuggling against Sohut, despite that it wasn't cold, a smile spread her lips.

He was hers and she wouldn't change all those horrible experiences now for the world.

In what felt like about half-an-hour, a spec in the distance began to form into something else—a residence of some sort.

The sight made her sit upright far too quickly and Wawa swayed on her shoulder.

"Is that..."

"The Sanctuary," Sohut answered, his voice holding a note of pride and trepidation, the latter of which pulled her gaze from the huge farm they were approaching to the man beside her.

Her spine stiffened a little. "What is it? Aren't you happy to be home?"

"Delighted." Sohut glanced at her and his green gaze softened a little. "It's just that...my brother is a bit..." He trailed off. "Riv doesn't like strangers."

Oh.

She didn't know what to say about that. She wasn't planning to stay in his brother's way anyway.

She turned her gaze back to the Sanctuary.

It looked...beautiful. Serene and beautiful.

There were huge trees on the property and she could make out several different fenced areas that held animals, but something, or rather someone, caught her gaze.

Cleo squinted.

Now that they were getting closer, she could make out the form of the person standing on the grounds.

It was a male, no doubt Sohut's brother judging from the blue skin.

He was shirtless and she watched as he lifted his head, undoubtedly having caught the sound of the approaching vehicle.

"That's Riv. He's seen us," she heard Sohut say but she couldn't pull her eyes away.

Sohut's family.

For some reason, there was anxiety building within her and she realized she really wanted this Riv to like her.

Sohut was obviously close to his brother. If Riv didn't like her, it would definitely strain their relationship.

Even as she watched, she saw Riv reach down and lift a massive weapon that was no doubt a gun from *Mad Max* judging from the size of it.

Riv lifted the weapon, pointing it their way.

"Sohut?" She glanced at her man. "What's he doing?"

Sohut squeezed his eyes shut for a second. "I think he thinks we're Geblit."

"Wha—"

Her words were cut off as something bright flew through the air above the hover vehicle.

Her mouth fell open.

"He's shooting at us!"

To her horror, Sohut chuckled. "Don't worry. He has great aim. He's just letting us, well, *Geblit*, know he doesn't want him to come closer."

Cleo pressed her mouth into a thin line and Sohut chuckled again.

"He's sane. I promise." He paused. "I wonder what Geblit did to make him react this way though."

As she turned to stare at Sohut's possibly insane brother, the hover car stopped at what appeared to be an energy barrier that surrounded the property.

On the other side, a female, a *human* female was rushing toward Riv. Cleo could only watch, her eyes wide as the female smacked Riv on the arm holding the blaster, pointing their way as she did.

She could feel the guy's frown even from where she was.

Sohut stood in the hover car and shouted something that didn't translate and his brother's head turned from the indignant female beside him.

In the next moment, Riv and the female were both rushing to the barrier.

"Sohut?" Riv said as the barrier stopped zinging. "Phek. I thought you were that excrement pipe, Geblit."

Sohut chuckled before hopping from the vehicle and touching his brother on the shoulder. Riv pulled him in and they touched foreheads.

"I thought..." Riv trailed off and Sohut chuckled.

She knew what he'd been thinking. His unspoken words were ones she'd forced away while she'd waited in that terrarium.

"You can't get rid of me so easily," Sohut said.

Cleo blinked.

Now that his brother was so close, she couldn't help but stare.

They looked like twins. The resemblance was uncanny.

When her gaze drifted to the side and met the human female's, her eyes widened a little.

The woman was smiling at her but not approaching, as if knowing this was all a bit to take in and she was giving her time for it all to settle.

When she glanced back in Sohut's direction, two sets of green eyes were now on her—his and his brother's.

Only, Riv was staring at her with a mixture of fear, disgust, and anger. "What the phek is that?!"

The female beside him moved closer, her hand at the back of his arm in a way that gave Cleo the impression she was pinching the large blue male.

She smiled at Cleo. "Hi, I'm Lauren and don't mind Riv. He can be a lot more hospitable."

Sohut grunted.

But Riv was still looking her way with the same expression and it took her a moment to realize his gaze wasn't pointed at hers but at her neck.

Looking down, she realized Wawa's face was visible from underneath the hood of the robe.

"That's not a slizz, is it?" Riv was still staring at Wawa, his blaster rising in the air again.

Sohut touched the weapon, pushing it back down.

"It's fine. He's her pet."

This time, Riv's eyes *did* meet hers and she couldn't read them.

Sohut moved to her side. "This is Cleo. My gnora." The pride in his voice was so unmistakable, she had to glance at him.

"Your *gnora*?" Riv moved to stand beside his brother, his face expressionless.

Sohut nodded.

For a few beats, neither of them said a word and Cleo could cut the tension in the air with a knife.

Out of the blue, Riv hugged his brother, patting him on the shoulder as he did.

"Brother," Riv finally said. "I am happy for you." He turned his attention to her. "Clee-yo, my brother's gnora, welcome to the Sanctuary. Any gnora of my brother is a sister to me."

Riv turned to look at the female beside him. "This is my gnora, La-rehn."

Sohut almost choked on air. "What?"

Lauren chuckled. "There's a lot that happened since you left."

Sohut glanced at her, his eyes twinkling. "Tell me about it."

It turns out the Sanctuary was exactly as she'd pictured it to be.

As they brought the hover car in, Cleo saw several enclosures with animals she'd never seen before in her life.

There were fat hippo-like animals they called oogas and tall giraffe-dinosaur-looking things called tilgrans.

There were umus that looked like little balls of fluff and a field filled with hairy fruit that she and Lauren joked about not chopping down lest the Lorax appear.

Needless to say, neither Sohut nor Riv caught that joke.

As she was being given a tour by Lauren, Cleo took her time looking around.

This was where she was going to live now.

She'd never lived on a farm before and this one reminded her of a lovely homestead.

There was something warm and welcoming about seeing the well-fed, happy animals, feeling the cool breeze, and the fact it was out in the middle of nowhere with people that were now to be her extended family.

"So, this is the Sanctuary," she murmured.

"Yep!" Lauren answered and Cleo's eyes widened in surprise a bit.

She hadn't realized she'd spoken loud enough for the other woman to hear.

Staring at her now, she still couldn't believe there was really another human on this strange planet.

"Do you like it? I know it's not much in terms of facilities, but we try hard and the animals are nice." Lauren grinned at her and Cleo got the impression she was the type that usually tried to find the sunshine on rainy days. "You can have Sohut's room."

Lauren's cheeks grew warm. "I mean, of course you're going to stay in Sohut's room. You're together." Her cheeks grew warmer. "Nia is using the spare room anyway."

"Nia?"

As she said the name, another human female rounded the corner, a bucket in hand.

"Nia!" Lauren exclaimed, waving the woman over. "Meet Cleo. She just arrived. I know we have a lot to talk about, but we can do it later after you come in."

"Nice to meet you," Cleo said, awestruck.

Nia smiled and extended her hand for a handshake before she grimaced and pulled it back.

"Hey! I'd shake your hand but mine is full of umu poop. Not the best of introductions."

Lauren chuckled and Cleo smiled.

This was unbelievable.

To meet not one, but two more humans, after she'd spent so long thinking she was alone.

"How'd you come? Did Geblit bring you in a box?" Nia asked.

"No, I came with Sohut."

She was about to ask about Geblit and the box before Lauren spoke up.

"She's Sohut's gnora." Lauren beamed.

Nia's eyes bugged out.

"Really? Wow." She smiled, but there was a sudden sadness behind her eyes. "That's...That's amazing." Nia forced her smile wider.

"Thank you," Cleo answered. The woman's response was a bit confusing and she couldn't help but wonder if Nia and Sohut had met before.

He hadn't mentioned her.

As if she summoned him, Sohut and his brother rounded the corner of another building.

"What are you ladies talking about?" Sohut's eyes found her immediately and he moved to stand by her side.

"Sohut, this is the other human I was telling you about." Riv all but growled the words. "She is called Nee-ya."

Sohut pulled his eyes away and they landed on Nia. "Nice to meet you."

When Nia met his gaze, there was no recognition there. Still, sadness lingered behind her eyes. "Nice to meet you too." She smiled. "Well, this is nice! You're all paired up!"

Sohut pulled Cleo closer against him.

"I'm delighted to be," he said.

There was a beat before Lauren spoke up.

"Well, it's almost dinner time! I hope you like rai and braised meat!" Lauren grinned as Riv pulled her small body against his.

"Everybody loves rai and braised meat," Riv growled, casting a serious eye their way that said they shouldn't protest.

Chuckling, the party headed into the house.

As the three beings walked ahead of them, Cleo slowed her steps and Sohut turned a questioning gaze her way.

"Clee-yo...is something wrong?"

Cleo moved her gaze from the Sanctuary and the view of the plain beyond to the man that had literally entered her life and turned it completely around.

"No, I just..."

Sohut moved close to her and pulled her into his arms. "I know it's not much, but—"

"It's perfect," she interrupted him. "It couldn't be more perfect."

Tears filled her eyes and she willed them back.

She wasn't the emotional type, damnit.

Sohut reached a finger to her face and wiped a tear away, just as Wawa pushed his head out from under the hood.

"I'm not making her cry," Sohut said to Wawa and Wawa bumped his head against her cheek.

Burying her face into Sohut's chest, she wrapped her arms around him.

"Clee-yo?" Sohut whispered.

"I just...that day when I escaped from the orc's cart, I never imagined I'd ever have this..."

Sohut was silent for a few seconds and when she looked up at him, there was a bewildered look on his face.

"But your eyes leak...are you not...happy?"

Cleo chuckled and sniffled at the same time.

"Oh, Sohut, I'm more than happy."

Sohut pulled her into him. "Sure?"

"Sure."

They stood like that for a few moments before she whispered into his chest, "I love you."

Sohut pulled her tighter into him.

"I love you too, my gnora."

And if that wasn't the best feeling in this alien world, she didn't know what was.

EPILOGUE

"KA'CIT IS COMING TO HELP ME GET THAT THING OFF YOUR NECK." Sohut walked toward her and massaged her neck.

Cleo leaned back into his touch. She'd begun to get used to the pressure there to the point that it was almost just a part of her existence.

The blue ring only bothered her when she had any sort of high emotion and being on the sanctuary, life was calm.

Still, that didn't mean she wanted to keep it on her neck.

"When will he get here?" she asked.

"Maybe after dinner," Sohut answered.

In the kitchen, she could hear deep chuckles that could only belong to a man and she knew Riv was in there laughing with Lauren. How the woman managed to do such a feat she didn't know.

For the most part, Riv only seemed to smile for Lauren and his brother.

She was thinking about that when a huge figure suddenly loomed in the doorway.

Instincts kicked in quickly and she reached into the boots Sohut had given her for her trusty piece of metal.

The intruder was male, and he was wearing a sort of welding mask.

"Ka'Cit. You arrived much sooner than I thought you would." Sohut smiled, moving over to touch the male on his shoulder.

"I was in the area," the stranger replied.

She didn't know how she knew it, but this Ka'Cit was staring straight at her. She could feel it.

She couldn't see his face because of the mask he wore but she could sense his gaze anyway.

"This is Clee-yo. I need that disruptor for her."

"A bio-tracker," Ka'Cit mused as he moved toward her, stopping just short of her. It was clear his complete attention was now on the intangible blue clasp around her neck.

"Yes," Sohut said. "Funny you had the disruptor with the right frequency to disband it." He paused. "Just how *did* you get a disruptor with that frequency, and so quickly, anyway?"

"Easy," Ka'Cit said. "Break a few fingers and a few toes...you can get anything."

She didn't know if he was joking or if he was serious. After all, she couldn't even see his face to determine his emotions.

Just as she was thinking that, he lifted the welding mask and smiled at her.

"Ka'Cit," he said. "Nice to meet another...*gnora* of my friends."

There was a note of bitterness there, she was sure. Only, she didn't know why.

He dropped on his knees before her then, taking tools from his pocket and Cleo glanced up at Sohut, who nodded at her.

Sheathing her piece of metal back in her boot, she turned her head to the side so Ka'Cit could take a look at the energy band that was there.

"Unique...such unique technology," Ka'Cit murmured as he moved his fingers in the air above her skin and she assumed he was touching the band.

"Well, time to get this phekking thing off you," he said, sending a smile her way and again there was a note of bitterness...or was it sadness...in his eyes.

He was working for maybe five minutes with tools and devices she'd never seen before, when Nia stepped into the room.

"Hey, Cleo. Wanna go check on the robots that are in the field? Gets a bit lonely when I do it myself," she said. Her gaze flicking over the room before landing on Ka'Cit.

The clang of metal hitting the ground drowned out Cleo's answer and her gaze fell on Ka'Cit too.

His mouth was slightly agape, wide enough for her to see his fangs and he was staring in Nia's direction.

"I—Yea, sure. I think he's almost done removing this thing from my neck," Cleo answered, her gaze still on the large male kneeling before her.

Nia smiled back. "Ok, cool," she said before turning and heading back toward the guest room.

"Ka'Cit?" Sohut broke the silence that enveloped the room and Ka'Cit shook his head a little before he picked up his tools.

"All done," he said. But he didn't meet her gaze or even Sohut's.

As Cleo rubbed her neck, it felt like nothing had been removed, of course, but the pressure that was there was gone.

Sohut moved over to her, his hands touching the spot.

"Is it gone?" she asked.

Sohut nodded. "How do you feel?"

Her gaze met his.

"Better, much better," she answered truthfully, tilting her head so she could plant a kiss on his lips. "Thank you," she said.

"For what?"

"For everything."

His gaze searched hers for a moment before he dipped his head and his lips touched hers.

"My gnora, I'd do anything for you."

"And you have."

She stood and Sohut straightened with her against him, their lips entwined.

Someone cleared their throat as Riv and Lauren walked in.

"Oh, you got that thingy taken off!" Lauren noticed immediately.

"Yes, Ka'Cit came and removed it," Cleo answered, clearing her throat as Sohut put a little space between them.

"Ka'Cit? He was here?" Riv asked and it was then that she realized Ka'Cit was nowhere in the room.

Sohut looked just as confused.

"He must have left when we weren't looking," Sohut murmured.

She didn't even get to thank him, Cleo realized.

"Aw," Lauren pouted a little, "we'd prepared enough for him since you'd said he was coming. Now, what are we going to do with all the extra food?"

Sohut raised his hand immediately. "I nominate myself to take that burden."

"You." Lauren rolled her eyes.

Cleo smiled.

This was her new home, her new family.

She couldn't have asked for anything better.

A NOTE FROM A.G

You reached the end!

I hope you loved Sohut and Cleo's story!

Sohut is a good-natured lad—the complete opposite of his brother—and I had a lot of fun writing him.

I'm beginning to fall in love with this little world on Hudo III and I'm pretty sure we will revisit it after Ka'Cit's book drops.

On that note, Ka'Cit's story is coming next in this series and I know a lot of you are dying to learn more about him. There's no date for his story yet, but it's in the works.

Also, keep an eye out for the Restitution series. I'm having the covers done and...omg, I'm in love with my own characters.

Shh...don't tell my husband.

Catch you on Facebook or at the back of my next book! Till then, happy reading!

A.G.

NEXT IN THE SERIES

Ka'Cit's Haven

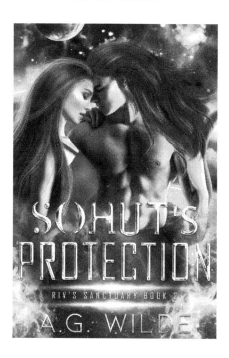

Join the mailing list for updates on its release!

OTHER BOOKS BY A.G.

Captured by Aliens

Xul

Crex

Yce

Kyris

Kyro

Riv's Sanctuary

Riv's Sanctuary

Sohut's Protection

Ka'Cit's Haven (COMING SOON)

ACKNOWLEDGMENTS

This goes out to all the readers of my books and to everyone who has loved them.

Thank you!

I would not be able to do this without you and I am truly grateful.

KEEP IN TOUCH

Join A. G. Wilde's Newsletter
    Join A. G. Wilde's Reading Group: The Wilde Side
    Like her Facebook Page
    Follow her on Amazon
    Visit her Website
    Follow her on BookBub

IF YOU ENJOYED THIS BOOK...

If you enjoyed this book, please consider leaving a review, even if it is only a line or two. It would make all the difference and would be very much appreciated.

ABOUT THE AUTHOR

A. G. Wilde is an avid reader, a gamer, a lover of all things space, alien, and sci-fi.

She is addicted to intense romance, irresistible heroes, and deliciously naughty things.

Printed in Great Britain
by Amazon

87666576R00162